Sweetwater Station

Malania E. Reynolds

THREE SKILLET

Sweetwater Station

◖❡◗ THREE SKILLET

www.ThreeSkilletPublishing.com

ISBN - 978-1-943189-10-6

v.4

One

"I see here that you're not married."

Sitting across the desk from the stage line supervisor, Josiah Jackson Hadley wondered how the hell the man thought he could have come up with a wife in the three years he'd been away at war. He'd only been back in Indiana about eleven months, and from what he'd seen, the farm had been taken over by his tyrannical older brother, Luther, and that was the reason why Joe wanted to get away again, in a hurry. He could see that the man was wanting an answer, so he guessed he'd better pay more attention to the conversation, else the fellow would give the position in Colorado to some-one else.

"No, sir, I'm not married."

"The appointment in Colorado Territory requires that a man have a wife. The female passengers feel more comforta-ble with someone of their own kind around, and the men like the soft touch of a woman's hand on a loaf of bread, fresh from the oven. Can't say that a man don't cook beans as well as a female, but as for bread, Mr. Hadley, well, you get the picture."

"Yes, sir, you're saying that I can't have the position, because I don't have a wife. But, what if I get a wife of my own, do you think I could hold down the job of station attendant in the West?" Joe looked expectantly at the man, who turned in his chair and spat a long trail of tobacco juice into the brass kettle at his side.

"You think you can find a bride before the fifteenth of the month? I can't hold the assignment open longer than that. Station couples are scarce as hen's teeth, what with the war just over and everything. Events will start to move fast, now that the transportation lines are opening up again. Everything was shut down tighter than a tick on a dog's back during the war. People in the East want to go west, and the people in the western places will want to see their families in the East, make sure they're safe and well. The owners of the passenger lines see a long migration of people moving across the country. Won't be no time before there's talk of building train tracks for the traveling public, but for now there's only the local stage lines." The man turned and spat again, this time missing the top of the kettle, causing a loud jangling sound, and the juice began to slide down the side onto the floor.

Joe hoped his work wouldn't require him to clean up after some uncouth tobacco spitter. He was good with animals, especially with horses and mules, but he could see where a woman's touch might be needed in cleaning up after the male passengers.

"Yes, sir, I think I know a gal that would marry me. She's a good cook, too. If you can hold the position open for a few days, I'll let you know how the courting turns out."

John Dempsey looked into the eyes of the young man with the sorrowful appeal in his eyes. According to his papers, he had just returned from the South where the fighting had been the worst. It was obvious that the man needed the work, and the isolated way station in Colorado Territory, near the high mountains, might help heal the dreadful wounds of war. If Hadley was half as good with animals as he claimed in his application for the assignment, he'd make a fine worker for the position of station manager. He looked mature and strong, in spite of the hardships he'd endured. It took a man of courage and endurance to wait around for the stage to come along once a week. Dempsey had seen many a man weaken, and in their sleep at night see the danger of wild animals or Indians, even when there was nothing to fear. They would then begin to imbibe heavily if they could get their hands on the liquor, and the end result was to neglect the animals in their care. He fancied himself a good judge of character, and he was certain that Hadley would hold up well under the pressure.

"There's one thing I haven't mentioned that might interest you. The Sweetwater station is near a large box canyon with high cliffs on three sides, I've been told. Never been that far west myself. The place has tall trees and plenty of brushy meadows nearby. Wild mustangs are known to drift into the area to water at the springs that give the place its name. Plenty of wild game comes to the springs, too, so you won't have to depend solely on the supplies to come on the freight trains. If you could maybe capture some of those horses and train them as draft animals, maybe to pull wagons or a stage, it would put extra money in your pockets, for the line is always looking for fine horses. Be a sort of side line, to build corrals and deliver those horses to the main line station or to Denver. 'Course, it would mean your woman and the animal handler would be alone while you're traveling with the horses, but we could perhaps see to sending someone to help with the chore, if you let us know in advance when they're ready for travel. Just a thought. See how the situation unfolds when you get there. First, you gotta have a wife."

Dempsey stood up and shook the hand of the young man and watched as he left the room. He sure hoped the man found a wife soon. He'd hold the position open like he said until the fifteenth of the month, but it was critical that the station have a manager before the stage started running along that route. They had already procured the services of a half-pay soldier out of the Army with a yearning to earn his keep as a helper. He was experienced in handling horses and mules, and the two would make a good partnership, if the young man could get over his chills and night dreams of war. Dempsey knew how it was for a man to have to turn his life from all the killing and sounds of war back to peacetimes. He had himself fought in Mexico in the last war and was still nervous of loud, popping sounds in the night. Well, he'd wait, but not for any longer than the fifteenth for the young man. He had positions to fill at the other stations. There were many former soldiers eagerly looking for work.

Two

Joe Hadley pulled the old brown felt hat down tight on his ears against the brisk north wind. The cold and dampness seeped into his soul through his threadbare coat. It was the first of March and the spring was late in coming to Indiana this year. He hated the coldness of winter. That was another reason why he had taken up the challenge of moving to the mountains or dry desert of the western country, but not the main reason, as he thought again of the changes that had come over his home since he had gone off to war.

It had been a thrilling sight, he supposed, for the towns-folk of Greenwood that day so long ago, when the fresh Union recruits had marched down the main street headed for battle. His brother was now dead; lying far away, in a mass grave near Gettysburg, in Pennsylvania.

He had chosen, instead, to volunteer with General Morgan's Southern troops. They had left town a month later to the jeers and mockery of the few merchants and farmers who witnessed their departure. He had held his head high and his shoulders straight and proud. But, glory and honor had not come to them. Only a few stragglers had returned to their homes.

His father, Peter Hadley, once proud and dominant, had

taken to drink during his darkest moments. Sometimes he sat with a vacant look in his eyes. Luther had no compassion or patience with him and wouldn't give him money to buy his way out of his grief. He had taken to begging from strangers. His mother, Ruth, had lost her vigor and hope, and although she tried to come to terms with the loss of her beloved son, she mourned with a deep sorrow. She sometimes ranted about the terrible times in which they lived.

Joe tried at first to understand and help the family, but he came up against the hard, unyielding stare of his brother, who couldn't be reconciled to the fact that James had died and Joe, the Rebel, had returned.

Joe had bent his back to the harsh labor of plowing and planting the crops, of tending the animals and garden, and it had served for a time as his salvation, but he, too, had passed the point of no return. The trial and execution of the conspirators involved in the assassination of the president, Abraham Lincoln, had awakened him to the danger of lingering longer under the control of his brother's influence. He must leave the farm or lose his self-respect and take to the bottle like his father. He had some money saved, but the funds wouldn't last long, especially if his brother knew about them. Already, Luther had hinted that he, Joe, must do more to pay for supplies and a new roof on the barn. His money was safe in the bank, and would stay there, secretly, until he was on his way west.

Since talking with Dempsey, Joe was now more determined than ever to leave the farm. Having read the small notice in the newspaper about the stage line building toward Denver, he came to town to apply for a career with the business. He didn't want a position as driver of the stage or lowly clerk in some office. He wanted and needed the isolation a way station offered, to gain once again a sense of duty and responsibility, for which he could challenge himself and win back his lost hope for the future. The family had done well without him for the three years he'd been gone to war; he doubted they would miss him once he was gone again. Now he must think of finding a wife.

He ducked into a small restaurant and ordered a piece of apple pie and a cup of coffee while he thought over this new setback to his plans. He picked up an abandoned newspaper lying on the table and read the headlines. With nothing grabbing his attention, he turned the page, hoping to find more interesting news but couldn't settle to the reading of it. He dropped the paper, took a sip of the hot coffee, left his pie unattended and thought of his situation.

The only young woman Joe had ever had an interest in had married someone else last year and moved away. He chuckled to himself when he thought of his brother James, teasing him about her lovely blue eyes. He sometimes believed that James had developed an interest in Mary Ann Butler but was too shy to approach her. He thought of that last time together, when he and James had donned their best suits and slicked down their hair to attend the harvest dance. They'd laughed and almost got into a fight over those sweet charms and blue, blue eyes. They'd danced with the other single girls, but it was she and she alone who had caught their attention. He wished her well in her marriage and future.

Joe let his mind drift over the other ladies of his acquaintance. There were not many single women of a certain age left in the town. There were a large number of widows, of course, grieving for lost husbands who had died in faraway places. Many orphan children needed the guidance and support of a new father. He snorted at that idea. He'd never been interested in taking over responsibility for some other man's spawn. He might have to choose a widow, but it wouldn't be his first choice. He lifted his fork with a bite of pie and placed it in his mouth. He almost gagged on the morsel as a sudden inspiration hit him dead on in the face of his dilemma. He quickly swallowed and took a sip of coffee to wash it down. The idea grew and took shape in his brain.

Hannah Edison! That was her name. Thinking back once again to that harvest dance, he remembered how Hannah had sat on the sidelines of the dance floor in her oddly-fitting brown dress, talking with the other single girls, who never were asked to dance. She had a certain glow in her eyes, a pink tint on her cheeks. He could see her now as her foot tapped to the music. He had thought of asking her to dance but couldn't bear the thought of the embarrassment, not if his two older brothers were to see him dancing with the ugliest girl in the room.

It wasn't her fault that the unfortunate red, puckered scar on her face detracted from her appearance as a young, healthy female. Two years older than his twenty-two years, she would be twenty-four now. As a small girl she had been caught up in the house fire that had killed her parents and younger brother, he seemed to remember. She had been taken in by her uncle, Claude Edison, and his wife, Ethel, as was his bound duty, the man made sure to say to anyone who asked. Although her father had left an estate to pay for her care, it was rumored the family treated her as a servant. James had been somewhat amused at the way she dressed and acted, following behind Edison's two daughters on their way from the church house. He recalled the way his brother, Luther, had sneered and taunted him when he had sought to speak with her. Joe always found himself comfortable when talking to her. Usually the aunt would call sharply to her and scold her for dawdling.

Yes, Joe thought, as he swallowed the last bite of pie and sip of coffee, she's ugly, but she's bound to be a good cook and housekeeper. And, she's educated. At least Claude had seen to that by allowing her to attend the local school with his own children. Joe wondered for the first time how far down the scars went on her body, to her neck, to her shoulder, her waist? She always wore drab dresses with high collars, with her hair bundled in a tight knot at her neck. Could he bear to touch her in the night as his wife? He laughed softly to himself, thinking she might be grateful for the chance to leave her uncle's guardianship and be the queen of her own household, for it might be the only opportunity she would have for marriage and children. Joe saw it as a challenge; an answer to the harshness of his brother's tyranny, his father's drunkenness, his mother's sorrow, and the stage coach line's strict rules and regulations. A wife might even heal his loneliness and pain. Yes, he decided. He would call on Claude Edison today, and to hell with the consequences. He picked up the check and walked with a new spring in his step to the counter to pay his bill. He even smiled at the pretty waitress who had served him.

Three

It wasn't going as easily as Joe had thought, this process of obtaining a bride. He had approached Claude Edison with high hopes and a slight degree of humor over the situation. As he sat answering the man's endless questions over his prospects for the future, his ability to support a wife and family, and about his integrity and his honor, he began to sweat and stammer in embarrassment. He found himself repeating almost word for word the advertisement of employment for the Overland Stage Line and the responsibility of managing the way station called Sweetwater in Colorado Territory. He rambled on about the mountains, the clear flowing streams, the beauty of nature, the plentiful game to be found, and minimized the dangers of hostile Indian tribes, the isolation, and the feeling of inadequacy that attempted to draw him into despair. He was careful not to mention an undying affection for the girl, claiming only his respect and admiration for her. His tale must have impressed Hannah's uncle, for he stood up, walked to the door of his office and yelled down the hallway.

"Hannah! Ethel! Come here!" Claude walked back to his chair behind the desk and waited for the women to appear. He silently stared at Joe as though he were some kind of unknown insect that had appeared in his line of sight. He knew as well as anyone how much Ethel would hate to give up the unpaid servant in their household. Claude could see, if his wife did not, that if their own daughters were to have a chance at an advantageous marriage, they must first remove the elder girl from the household. It wasn't as though she would detract from their charms and startling beauty, but that the neighbors and family members would expect some attempt to find her a husband in spite of her appearance.

It occurred to Claude that if the truth were known of his niece's modest wealth, certain untoward men would flock to her like bees to a hive. He'd been in fear that somehow the knowledge would seep out through the lawyers and accountants, and with the discovery would come the revelation of how the family treated her. Eventually, he cleared his throat and sat with a stiff and frozen face.

Joe, nervous about Claude's intent, rose from his chair and stood perfectly still. Once erect, he waited as he would have appeared before his commanding officer, expecting a reprimand over some unacknowledged misdeed on the field of battle. Even so, Claude Edison didn't intimidate Joe. He'd been set down by experts in his three years as a soldier. He had tackled challenges that would have frightened Claude until he squealed with horror. He had killed with his rifle and fought hand-to-hand with expert knife-wielding enemies. Aroused to empathy for the older man, Joe caught his antagonist's eyes and smiled. And, surprisingly, Claude seemed to relax and enjoy the challenge.

Ethel rushed through her husband's open office door and stopped with such suddenness that the woman behind her almost knocked her down. They both had large white aprons over their gowns, and Hannah had a smudge of flour in her hair. They had obviously been baking bread. Their hands were white with the sticky dough. Following closely behind was the eldest daughter, Claudette. She quickly assessed the scene, and pushing Hannah aside, marched to her father's shoulder and turned, her keen gaze fastened on Joe. Short and stout like her mother, she had blonde hair and blue eyes, while Hannah had dark, almost black hair and brown eyes.

Ethel was the first to recover from her surprise, and demanded to know the meaning of this interruption to her household chores. She moved closer to the young man standing at attention and pretended that he was unknown to her, although they had been neighbors for the whole of his life.

"Well," she demanded. "What have you to say for yourself, young man?" As though her husband were not even in the room, she silently accused him of interrupting her work.

"Please, Ethel. Sit down, my dear, and calm yourself." Claude asserted his authority.

Ethel turned to her husband and sat in the chair recently abandoned by their visitor. She was careful to keep her dough-smeared hands from her apron, but it was clearly a lost cause. She finally dropped them into her lap. Hannah stood near the door. She darted one glance toward Joe and dropped her eyes to trace the pattern of the office rug at her feet. Claudette twittered and smiled, for she couldn't ignore the presence of a young man near her. She started to say something, but her father raised his hand and gestured for silence.

"Ethel, Mr. Hadley has surprised me with an offer of marriage for our niece, Hannah, and I've decided to accept his offer." Claude eased back in his seat, prepared to enjoy the reaction of his womenfolk. As the girl's guardian, his wife couldn't dispute his decision.

There was a gasp from Ethel and a squeal from Claudette, but Hannah made no sound at all. She gawked at her uncle, shocked at his words. She looked at Joe, puzzled, and quickly returned her gaze to the pattern on the rug. She'd known Josiah Hadley since childhood and never found him to be impulsive. Her heart skipped a beat. Marriage? He wanted to marry her? Surely it was a mistake. She looked again. He seemed so much more mature and solemn since the last time she'd seen him at the harvest dance, before he'd marched off to war. He had smiled and appeared carefree and gay back then. Now, he appeared ill at ease and embarrassed.

Joe himself was taking deep, silent breaths, having suddenly realized what the significance of his offer truly meant. He was now committed; he couldn't escape if he were to be proven an honorable man. The saliva slid down his gullet, while his Adam's apple quivered under his neck piece. His hands trembled, and he wished he could put them in his pockets. He took a quick peek at the girl, standing so still and quiet. He was struck by the contrast between her and Claudette. They were as different from each other as night from day. He brought his wandering mind back to Hannah's uncle, who was speaking.

"Well, what do you have to say, my dear? Shall we leave the young couple alone to discuss the situation?"

Both Ethel and Claudette screamed at once. The sounds came so suddenly that Hannah jumped. Ethel screeched with resentment and anger, while Claudette wailed with a hatred that had hardly been concealed before today, but now resounded in a tantrum of immense proportions. They shrieked. They yelled.

"Get out! Leave my house at once. The very idea of your conniving dishonesty sickens me." For a split second it was undecided whether Ethel was speaking to Hannah or Joe. Her face was puffed and red, her eyes glowing with the unholy fire of anger. Her sharp words echoed around the room like a thunderstorm. Ethel seemed to have been released from years of built-up tension. Although she was more subtle in her approach than her daughters, she was nevertheless the more dangerous. She sprang toward Hannah, as though to claw at her eyes with her long nails.

Joe was about to spring to the aid of his future bride and take her from the room, when Claude asserted his power as head of the house.

"Stop that bellowing at once! Remember your position,

woman. How can you set an example of dignity and grace for your daughters, when you act like a fish wife at the market? You are a lady, my dear."

He grabbed the woman's hand as she began to strike Hannah and gently led her back to her seat. With a degree of dignity that surprised Joe, he supported his wife by placing his hand on her shoulder. His daughter, he ignored. He turned to Hannah with a soft and gentle voice.

"Go upstairs, my dear, and pack your clothes. I believe there's an old valise under the attic stairs that you may use. I'll see that your mother's jewelry and your father's papers are removed from the bank and returned to you." He turned to Joe with a frown on his face.

"I apologize, Mr. Hadley, for my wife's unseemly behavior. If you'll but wait a moment longer, I'll speak to you of the bride's price and her dowry." He ushered his family from the room.

Released from his stiff posture, Joe soon found himself sitting in the large leather armchair, alone with his troubled thoughts. It was as he had expected. Hannah had been abused, if not physically, then certainly emotionally by her female relatives. He supposed that the younger daughter, Margaret, must be out, or she would have surely lent her ranting to the other women. He was relieved that he hadn't chosen Claudette for his wife, for the thought had crossed his mind. He couldn't visualize her in a rude cabin in the wilderness as servant to a group of cantankerous stage passengers.

He looked closely for the first time at the furnishings in the room. The furniture was of the latest and best style; the lustrous rug of a colorful wool blend; and the pictures and painting on the walls reflecting the taste of a collector with imagination and daring. He sighed. He wondered if Hannah would miss the splendor of the environment in which she now lived. Would she come to resent his interference in her comfortable if restricted place in society once she was forced to endure the hardships of the wilderness?

As though in answer to his doubts and questions, Hannah appeared in the room, dressed in a clean, drab gray dress, with freshly combed hair. She seemed shy, and Joe could see her trembling. He went to her and led her to the chair, while he stood before her and smiled.

"I'm sorry it hasn't turned out exactly as I planned when I arrived, but I'm sincere in my offer of marriage. It seems that through circumstances out of our control, you now have no choice but to accept my offer. I had hoped to explain about the position I've undertaken as manager of an overnight way station on the Overland Stage Line near Denver, in Colorado Territory. I wanted to explain that we'll travel to New Albany, ride by steamboat on the Ohio River to the Mississippi and transfer to another steamer west at St. Louis, on the Missouri, where we'll transfer once again to a third or fourth steamer to the end of the line, then go by stage to our new home." Joe paused to catch his breath and saw that Hannah was listening to his every word, her eyes as large as pumpkins.

"It'll be a long, tiring trip, and at the end, I'm not sure whether our house will be ready or whether we'll have to sleep in a tent while it's being prepared for us. I have to leave that to the decision of my superiors. I can't emphasize more clearly that the work will be hard, the isolation demanding and harsh, the threat of Indian uprisings ever present, the animals, both domestic and wild, dangerous. It'll be especially tedious for you since you'll need to cook and clean for the overnight guests."

"Is this true? You're planning to go to the western territory, and leave your family behind? How can this be? You have a settled farm and property here." She looked at Joe with concern on her face. Her eyes were wide with surprise and wonderment.

"Yes. I'm going away." He walked to the window and drew aside the curtains, as though the stifling atmosphere of the room was uncomfortable, and he must see the open sky to relieve the pressure. He dropped the curtain and returned to her. He sat down.

"I've come to realize that I'll never have peace with my brother. We're too much set in our own characters. It was different before the war, when Father was strong and in control, but he's lost the will to live with my brother James not returning from the war. And my mother is despondent. I cannot remain."

His eyes held a fierce look of anger and resentment. "My brother's always been arrogant and overbearing, even when we were children, but it's worse now. I fear I would end up killing or maiming him in the end, if I stayed. I've seen enough violence. My parents will be watched over by the servants and neighbors. It'll be better if I'm not around to remind them of their loss. I plan to give my portion of the land to my brother. He's been running it as his own during the war, anyway."

Joe rose and began to pace the floor, trying to gather his thoughts. Before he had circled the room once, Hannah rose and took his hands in her own. He saw the compassion in her eyes.

"No, don't continue. I understand, and I accept with deep gratitude your offer of marriage." Her eyes twinkled, and she giggled like a school girl. "In truth, I'll be happy to leave this house, whether in shame and disgrace or with a large, previously planned society wedding. Oh, Joe, I'm so happy. To think that just this morning, I was weeping in my pillow over the monotony and tedious duty of my position. Now I'm to be a bride." The side of her face that wasn't damaged glowed with the pink tone of embarrassment. She dropped her eyes to the rug, and became instantly serious.

"Joe, can you truly take me as your wife, and do so without regrets? I don't want you to be unhappy. You've suffered so much with the loss of your brother and the wounds of war. I know you've changed since you've returned home. You seem so sad at times. Has it been so awfully bad that you must leave again so soon? Will your mother and father not feel the loss of another son?"

There were tears in Hannah's eyes, but she blinked to keep them from falling. Joe moved to take her in his arms. He could smell a sweet perfume in her hair, and the faintly pungent scent of yeast from her baking chores. For the first time, he felt a compassion and gentleness he hadn't known before for another human being. Not even his mother's sorrow and pain had appealed to him in such a deeply tender way. It surprised him that Hannah could feel sympathy for him, when her own doubts and fears were equally as troubling. He raised her face to his and kissed her gently on the lips, then the puckered skin of her cheek. It felt rough and dry to his lips. He stepped back and smiled.

"Thank you for your understanding. I can't guarantee that I won't become grumpy and melancholic at times, or scream out with pain in the middle of the night, for the emotional wounds are truly deep and the memories still fresh. I'll try to be a good husband and protect you with my life, if necessary. We'll have plenty of time to get better acquainted and deal with each other while serving the needs of others."

"Serving the needs of others? What do you mean?"

It was clear to Joe that Hannah had not yet grasped the responsibility of running a way station between two points of the compass for the stage line. He didn't have time to explain, for at that moment, her uncle returned, wearing a frown on his face. The conversation upstairs with his wife and daughter hadn't gone well, Joe decided.

Claude stepped fully into the room and didn't seem to notice that the couple drew back quickly from each other. There was a pink blush on the face of the girl. His mind was still on the problem of the moment.

"I'm sorry. You must leave quickly and make arrangements to live at a hotel, Joe, or at your parents' home until you can be married. I'll send my lawyer to you with the financial details that I wanted to discuss with you privately, when you send me word of your address. Hannah, I would wish that you be wed here in your home, but Ethel cannot be persuaded. She feels betrayed for some odd reason. Don't let it concern you. Don't let it interfere with your future happiness. I'll make arrangements for your possessions to be sent to you as soon as possible. I wish you well, for you're like a dear daughter to me."

He took her in his arms for the first time that she could recall and kissed her forehead, then released her and shook Joe's hand. He left the room before they could detect the tears in his eyes.

Left alone, the couple had no choice but to leave the house. It was fortunate that the morning mist had disappeared and the wind calmed, for she left with no wrap or outer garment. She had no hat, nor gloves. She paused a moment on the walk to look back at her childhood home and glanced up at Claudette's window in time to see the girl draw back. Hannah knew in that moment that she would never see her relatives again. She was totally dependent on the man walking beside her, come good or bad, whether they were truly married or not. She wondered whether it would be best if she released him from his obligation to her and found her own way in the world, but she didn't have the courage, nor did she have any experience of the world. She had nothing to contribute to society, nor did she know anyone in a position to help her if she asked. She sighed deeply, placed her hand in the crook of Joe's arm, and walked toward the future.

Things were moving too quickly for Joe to understand. He had thought to ask for the privilege of courting Hannah, and after a short length of time, to be married in the church he attended on Sunday when he came to town, then return to his parents' farm until he heard from John Dempsey, or someone with equal authority in the stage line. That was now out of the question, for it was plain the family wouldn't accept the idea of a public wedding. He seemed to be waking from a nightmare, not knowing where he was or how he came to be walking on the street with a young woman clasped to his side. He looked around to get his bearings and noticed that they were a few blocks from the church. He impulsively decided to take a chance that the pastor was there.

It was silent and dim inside the church. Joe had never been in the building during the week days without the chatter and laughter of many people. He waited a moment for his eyes to grow accustomed to the gloom, entirely conscious of the curiosity of the woman standing silently beside him. He noticed there was someone at the front of the room near the altar railing so began to walk that way.

Hannah didn't follow, instinctively knowing perhaps that she wasn't wanted at the moment. She sat in the last pew and bowed her head. She wasn't one for seeking the assistance of the Lord in matters beyond her control, but she didn't know what else to do.

Joe saw as he drew near the altar that the preacher was standing quietly as though waiting for him. He thought that was very odd. How could the preacher know that he needed assistance?

"Hello, Preacher Johnston, I'm glad you're here, for I'm in desperate need of advice."

"Josiah Hadley, how can I help you?" The preacher, had it been acknowledged, was as puzzled as Joe, for he had had a dream last night that someone was troubled. He had told his wife after breakfast that he must go to the church and wait. She had frowned but didn't object, for he often seemed to have a mysterious feeling towards these things.

"Sir, I have for some time felt restless and uncomfortable in my own home, so talked with the supervisor of a stage line about a position in the West. Since the war is over, and the transportation sources among the several states more easy, I feel that a great migration will start westward, and I want to be a part of it." He paused for a moment, trying to gather his thoughts and jump into the heart of the problem, what to do with a young woman who now had no home and no other person to rely on but himself.

The Reverend Mr. Johnston waited patiently for him to continue. He felt his heart quicken in anticipation of some great turmoil in the mind of the young man, whom he knew only slightly, since he had not been the preacher when Joe had gone to war.

"I asked for an appointment at one of the way stations on the Overland Stage Line and was shocked to find that they don't take men without a wife, because of the cooking, and tending to the passengers' needs, you understand. If they are staying overnight, they must have clean beds and food."

"Yes, yes, I understand that you need a wife." He looked toward the woman sitting with bowed head at the rear of the room. He didn't recognize her.

"I went this morning to Claude Edison to ask permission to court his niece, Hannah, and suddenly I find that she's now dependent on me, for they have tossed her out of the house. You would never believe the uproar over a marriage offer. They commenced to yelling and screaming at her and calling her all sorts of vile names, when she's entirely innocent of their charges."

"They? Her family was upset?" Homer Johnston didn't know the household involved, for they no longer attended worship services at his church, but he had seen situations of a similar nature before. He didn't think the woman was guilty of sin, so why the abuse? Was she with child? He wondered.

"Yes, sir. Her aunt and cousins have become accustomed for most of her life to treating her as an unpaid servant, a slave, really, I think, but I can't be certain of the matter, since I've been away so long. I've known the family for years and heard only rumors. When Claude accepted my suit and agreed for us to be wed, the womenfolk went crazy, heaping their anger and bitterness on her head. I suppose they saw her getting away from their clutches, and they didn't accept the new situation." Joe looked back at Hannah, hoping she couldn't hear the conversation.

24

"Her uncle gave his consent to the marriage? Is she of age?" Reverend Johnston now thought he understood the problem. The family had discarded the woman as though she were an animal that they no longer wanted.

"Yes, sir. He accepted my offer of marriage. That's when the screaming tantrums began. She's twenty-four years of age, I believe. I'm not sure when her birthday comes."

"I see no problem. I can call my wife and mother from next door at the parsonage as witnesses, and you can be married today, if you wish. Since she's of age, you don't need the consent of her guardian. Of course, to make it completely legal, it will have to be registered at the courthouse, but I can take care of that for you. It's a matter of formality to satisfy the law, you see. If you'll wait with the young lady while I fetch my wife, we'll take care of the matter." He was already moving down the aisle toward a side door before Joe realized the significance of his suggestion.

Joe, his heart racing madly, strode toward the back of the church in something of a panic. He was frightened of the future. He had made a quick summation of his problem and acted impulsively. He wanted this opportunity for employment in Colorado, but did he want to marry a girl with whom he was barely acquainted and who appeared unattractive to most people? Oh, God, he prayed. Help me. He could do no more, for he was standing in the aisle, and she rose to meet him with a frown on her face. Did she think he had changed his mind? He smiled.

"All is well. The preacher can marry us today." He paused and took a deep breath. "That is, of course, if it's your desire, for I won't force you to marry if you do not wish it. I can tell him you find me too repulsive and have changed your mind. I'll take you to the hotel and leave you there until your uncle can make arrangements for your future. It's your decision."

Hannah's eyes sparkled, and she smiled with her whole face, and suddenly Joe didn't find her ugly at all. She reached up to kiss him softly on the lips. He couldn't help his reaction. He held her close and deepened the kiss, until they were both out of breath. He looked into her eyes and kissed her again. Aware of where they were, he drew back, but he smiled. They sat, quietly and with reverence, waiting for the preacher to return with his wife.

It seemed to take so long that Joe began to explain more fully the job he was undertaking in the western country. He explained how she would have to cook and clean for the passengers. It would be a lonely life through most of the week, and he would be gone occasionally, but they would have an assistant to help with the chores and tend the animals.

Hannah was most impressed when he began to tell of the mustangs and how he could make extra money if he could capture and train them for the stage line. She saw how his manner changed when he spoke of the horses. He was no longer sad and sorrowful, but alive and enthusiastic about his future plans.

Hannah and Joe left the church a married couple, with an official-looking paper in his pocket. He would have given the license to her, but she had no pockets, nor a handbag. He promptly took care of that problem. They visited the local clothing store and bought her a complete set of clothing and shoes, including a heavy wool coat, a small handbag, gloves, and a hat. They laughed when they ran out of the store, for the sunshine had disappeared, and a cold rain was falling. He suggested a return for water-proofed coats but decided that the hour was late, and his family would wonder at him staying away so long. There were chores to be done at the farm.

Four

It was their last night aboard the steamboat, and Joe paced the floor in nervousness and worry over the freight. It had been a surprise when the lawyer announced with a pretentious voice the total amount of Hannah's inheritance. He had droned on and on about the details, which Joe could easily have done without, since his mind was in shock. He had spent hours filled with anxiety over whether his own limited funds would last until winter, and now he was a wealthy man, going into the desert where there were no stores or restaurants to spend the money. He could have laughed out loud, it was so odd. He wanted to rush home and tell his brother, but that would have only caused trouble among the family. Luther would surely have found a way to demand that he buy the new barn roof he had complained about since Joe had returned from the war. He didn't feel that he should use Hannah's money for such a purpose.

The shock was even greater for Hannah, who had been made to feel that she was a financial burden to her uncle and aunt. She burst into tears, and it took Joe a long time to calm her. It turned out well, for they had gone on a shopping spree in New Albany that would make their lives at the stage station much more comfortable. They had bought bedding; and linens; dishes and kitchen utensils; two high quality and fashionable carpetbags for their personal luggage; and farm implements and seeds. Hannah insisted a kitchen garden was essential to the serving of good, nourishing meals to their guests. Joe had laughed but agreed with her on that point. The whole of the luggage and barrels and boxes was now somewhere in the bowels of the boat, and he was anxious that they get safely to the Sweetwater station.

As soon as they docked, he would ask around first thing to see if a freight train was headed that way, and should one not be available, he would purchase a wagon and pay a driver to haul the freight to the station if necessary, although it was possibly not safe for one wagon to travel alone for a long distance. He didn't know yet how the supplies for the station provided by the company would be shipped. If the stage agent could add their personal items to the other goods promised by John Dempsey, then he would no longer have to worry so much about it. They would travel west by stage themselves, and they were restricted to only one item of luggage on the trip just like the other passengers. That would only allow for one change of clothes and a few personal items. Joe understood that the passengers' weight and the luggage made it harder for the horses or mules to pull the stage with any speed over the rocky hills and mountain passes.

Hannah stood beside the rail and watched as the foaming water encircled the lower boards of the boat. She looked up at the white fluffy clouds in the sky and was grateful that it wouldn't rain on their first day on the open prairie. She couldn't believe her luck and pinched her arm to make sure it was all real. Only a few weeks past she'd been weeping with tiredness and pain over some expression of her aunt's temper. She thought back to the last day of her life there and the excitement she felt when Joe had asked her to marry him.

Her mind wanted to skip over the remembrance of the awkward first night of their marriage, but Hannah forced herself to examine once again her chagrin at discovering that Joe didn't love her. It was silly in the extreme to imagine that he had, for he'd never shown a desire to dance with her at the social events they attended as youths. She had waited, freshly bathed and powdered, in her virginal white gown for him to come to her. He was polite and charming, but she could sense that he was uncomfortable in the situation. He had blown out the lamp, raised the covers and climbed into bed beside her. He lay for some time on the edge of the bed before turning to her. It wasn't the passionate and exciting mating that she had dreamed of, but a cold, unemotional coupling. He'd continued until his breathing was labored and his body wet with perspiration, then rolled off her and onto his side, his back to her, and gone to sleep.

The next morning, he appeared as though the night's activity hadn't happened. He had explained at breakfast his plans for the day, and treated her with respect and dignity, but there was no affection or desire in his eyes. A smile, a friendly greeting, even a helpful hand when she needed it crossing the road were not a substitute for love, but perhaps, she told herself hopefully, he would come to love her in time.

As the nights passed by, one after another, passionless, unrelenting, she questioned her own feelings for him and decided that what she felt was only gratitude. All the books and poems that she had read were a fraud, an attempt by the writers to sell their merchandise. Love did not exist. She buried her dreams and desires deep in the past and determined to live with the simple pleasures she would derive from being a good hostess and servant at the way station. Perhaps, when the troubling memories of the war years were passed, Joe would find peace and contentment in the wilderness of their new home. Hannah told herself that she must accept that which she could not change. She would be his partner, not his lover, and if they should be blessed with children, then she would find the love she craved with her heart and soul.

The last few weeks in Indiana had been hard, trying to keep peace in Joe's family until their boat left the farm far behind. Joe's parents weren't at all as she had remembered from her youth. His father had been kind and trusting; his mother charming and pretty, but the years of war and the loss of a son had changed their characters beyond recognition. Mr. Hadley had been drinking and staggered into the room, pulling the scarf off a table and causing the vase of flowers and water to leave a puddle on the rug. Oh, how he'd been scolded by Luther when he came in for supper. Hannah put her hands over her ears, for even now, she could hear the harshness in his voice.

She'd cried for Joe and his family that night as she'd walked to the outhouse. She'd stood looking up at the stars, momentarily consumed with disappointment, and only now fully understanding why Joe wanted a new start in the western country. Her heart went out to his parents also, for they deserved better than to spend their last years in such a manner. She'd timidly suggested giving up some of her wealth for their comfort, but Joe said that Luther would have found a way to keep it from them, and she believed him. Standing silently on the boat deck, she looked around, breathed the fresh scent of flowers in the air, and felt the slight mist coming from the river on her face. In that moment of private silence, she prayed that both families, his and hers, would find a type of peace in the future.

Hannah felt rather than saw her husband come up behind her. She turned into his arms and smiled. He was a strong, yet surprisingly gentle man, always pleasant when they were together, and very intelligent. She felt she could discuss anything, and he wouldn't think her ignorant and unschooled. They had already spent many hours reading the old newspapers and magazines left behind by other passengers. They had purchased two boxes of books for their new home. Bought by weight, not by author or title, she knew that one of the joys of the enterprise would be to open the boxes and discover the contents.

Joe was interested in the political views of other men on

board the boat, and she watched each night with amazement and amusement when he talked with the men of many things, without rancor or argument, especially when the recent war or the character of the late president Lincoln was discussed. He seemed to have no bitterness toward his former enemies, although twice in the night he had awakened with nightmares of the bloody battles in which he had fought. One night he had been crying, and when she asked, he told her of a young man only seventeen years old who had died beside him, his face unrecognizable. He wouldn't discuss the details of the battle at Gettysburg when his brother James had died. It had been too painful, and she hadn't tried to push him further, thinking maybe someday he would be able to recall the loss without pain.

"All is well, my dear?" Joe gazed into the far distance, seemingly distracted.

She answered him anyway. "All is well."

He blinked and brought his attention back to her. She smiled. "It won't be long now. I talked to the purser, and he thinks about another hour and we'll see the landing around the left bend of the river." He stretched with his hands high in the air and took a deep breath. "I, for one, will be glad to be off this slow-moving vessel and on our way across the prairie grass, where a body can feel the ground beneath him."

"Ah, but my husband, there will the dust blowing and bumps in the road and the rattle of the horses' harnesses to keep us awake."

Hannah's eyes were twinkling in that way that made Joe's heart flutter madly. He laughed and agreed that each sort of travel had its own problems. "Come, darling, if you want a bite to eat, it had best be now, for they will be closing the kitchen down while in port."

He gently led her from the rail and into the large dining room. Hannah was not deceived. She knew that it was Joe who was hungry, and he wouldn't admit it to her.

They ate a quick meal of sliced bread, goat's cheese, paper thin slices of roast beef and sour pickles, washed down with hot coffee. Hannah would have preferred tea, but she didn't object to coffee. As they were finishing, the waiters were clearing the tables for the stop in port. The kitchen staff was clearly working in a frazzled attempt to put everything away before the stopover. Hannah wondered if it would be the same for her and Joe when the stage passengers departed their station dining room. She laughed. Of course, she would have a whole week to clean and prepare for the onslaught of new guests. The stage would come through once a week when the line was finished. In the future, it would attempt the trip more often, when more horses and mules were purchased, more stages built, and more drivers hired to drive the route. For now it was in the experimental stage, for no one could estimate how many people would be traveling to Denver.

All was excitement on deck, and as the passengers prepared to depart, the luggage was sorted and the freight separated for the trip to shore. Joe looked closely but couldn't identify their baggage, so he tried not to be overly concerned. He had had a clerk in New Albany identify it with large black lettering on the side of each case, announcing that it was going to Sweetwater Station in Colorado Territory. He put his hands in his pockets to calm the shaking he could not control; the excitement was building inside him to the point where he thought he would scream in frustration. His nerves were at high alert, as if he were going into a battle with an unknown enemy. It was the waiting that always bothered him. Once they were ashore, and he had a chance to speak with the local transportation official, he would be calm, he told himself. He must be patient. His fingers felt the solid surface of a minted coin, and he rubbed the slick shape gently between his thumb and forefinger. The repeated motion—the familiar shape, one that never changed, he guessed—filled him with a sense of security.

As the couple descended the gangplank, there stood a

tall, slender, rather forceful-looking man dressed in a black suit and stark white cravat, looking up toward the deck. As Joe moved farther down the ladder, he was surprised to hear his name called out by the same man. He raised his hand to draw the man's attention and received a tip of the hat for his effort. On the ground, the man smiled and walked toward them, his motions hampered by a limp in one leg. He took his hat from his head and held it tightly with one hand against the strong wind. Papers and trash from the street swirled at his feet, the larger pieces eventually coming to rest against carriage wheels or the sides of nearby buildings. The sour wharf smell of bird droppings and rotting fish distracted Joe, and he wrinkled his nose. He glanced at Hannah to see her holding a cloth to her mouth, and when he caught her eye, they both smiled.

"Welcome. Welcome. I'm Ned Baldwin, Overland agent for this section of the route." The nattily-dressed agent chuckled, as though at an old joke. "Actually it's Theodore, but no one but my mother calls me by my true name. You must be Mr. and Mrs. Hadley." He shook hands with Joe and turned to Hannah. He paused at her face, seeing the scar for the first time, but after a moment covered the near gaffe with a cough and continued speaking. He kept his gaze turned toward the dark water beneath the boat's paddles. "I have my wife waiting at home to welcome you. She'll be so pleased to hear of the latest bonnet styles in the East. Very fashion minded, is my wife." He shook his head at the foibles of females, and placed his tall silk hat back on his head. "Come, I have a carriage waiting for us."

"What about the baggage, sir?" Joe frowned anxiously as he looked back at the ship, hoping to see the bold lettering on the boxes and barrels he had purchased in New Albany. He really wanted to punch the stranger in the face for staring at Hannah's scar, but knew it would be better to ignore the insult. He didn't want to get into a fight on his first day in Davidson County. Men on the boat had stared at her in the same way. It made him uncomfortable, as though he should do something to protect her, but she seemed to ignore the stares with a dignity that impressed the spectators.

"All taken care of, Mr. Hadley. The freight caravan was scheduled to begin the journey to the western way stations this morning, but when I received the telegram that you were arriving on the River Queen, I asked them to delay to board your baggage. The men will see that it's placed in one of the wagons. You'll find it waiting for you when you arrive, if all goes well and the Indians don't attack." He laughed at the expressions on the faces of his audience. He enjoyed setting the eastern passengers on edge at the beginning of their journey. There had not been an Indian attack on the route for several years, but the eastern strangers seemed to expect it. The small suggestion was just a joke to him, and he discounted the occasional complaints to his superiors. He was an important man, and vacuous objections from passing strangers came to no avail. He would continue to make his little jokes at the strangers' expense, for it was worth the humor it brought into his ordinary life.

The group stopped at a fancy carriage, pulled by four of the finest horses that Joe thought he had ever seen. He would have liked to examine them more closely, but Baldwin was helping Hannah onto the bench seat at the back. He turned and swung himself aboard the passenger seat in front. Baldwin took his place in the driver's seat and lightly flicked the hair of the left wheelhorse with the whip he drew from its place near the brake.

"Gedup, you lazy critters," he yelled, and the lead horses pulled ahead, guiding the wheelhorses as they moved out at a trot behind a large freight wagon, almost overturning a vegetable cart stopped at the side of the road. The angry cart vendor lifted an arm and cursed, but Baldwin paid him no mind. He continued to guide the horses in and out of traffic as though he were racing with an opponent.

Hannah, on the back seat, held on to her hat with one

white-gloved hand while holding tightly to the side rail with the other. The carriage was moving so swiftly she barely noticed the buildings flashing by on either side or the people walking on the sidewalks. She could feel the breeze on her cheeks, and the smell of rotting fish was overpowering. The men seemed to be conversing, but the sound was drowned out by the noise of the city. After what seemed an hour, Baldwin stopped the team before an imposing whitewashed house of two stories some distance from the river. It was nestled on a tree-lined street with about a dozen similar houses set back from the dirt curb with bushes and trees and flower gardens. Hannah was impressed with the neat, tidy appearance of the whole scene.

"Here we are, all snug and safe." Baldwin dropped from the carriage and turned to help Hannah from the seat.

Hannah already had her hand in Joe's. He had beaten the finely-dressed man to his wife's side, and she stood, poised in momentary surprise at the sudden activity from the house. From the windows of the top floor, a very pretty woman of uncertain age leaned out and whooped a greeting, then pulled back and shut the window. The dark green painted door flew open, and what seemed to be a small army of children trooped out, followed more sedately by a large woman carrying a babe in her arms.

Baldwin indicated they should move up the walkway, and turned to take the horses and carriage around to the back shed. Hannah was surrounded by toddlers and young people, all chattering and staring at the strangers. Joe remained at her side as though to protect her from the danger, but she went straight to the woman and held out her hand.

"Good morning, you must be Mrs. Ned Baldwin. I'm Hannah, and this is my husband, Joe, the new manager at the Sweetwater Creek station. I hope we haven't inconvenienced you by coming here straight from the boat." At that moment, the young woman who had leaned out the window rushed from the door and joined them on the sidewalk.

"Oh, I'm so glad you're here. Papa said you were coming, all the way from Indiana. I've never been outside Davidson County. Please tell me, where did you get that hat? It's so pretty. Do you have more like it?" She moved to Hannah's side, reaching for the hat, but Joe stepped in her path.

"Gladys, mind your manners. Let the poor woman at least enter the house before you go on about the latest fashions. Please, forgive my daughter her impulsive habits, Mrs. Hadley, but it's so seldom we see someone of society from the East." While she was talking, Mrs. Baldwin moved them toward the front door, although the gaggle of children, having lost interest, was separating to go in different directions. "Mostly around here all we see are the stage drivers and the freight men, come to call on Ned about business. The children keep me busy at home, but you're welcome to stay the night. I've prepared a room for you."

"Oh, really, I thank you, but we could stay at a hotel in town." Joe tried to insert some manner of authority into the situation. He had certainly not expected to stay in a private home, especially one filled with a dozen children. He was uncomfortable around small children. He never knew quite what to say or do around them, but Hannah had already taken the baby into her arms and was laughing with it. The baby leaned over and did what the daughter, Gladys, had not managed to do: He tipped the hat off Hannah's head. Gladys swooped down, placed it on her own head, and ran to a mirror in the parlor.

Joe had completely lost control of the situation and was glad when his host entered the room through a side door, motioning for him to follow. He took one last look at the chattering women and was relieved to walk down a short hallway and enter a library where a thin, almost starved-looking youth with blond hair and what appeared to be the start of a shaggy mustache quickly rose from a chair. In that clumsy motion, he hid something behind his back, looking guilty. Joe suspected it was a cigar, or a drink of liquor. The faint smell of tobacco lingered in the room. He looked at his host, but Baldwin ignored the young man's minor transgression, just as his wife hadn't taken much notice of her daughter's rudeness. Joe thought them an odd family. He gazed quickly around, admiring the shelves of books, hundreds of them, and the fine leather furniture. He wondered how the Baldwins had managed to amass such excellent furnishings; surely he didn't receive so large a salary from the stage line position as no more than a regional manager.

Baldwin moved to the side of his desk and held out a box of cigars. He looked suspiciously at the thin youth but didn't rebuke him. Joe shook his head. He hadn't yet succumbed to the habit of smoking the fat long weeds. Baldwin offered a drink, but again Joe refused. He took a small drink in a fancy clear glass for himself and swallowed it in one long gulp. Joe's stomach rumbled from hunger. He would have liked a drink of water instead of liquor, but didn't want to impose. He kept quiet and watched the youth, who was trying to be discreet, but not very successfully. His face was a perfect picture of guilt and shame.

"Joe, this is my son, Matthew. He's a student at the moment, but fancies that someday he'll be a driver for the line. Maybe so. Maybe so. It'll be time to decide when he finishes his education."

Joe could feel the contention between the two, for Matthew looked at his father with frustration. He came over and shook hands politely and muttered some kind of greeting before hurrying from the room. Joe suspected he intended to finish his cigar in the backyard. It was none of his business. Tomorrow, with a little luck, he and Hannah would be catching the early morning stage for the next portion of their journey west.

"Sit down. Sit down, Joe. At last we've begun to hire men for the far western relay stations. I'd begun to despair of having the stations open on time. I haven't heard in some weeks how the building of the station is progressing, so you might have to stay in a tent a few days or possibly several weeks until they finish your house. We'll provide at least that for you. The corrals and stables will take longer, and it'll be helpful if you're good with carpentry work. Make it go much faster, if you can help in that respect. Your station will be an overnight stop; about halfway between Denver City and Colorado Springs; relatively flat land on the east, forests and mountains on the west." He looked at Joe inquiringly, took a puff of his cigar, and blew the smoke ceiling ward.

"Yes, I can do carpentry work, and we've brought seeds and tools for a garden vegetable patch, and if possible, I hope to have time to plant and cultivate some oats, corn and wheat. My wife says she wants to provide as much variety to the meals for the passengers as possible. Of course, it won't happen this year, the fresh vegetables, because of the late season, but for the future. The company has no objections to that, do they?" Joe hadn't thought to ask for permission to grow crops on company land. He anxiously looked at his boss.

"No. No, objections." Baldwin gazed at this new station manager, pleased with what he heard. It appeared the man planned to stay. It was hard to keep station attendants on the frontier. "Do whatever you think best for your own comfort. These isolated stations are in somewhat of an experimental state; haven't been able to expand to the western and northern territories like the owners wanted because of the war, but I'm sure they'll have no problem with your wife serving fresh vegetables to the guests. Fresh oats for the animals would be better, in case the supplies get caught in a rain storm or stolen by the Indians. We haven't had trouble the last few years, but there are bandits as well as redskins on the trails. Had many caravans robbed on the Santa Fe Trail before and after the war with Mexico. We'll try our best to get your supplies to you on time, but I like a man who thinks for himself."

He leaned forward and smashed his cigar into a small

glass bowl on the desk, extinguishing the flame. He paused and looked out the window at some children playing on the lawn with a dog. He smiled at their antics and then continued. He turned back to Joe and coughed as though embarrassed, but Joe couldn't understand why he would be uneasy. He was the one who made the decisions, after all. Joe was just an employee.

"I've hired a man to help you with the animals. Name of Zedediah Jones. For some odd reason he's called Buck. Don't know why; didn't ask him. I suppose at one time, he must have been thrown from a horse, or some such nonsense. An ex-Army man. Has an Injun squaw name of Rosie. That going to be a problem with you?"

Joe knew that he would have a helper with the animals, and John Dempsey had hinted that he would be an ex-soldier, like himself, but then there were hundreds of men looking for work, good men who had fought in the war on both sides of the fence. Which side was the question. He knew it was too late to matter, but he needed to ask so he would be prepared in advance. The man's choice of woman didn't concern him.

"Yankee or Southern?"

His boss looked him in the eyes, with a speculative frown on his brow. "Union, of course. He spent thirty years in the service, mostly in the Southwest. A little long in the tooth, but experience is useful in this business. He'll be staying in his own room, part of the outbuildings; don't know if it'll be ready for him when he gets there. Said he didn't want to come between you and the missus. Retired on a half-pay pension, which, from what he says, is a long time in coming. We've put in a bid for the mail service. If we can get that, he'll receive his pay sooner."

Joe thought he had better get off the subject of Buck Jones fast. It wouldn't do to fight that war all over again with his superiors in the business. He'd wait until he met the man before he judged his character.

"You think there's a chance for the mail contract?"

"Bound to, what with the passengers and freight moving along the established trails in increasing numbers. Someone is sure to start building the railroads west. I heard about an East Coast to West Coast line to connect the whole continent."

"How does that impact your stage lines?" Joe needed this to be a long-term position. If the railroads took over, that might be a problem.

"Don't you worry. Stage coaches are here for a long time. The more immigrants that travel, the more imperative the need for the railroads, and the territories will be made into states as soon as the population grows, but the short routes will still be necessary between towns and small villages. The world is changing right in front of our eyes, Joe." He paused, then continued in a different voice as if saying something that some might consider counterintuitive to a stage man's good sense. "A wise man would be smart to invest in railroads, if he had the money."

Joe thought about Hannah's money in the bank, even now being transferred to Denver City. He'd never been much of a gambler, so he'd leave it where it was, railroad or no railroads.

There came a short rap on the door, and the daughter Gladys came in. Joe saw that she had changed into a pale pink wool dress. "Papa, Mama says you've been holed up in here with the guest long enough; time to come eat."

"Thank you, daughter, we'll be right there." He rose from his chair and led the way from the library to the dining room. Nothing more was said between them about stage lines or railroads or Indian squaws.

At first glance, Joe thought there were a dozen children in various sizes and ages sitting around the table, but in reality there were only six, and they were introduced to him one at a time. Hannah seemed to be already well acquainted with each one. The baby was not among them, and Joe was later told the child had been given to the nurse for the night. All through the meal, which was lavish and well cooked, the chattering of children interrupted the adults at will. The larger ones helped the younger with his or her food. Joe was overwhelmed, and his eyes met with Hannah's over his napkin. She smiled. "Later," she seemed to say to him.

At last, when Joe was ready to explode with impatience and frustration, the children were dismissed and sent to bed. The silence was intoxicating. The four adults sat in the parlor as old friends, discussing everything from the weather, here and during the coming trip; politics; and the latest in women's fashion; interspersed with plans for the new stage line. The men sat at one end and the women at the other, and a game of cards was soon introduced. It was very late when the couples separated to their individual rooms for the night.

Joe awoke with the remains of a horrible dream still in his mind, of men dying on the field, and him as a youth trying to catch a butterfly that flew from flower to flower. It was pure fantasy, and he was troubled over its meaning. Hannah was fast asleep beside him, her breathing calm and steady. Somewhere in the house, he heard the baby crying, and the sound of a woman's voice. The crying stopped. He wondered if Hannah wanted children; they hadn't discussed the matter. He wasn't sure, after tonight's experience with the Baldwin clan, whether he wanted them himself. It was something that would take care of itself in time, he supposed.

Hannah's profile was visible in the window's dim light, her neck scars hidden under the covers wrapped around her shoulders. Her long hair spread across the pillow. Joe was now accustomed to having her in his bed, and the scars on her face and neck were not nearly so prominent in his mind. He even accepted that she was beautiful when she was asleep. He felt himself quicken to her warmth and the soft whisper of her breath coming toward him. A strange new feeling of desire came over him. It was relief from his unwelcomed night of troubled sleep, surely brought on by the day's unusual tensions, he guessed. What would she do if he took her in his arms and overwhelmed her with his kisses and passion? Would she reject him? No, he decided. She would lie under him with her usual calm acceptance of his manhood. She never complained or turned aside from his advances. He forced himself to turn onto his back so he couldn't see her face.

His mind moved on to the conversation with his superior and the responsibilities that he had taken on himself. What would he find when they arrived at the station? Would he be able to get along with a career Union Army man? Could they discuss the war without rancor or bitterness over the outcome? Slowly his mind began to drift into an incoherent scramble of ideas, memories and dreams. He turned and covered Hannah with one arm, listened to her soft, feminine snore and slept peacefully the rest of the night.

The next morning was a mad dash against time. The children were constantly underfoot as the adults ate breakfast and prepared for the day. Joe and Hannah dressed for the trip and packed the essentials of life in their brightly colored carpetbags. The carriage was brought around, hugs were shared among the two women and the children, and the goodbye sounds lingered in the air of the house long after the guests were gone.

Baldwin drove in the same manner as the day before, and Hannah wasn't sure that she was prepared for the trip, if the stage driver was cast from the same mold as the regional manager. Joe had his mind on the baggage again. Although he'd been assured that it would arrive safely, he couldn't give up the notion of bandits or Indians attacking the supply wagons. At the last moment, standing outside the door of the stage station, Baldwin took a small covered basket from the back of the carriage and placed it in Hannah's hands. She heard the whining sounds of an animal and inside the basket found a brown, black and white pup.

"Oh, what a precious puppy!" She looked questioningly at their host.

"A gift from the children. They insisted that he's well trained. I've brought a bag of food for him. If the stage driver objects to the extra weight, I'll speak to him. They said his name is Jack, but you can call him what you want." He stepped back and laughed indulgently at his children's strange notions. It was clear he was a good father, Joe thought, although too permissive by far with their rudeness and habits of dress.

Standing and watching Hannah with the pup, Joe could imagine trouble later for the Baldwins if their children were left uncontrolled, but the family was a happy one, so who was he to judge, since he wasn't a father himself. His thoughts drifted to his own father and mother and how the war had changed their lives. They had been happy, once; when the three boys were young and carefree and their only concerns the weather and the crops.

Baldwin remained until the coach arrived in front of the station. He explained to the driver that he'd given permission for the dog to travel on the stage. He carried a lot of weight in the Overland Stage Company, and the driver found no objections, although he was later overheard cursing officials who allowed dogs on coaches. Finally, the horses were hitched, the passengers leaped aboard, the luggage was stored in the rear boot, the driver took his seat in the box, and Baldwin shook hands with Joe one final time and wished him well in his new livelihood. The door closed, and the coach moved toward the edge of town. The wheels caught in the rutted street and tipped roughly to one side as it met a puddle of water. A young girl screeched at the new wet spots on her calicos, only to be jerked back to the wooden sidewalk by a craggy, clean-shaved man. The horses' shoes threw clods of unwelcome mud for a moment as the coach's hard, spinning wheels churned by. After a short time the wisps of fine brown dust settled, and the people went on about their business, the arrival and departure of the stage no concern of theirs.

Baldwin walked slowly toward his carriage, shaking his head at the loss of a potential friend, and the thought of a mischievous puppy inside the coach.

Five

The first leg of their journey by stage was uneventful. There were three other passengers, two of whom were an elderly couple going to the next town to visit their daughter, who was expecting a child any day. The woman talked endlessly about whatever subject crossed her mind. Occasionally, the men interrupted out of self-preservation and discussed politics and farming. The other passenger was a traveling salesman, who hunched unhappily in his corner, complaining the whole time about the presence of the puppy in their midst. Since the animal slept through most of the morning, no one took his complaints seriously.

The meal at noon was good, although not as pleasing as the one enjoyed the night before in the Baldwin household. However, it served to give the young couple an example of how to serve their future customers. The building was small, made of adobe with large wooden beams across the ceiling. It was cool and dim inside, with the only light coming from two kerosene lanterns and a few candles on the bare dining table. The corrals were well attended, and the water drawn from a deep well. It started Joe to thinking whether he should dig a well to supplement the spring water at their station, in case there was a drought. He spent the afternoon making plans in his mind for his place.

In the late afternoon, they arrived at their next station and the elderly couple left them with a mutual wish for their well-being. Except for the salesman—Delaney Shelton, Joe was told by the station manager—who continued to grumble about the food, the dust, the dog, and the rocky road, Joe and Hannah were alone. Shelton complained about the heat and opened the curtain for some air, then closed it complaining about the dust.

The station was not very different from the first, and Joe could see that the pattern was set for the whole route. He decided he'd have trouble remembering all he was told, and he took out his pencil and small tablet and began making a list of facts. Whether they were important or not would wait to be seen. There was a small creek nearby, and no well. He asked the attendant about the water supply and was told the creek never ran dry, even in drought conditions. The meal was beans, salt pork, and dry biscuits, but satisfactory. Hannah was glad they had brought the seeds and extra cloth for curtains. They picked up five more riders, all men. Three climbed inside and started a conversation with the salesman. He seemed to be more content and friendly on the next leg of the trip. The other men sat on the top of the coach.

On through the long night and the next day, and another night, the coach moved, stopping only for short breaks to change horses. At different points, the men left them, even the disgruntled traveling salesman, and they picked up two soberly dressed women who seemed friendly after a few moments' hesitation, and Hannah welcomed the feminine conversation, since there weren't many ladies traveling west.

The early morning stop at Mozier Station was the last before arriving at their own station, and currently as far as the coach would travel west, except to drop off Joe and Hannah. The two friendly ladies left them to continue their way south.

The sun was barely above the horizon, but Joe could see that the building was much larger than the others, being currently a major artery from north to south. It housed, besides the manager, his wife and small children, an animal handler named Tim, and the drivers who were resting between stops.

Standing beside the corral in the half-light of daybreak, Tim explained to Joe that it was the general tradition that a driver drove from one site to another, rested or spent the night and then reversed his route, back to where he began. He was awarded his own bed at these layover stops. Sweetwater Station would be such a place. They would use mules at this final stop instead of horses, Joe was told, for they were stronger to pull the vehicle through the deep sand in which they would soon be traveling once they left the river behind.

Joe spent the whole time jotting down notes in his tablet, and making a diagram of the building, corrals, and other ideas that came to him. He sketched in simple mountains as far away clouds on the distant horizon, recognizing them from the maps he had been given in Indiana.

The information was confirmed by the animal handler, who gazed at them with a wistful look in his eyes. The great Rocky Mountains could be seen in the distance and Indiana seemed far away. Joe wondered if he should write a letter to his parents and to Hannah's uncle, to let them know they had arrived. There was no regular mail service, but maybe the letters would get through somehow. The thought was as good as the action, and he tore a few pages from his tablet and began to write.

Hannah took the puppy, Jack, for a walk, and smiled at his antics, remembering the Baldwin children who had named him. She made some sandwiches of beef and bread and asked for a jar of water for them to eat their last meal in the coach. She noticed that the woman had a small garden area with a few root vegetables. They discussed what grew best in the altitude and soil.

Since they would be neighbors of sorts, the woman was friendly and the man cooperative with Joe, first giving his name as Sam Mozier. With an apologetic smile, he agreed to send the letters out, but wasn't sure if they would get to their destination. "Rustlers," Sam explained in an offhand way, with a shrug of the shoulders. "They sneak up on a man at night."

"Cattle?" Joe frowned. He didn't expect to keep cattle.

"Not so loud," Sam hissed, looking at the distant mountains. "Horses. Some people say the red man ain't got far without he has a way to get back to his paints. There's wild horses out there, but you catch 'em, and the injuns come after 'em."

"Paints?" Joe was intrigued by the man's secretive manner, and wondered if he was overly sensitive to the lonely atmosphere of the desert.

"Spotted horses. Mostly white with brown or black spots. Comanches especially like the loud coat coloring. But, the plains tribes'll take anything with four legs."

"What do we do?" The free roaming horses were part of Dempsey's plans for Joe's station. This was a setback if the Indians caught the feral horses before Joe could nab them.

"Branding works, but there's the missus." He lowered his voice. "She don't like this talk. We'll speak of it another time."

"Hello, I'm Rebecca, and you must be Joe. I'm pleased to meet you." The pleasant-faced woman had a short, clipped Eastern accent, although Joe was certain he could detect a hint of a Southern drawl. Sam's speech pattern was pure Southern.

"Joe!" Hannah was right behind Sam's wife. "Guess where Rebecca and Sam last lived?"

"Um, California?" He took Rebecca's hand and as quickly released it. What really interested him was the idea of branding the horses. Wouldn't the Indians take the horses anyway? Brands would have no meaning to the tribes. Hannah brought his attention back to her.

"No, Joe, they lived in Kentucky and before that in Vermont," thus confirming Joe's assessment of the woman's accent. "You remember the Jenkins family that attended the church for a while came from Kentucky. They had a son named Sylvester, and the boys teased him unmercifully about his stutter." She sighed. "They didn't stay long."

"Yes, I do remember him, Hannah; tall, overly thin. Brown hair?"

Rebecca impatiently looked from one to the other, and took Hannah's hand. The dog gave a growl and jumped down. Joe grabbed him before he could get away and handed him back to Hannah.

"Oh, it's so fine to have neighbors again," Rebecca exclaimed breathlessly. "We've been here two years, and it's sometimes lonely with no woman to talk to. Hannah, dear, do come into the house and write down that recipe for baked squash that we discussed when we were in the garden."

With the women gone, Joe opened his mouth to ask about the branding of the horses, but was interrupted by a commotion from the house.

The driver, an old timer with a long gray beard and bald head going by the name of Rusty, a nickname for Russell Backgammon, was not happy driving the extra miles. He stomped down the steps and came to a halt in front of Joe and Sam.

"You folks keep adding more line, but I don't get any younger. Don't get no extra pay, either." He huffed, but he sported a rough smile as he gave a puff on his cigar.

He took the stogy from his lips and pointed toward the south. "I heard tell yore animal handler's coming from the south. Don't envy that driver. That's a rough route coming up from the Springs; dry and dusty all the way. I saw old Buck Jones once at Fort Laramie when he was in the Army. Big fellow; got a temper. You got any fresh cigars, Hadley?"

"No. I'm sorry. I don't smoke."

"Shame." Rusty shrugged his disappointment. "Best get the missus out here soon. Time's a'wasting. Hey, Scrappy, time to go!" He bellowed to his partner, who was still at the

49

table eating. Phineas Knell, the stage guard and relief driver, was known more familiarly on the stage line as Scrappy for his way of surviving with little more than a rabbit-skin bag holding some jerked beef and a canteen of water.

The ladies came from the house, Hannah carrying a small basket of fresh vegetables from Rebecca's garden on her arm. She let the dog ramble around, sniffing the wagon wheels.

The driver checked his mules' harness and the coach's axles. He made sure they were ready for the extra miles of travel. He lobbed some grease on the axles, explaining to the newcomer that the dry desert soil was hard on the axles and wheels, and there was a danger of breakdown at any time if they were not soft and damp with the grease. Joe jotted it down in his notebook: "make sure the axles leave the station with grease".

Scrappy finished his meal as he left the house and walked to the coach, his shotgun hoisted over his shoulders. He threw his rabbit-skin bag carelessly on top and climbed aboard to the high seat.

Joe picked up the dog and thrust him into the coach. He lifted their carpetbags and the bag of sandwiches that Hannah had made and tossed them after the puppy. He and Hannah stepped into the coach and shut the door. The dog sniffed at the food bag and wagged his tail. Joe leaned from the door and waved at Rebecca and Sam, thinking his curiosity about the horse branding was never answered, and unsure if it was important.

Rusty took one last look at his mules and leaped aboard, unfastened his whip, let go of the brake, and the mules burst forth and on their way at a trot. Rusty drew them back to a walk, for there was no schedule to keep to this last stop on their way. He had heard a rumor that the horses and mules had arrived at the station but the corrals were not finished, and the house had no roof. It was not his problem, though. He had his tent in the coach, and his possibles bag with some beef jerky if he needed some food. He knew that Knell always came prepared too, for a body never knew when the coach would break down, or a horse or mule go lame between stops.

The excitement inside the coach grew with the miles passing behind them. For the first few minutes, the couple discussed the sights and sounds of the last station, while Joe ate his food and took long sips from the water jar. When he finished eating and gave the few bits of meat and crumbs to the dog, he leaned back and relaxed. Eventually, he burst forth with his plans for the site, and Hannah joined him in his enthusiasm. The puppy jumped from Hannah's lap and barked, as if he, too, wanted to take part in the conversation.

They were grateful that they were alone in the coach. The miles disappeared in the dust and bits of bison chips flung aloft by the wheels. On the left side of the stage was a line of trees along the banks of the river. With the beauty of the passing scenery, silence soon filled the coach, each partner deep in personal thoughts, and they watched in fascination as the coach came within fifty yards of the water. The sun glistened on the surface of the river as it passed between the tree branches. Suddenly, the road curved out away from the river, and Joe looked at Hannah with disappointment. In another hour, they were crossing the deep sand, and Joe wondered aloud to Hannah if he should get out and walk to lighten the load, but Rusty didn't slow the coach's momentum.

More than two days and nights on the road and the constant droning of the animals' hooves took their toll, and Hannah leaned on Joe's shoulder and began to doze. She was startled awake by a yell from the top of the stage, and the dog jumped from the seat and shook himself.

"Thar she is, just ahead!"

Joe couldn't see anything on the right side of the coach. He moved to the left, but there was nothing visible outside that window, either. Another ten minutes of waiting, and

Hannah pointed to the trees growing thickly along the Sweetwater creek, formed from the springs that gave the station its name. Joe sat on the end of the seat, gazing in awe at the sight of a forest of green, after so many miles of scrub bushes and desert cacti. His heart was beating fast and his palms were damp inside his leather gloves. He was here at last; his and Hannah's new home.

Rusty eased back on the reins to bring the mules to a slow walk and pulled on the brake, which gave a squeal of protest. They moved cautiously across the shallow creek crossing. The water danced under the mules' hooves, splashing the front of the coach, and it dipped slightly to the side as the water rose to the hubs of the wheels. Hannah hung on tightly to the leather strap, fearing they would tip over. She could see the rushing water on both sides of the coach, and for the briefest moment she was reminded of the ride on the steamboats. Rusty brought them safely up the bank to the far side and then let the animals have their run for the last one hundred yards of the road. He pulled out his brass trumpet and gave a loud long toot that startled Jack, who set up a frenzied barking and scrambled into Hannah's lap in fright.

The coach stopped under a cluster of cottonwood trees. Joe turned to Hannah, his eyes glowing with excitement.

"Do you see that? We have trees. Who'd have thought we would be blessed with trees like in Indiana?"

He could hardly suppress his excitement and opened the door without waiting for Rusty or Knell to dismount from their seats high in the box. He stepped from the coach onto a soft cushion of decaying leaves and broken twigs. He gazed in awe at the sight of maybe two dozen tents, spread out in a vast clearing near the spring. Men swarmed around the building and grounds of the place. The large house itself was near completion. The men, having finished the roof, were working on the windows and doors. Half hidden in the ground along the bottom of the walls was a line of flat stones, a solid foundation for the building's construction. The dominant trees filling the bulk of the landscape seemed to be Ponderosa pines and Douglas firs. The cottonwood and willow trees near the creek were tall, stately and green in color. He thought he recognized piñon pines, junipers and spruce trees as well.

The contractor had chosen a site for the house under the greenery's leafy overgrowth and to the left of the springs, within easy walking distance. Joe began to walk toward the men, who hailed the coach with interest. He saw several wagons parked near the tents, and assumed they were the source of travel for the men, but Baldwin was as good as his word, and the supplies had arrived only a few hours before, waiting to be unloaded. The horses and mules were gathered in a corral made of split logs. There was an assortment of chickens clucking around the house's yard. Joe was certain he caught a glimpse of goats in a rope corral under the shade of a great cottonwood tree.

The men stopped work at the sight of the old brown stage coach in their midst and gathered around the stranger.

A shout of raucous laughter erupted from the crowd and several other men ran from the site along the road they were carving through a portion of the forest for the stage coaches to go through to the other side. Maybe forty men altogether, tough hard-working men with beards and dressed in dirty and sweat dampened clothes, were working on the station and the road. The planners had decided to cut through the forest for a few miles instead of circling around and crossing the river twice. It would be better to build one bridge than two. The extra lumber from the forest would be used to build additional stations along the road to Denver.

Hannah sat alone in the coach, the only woman within twenty-five miles. She slowly gathered her skirts and stepped from the protection of her enclosed carriage. Jack darted down the steps, at first hidden by her wide skirts, but she pulled one leg back to let him pass, giving him permission to roam, sniffing here and there as he followed some secret trail of his own. She stood at the side of the coach, the bite of the afternoon sun on one side of her face and a small breeze caressing the other, wondering whether she should join the men's group or wait for Joe to discover he had abandoned her. She pulled her wide-brimmed hat more securely on her head to provide a bit of relief from the sun's glare.

The shade of the trees called to her, and after a minute's hesitation, she accepted that if Joe spent all his time fawning over her, there would be no one to run the station.

She found a soft bed of grass and sat under the heavy overhang of the tree, grateful for the cool breeze that passed by and worked the fabric of her blouse. She closed her eyes for a moment in pleasure. She spread her skirts modestly across the long blades and leaned back on her arms, letting the peace of the moment calm her nerves. A screech was heard overhead, and she straightened and squinted up at the clear blue sky through the leaves of the trees. She saw what she thought was a hawk circling in the air above her. She smiled at the bird. For the first time in her life, she felt free; this was her new home. There was the building, and sitting underneath the tree, her joy was complete. She bowed her head in prayer.

A loud bark brought Hannah from her meditation. It was Jack, drawing her attention as he worried a small creature he had discovered in the bushes. She called to him to quiet down, but he barked the louder, breaking away and running across the yard.

Immediately, a loud yell arose from the men.

"Come, Zig!" A voice rang out, filled with the lilt of enthusiasm, although there was no suggestion of the speaker. "It's a womanfolk!"

"Ah, Beaker!" The source of the reply was more obvious, as a heavyset, bearded man slammed the tip of a long-handled shovel into a patch of broken soil and spat into the dirt before continuing. "What do you know of a woman? You ain't never held one since your momma suckled you last, you being the runt of the litter."

Joe frowned at the yelling men as he passed them, his baleful glare bringing the full gathering's attention to the woman sitting near the stage coach. He walked straight to her, while Rusty the driver explained this strange sight in the middle of the wilderness.

"What you'all looking at there? You ain't never seen a genteel lady afore now? You treat her kindly now, you hear, and spit in your tin cans instead of the dirt, 'cause nobody can expect a lady to walk around in yore spit spots." He pushed his hat to the back of his bald head and spat on the ground. He grinned at the men's wonderstruck faces as Hannah rose and dusted off the back of her skirts and prepared herself for the glances of the men.

Joe took her by the hand and guided her to the men. She noticed the embarrassed glances and cautious whispers of the men as they first looked at her damaged face. Some turned away, while others coughed behind their hands or shuffled their feet.

Joe walked boldly up and declared in a proud voice, "This is my wife, Hannah, who cooks the best apple pies in Indiana." He dared the men to reject her presence in their midst, and with shamed glances, they ceased to stare.

Surprised laughter arose among the men, as Jack came to the front and barked loudly at the unfamiliar faces. One of the men, average height and with the beginning of a paunch, tried to grab the dog, but he ran away. Shouts of encouragement echoed among the trees as more men noticed the presence of the mischievous puppy, running with his tail wagging with happiness, followed by the young man.

The man leaped after Jack and caught his foot on a fallen branch, going down on his left side. He held his right hand up, smiling sheepishly as another worker helped him stand. With the advent of the puppy, his tail wagging in triumph, followed by the antics of the young man, they all turned and became a friendly bunch of workers, instead of shocked bystanders.

One man stepped forward, a giant with blond hair and gray eyes, and bowed over her hand. There was a twinkle in his eyes. "Mrs. Hadley, welcome to Colorado and to Sweetwater Station. We'll have your cooking stove ready for you in a few days, and I hope you'll let us find out for ourselves if your husband's boast is true. I'm Clifton Taylor, the boss of this mangy group of tent dwellers. I apologize for our delayed reception and uncouth welcome. We're not used to seeing a woman in our midst, you understand."

"Of course, Mr. Taylor. I can see that we have interrupted your work." She smiled at the group, trying to notice individual characteristics that might help her untangle the identities of each man. "A real stove, did you say? Oh, that will be most welcome, indeed. I had thought that I would have to cook in a fireplace."

Taylor pointed toward one of the wagons. "There she is, ma'am, straight from St. Louis, forged from the best iron smelters in Missouri. Just came in with the freight wagons this morning. We'll have it set up for you by tomorrow morning, for sure. If you don't mind, I'll introduce you to some of the men. This red-haired jack-of-all-trades is my foreman and stonemason, Odell Graham, from Ireland, who washed ashore in Baltimore, and was determined to see the Wild West and the Red Indians of the plains."

"Hello, ma'am. Pleased to meet you. Your foundation stones are my handiwork." Graham smiled with a degree of pride as he politely shook her hand and stepped back for the next man. He wasn't embarrassed to look at her face for he had known a child in his village in Ireland with similar scars who had been burned by a boiling pot of water fallen from the stove. The child had died within the year of infections. He felt compassion for Hannah and respect for Josiah Hadley for his strong defense of his woman.

One by one, the men moved forward, each with a word of encouragement and a hand shake. She spoke to them graciously and repeated their names when they called them out. They shook Joe's hand and some paused to talk with him a few minutes. All the while the other man was chasing after Jack, who seemed to enjoy the game immensely. Finally, they both collapsed under the shade of a tree, exhausted. The dog was content to be petted by the stranger. Hannah's hand was tingling and red when the last of the workers passed by and returned to their work. It was a good beginning, she thought later.

Even before the introductions were halfway advanced, Rusty, the stage driver, and Knell, the guard, had unhitched the team and driven them into the temporary corral, then selected six of the fresh mules to pull the stage back to the Mozier place, and hobbled them apart from the others. They would start back later on their return trip. They pulled their bedrolls from the top of the stage and ate a supper of dried beef and drank from the cool waters of the spring. Rolling their blankets under a tree, they slept undisturbed by the sounds of the workers hammering and sawing in the court-yard of the future station.

Graham went to the supply wagon and selected a large, surplus canvas army tent for the station manager and his wife. Calling on two of the men for help, they soon had a temporary home set up for the couple. A table and a few hand-made chairs from their own camp were placed inside the tent, along with their personal luggage. One of the car-penters was ordered to make a bed. They uncovered the wood-burning iron stove, and by nightfall, it was installed in its place in the house and ready for cooking. One of the road builders was chopping firewood to feed the stove. Graham's final act of the day was to dig out the tools necessary for making pies.

Joe spent the rest of the afternoon looking over the ani-mals, accompanied by two other men, who professed to be experienced horsemen. He examined each animal closely and selected certain ones to be separated from the others. He counted eighteen horses and thirteen mules, enough for several teams to pull coaches.

He moved from the horses to the mules and discovered, to his amazement, in a small clearing under a willow, two donkeys, a male and a female. He gazed at them in awe. He remembered what Dempsey had said about the mustangs, and wondered if he expected him to breed some of the wild horses with the donkeys.

After looking them over carefully, he moved with his two friendly comrades to the six goats: three females, and three males. Along with two dozen or more chickens, he could see that Baldwin had planned for a long stay. A sense of almost overwhelming responsibility attacked him. For the first time since taking the position of station manager, an occupation for which he had no experience, he began to wonder if he was capable of the work. He had grown up on a farm, and was experienced with animals, but always there had been his father and two older brothers to guide and help him. Once the carpenters and road builders were gone, it would be just the Union soldier and him to care for the animals.

Hannah was having a similar panic attack of her own, once Graham had uncovered the huge two-oven wood-burning stove in the wagon and set it up on the platform in the house. She had cooked on her aunt's kitchen stove many times, but it was half the size of this black and silver monster. She examined with bewildered awe the burners, the ovens, and the smoke stack. It would take a mountain of wood to keep this great beast alive. She glanced nervously at the men working on the windows and doors, certain they expected her to bake them apple pies before the sun was gone from the sky. She wanted to sit down and cry. Instead, she enlisted the help of one of the men and began to sort through the supplies for her utensils and knives.

Rusty and Knell rose from their naps and after a quick meal from the carpenters' communal kitchen, hitched the team and started back for the eastern station. He reminded

Joe to expect another coach within a few days bringing Buck Jones and his Indian wife. He conferred with Taylor and was assured that the next station would be built within the month. After finishing a few more details, Jackson and his men would be leaving in a few days to start west, pushing the road building farther that direction. Blowing a last farewell on his brass bugle, Rusty pulled out for the Mozier station, carrying in his shirt pocket a second letter to Joe's parents in case the first one got lost in transit.

It was a noisy group that sat around the campfires that night. One of the men pulled out a fiddle from his pack and played a mournful tune, until someone complained and he switched to a cheerful ditty. Guards were set up on the out-skirts of the camp to watch for Indians or bandits. Although occasions of a violent nature were rare in the Territory, the building crew was nevertheless cautious and prepared for trouble. There were expensive supplies and equipment that would tempt the lawless if it were known that they were there. The horses and mules would provide a tribe of Indians with transportation to raid their enemies, and the other ani-mals would provide winter provisions.

Joe and Hannah spent the first night at Sweetwater Sta-tion in the canvas army tent. The bed was rough-hewn and hastily built. The carpenter, a man called "Carp," strung lengths of rope across the sides from left to right and from top to bottom. Joe, who had supervised the packing of their personal goods, knew the right trunk in which the mattress of soft goose feathers and the blankets and pillows had been placed to keep them dry and clean. He spread them out on their new bed and soon they were fast asleep, lulled by the sound of hushed men's conversations and the strumming of the fiddle. Jack lay content beside the bed, curled in a ball of soft brown, white and black fur.

Hannah was up before the cock crowed and started a fire in the huge iron stove, building up the initial blaze with a handful of small pine cones she'd picked up the day before.

Jack followed her every move with watchful, intelligent eyes and his tail hanging low at his back. After carrying the table and two chairs into the kitchen for Hannah's convenience, and the bed and bedding into the first bedroom in the right hand hallway, Joe went out to the temporary corral to check on the animals and visit with the night guards. Jack followed him, barking at imaginary critters. They walked around the perimeter of the grounds, careful not to intrude on the affairs of the workmen.

A heavy fog lay on the ground near the creek, casting a ghostly gloom over the scene. Joe took a deep breath of satisfaction, and walked to the chicken coop for eggs. He brought a half dozen into the house.

The dog rushed inside the house ahead of him as he opened the door, almost causing him to stumble and fall. It was warm inside after the early morning chill. He glanced at Hannah, standing by the table, her hair neatly combed and her clean dress of a pink gingham material. Joe liked Hannah in pink; it seemed to suit her. He badly wanted to go and kiss her but refrained.

"I believe the animals have spent a restful night. I think I'll do some exploring after breakfast to see if I can find the box canyon Dempsey told me about. No telling if Buck Jones and his woman will be on the stage today. Probably be best to do the exploring while you have the protection of the other men about. Dempsey said it's about ten miles away. Shouldn't take me long to ride up and see what I can find before Jones gets here."

"That's fine, Joe." Hannah adjusted the damper on the hulking behemoth in front of her. She pulled up a bowl from earlier. "Eggs and bacon, will that do?"

"And coffee? I think I smell coffee." Joe stood at the side, unsure of himself. He wanted to help by taking the bowl, but this was something he had no sense about, personal relationships with a woman. It was enough that the animals outside now depended on him, but Hannah seemed so confident of her skills. "Is there something I can do before I leave?"

"No, thank you. I'll bake the pies and some bread while you're gone. If the men finish the windows, I'll have Mr. Taylor ask one of them to bring in the rest of our supplies."

Hannah was flushed with the heat from the stove, and she worried her hand where a splatter of bacon grease shone on her skin. She didn't look up, so missed the expression of anger on Joe's face. He was surprised at the sharp pang of jealousy that crossed his mind as he thought of some stranger in his cabin with Hannah. If anyone had asked him, he would have denied the emotion, but in the last few weeks, he had grown accustomed to having her alone with him. He was only now realizing that she was an individual of courage and integrity. At home in Indiana, she had been overshadowed by her cousins and her aunt Ethel. He was pleased that she had come with him to Colorado; more pleased than he was comfortable admitting even to himself.

"Joe, have you given thought to where Buck and his wife will sleep? We'll have four rooms, but we might need three of them for the stage drivers or the passengers. And, the barn hasn't been built yet for the animals."

Joe thoughtfully added intelligence to his list of praises for his wife. He had not taken the time to think about the prospect of Buck's actual arrival. Now that it was brought to his attention, he considered prejudices many people held against Indians. There could be recriminations if he housed the couple in one of the rooms next to the guests.

"Thank you. I hadn't thought that far ahead, but of course, if they arrive today, they'll need a place to sleep. It would be only right that they take one of the rooms in the house, since he's an employee of the company, but I don't think the guests would appreciate the honor of it. I'll talk to Taylor about buying the tent from him. At least that would solve the problem until we can build either a separate cabin or the barn. Maybe I should postpone my exploring for another day." He frowned as he considered the perplexing problem.

"Sit down and eat your breakfast, Joe. Talk it over with Mr. Taylor, for I'm sure he has experience in these matters, but I don't think you should postpone your explorations today." Hannah placed the heated plate of crisp bacon and fried eggs in front of him. She turned to pour a cup of coffee just as a hail came at the door.

"Hello, who goes inside! Hadley, are you in there?"

"Come on in, Mr. Taylor, and join us for breakfast." Hannah placed the coffee pot on the stove and turned to get another cup as Taylor walked in the open doorway. He looked like a man who hadn't slept; his face was red on one side, and his hair not yet combed. His clothes were wrinkled and dusty.

"Thank you, I'd like that." He sat down in the only other chair in the house, its mates still in the tent. He took a sip of the hot, fragrant coffee and leaned back with a sigh. "Had a little trouble this morning with the road crew. 'Couple of fellows got into a fight over the war. It happens sometimes, even though the official fighting is over. Folks from the South are extra sensitive to remarks from the Northerners, and Northerners like to tease the Southerners about their slaves. I don't reckon most of those Southern gents even owned slaves. Some of the tougher men lived west of the Missouri all their lives, never once crossed the Mississippi." He sighed and drained the coffee cup. Hannah refilled it and poured the rest of the dark brew into Joe's cup. She filled her own plate with eggs and bacon and placed it on the table in front of the building crew boss. Taylor took the spoon and dug in, as though he hadn't eaten in a month of Sundays.

"How'd the battle come out this time?" Joe had been watching the tableau and wondered what Hannah would eat. Maybe he would have to borrow some more eggs from the chickens. She began to gather a couple of bowls together and placed the tins of flour and salt on the table. He turned his attention back to Taylor, who was talking as he ate.

"South won, which will give 'em more reason to fight next time. I gotta admit those men from the South know how to swing a punch. I had to punish both men, or I'd have had a riot on my hands. I put 'em to work felling the trees. That'll quiet 'em down for a while. Most of the men've lived tough, hard lives. We're lucky to get 'em. Have you thought of where you'll put your animal handler when he comes?" Joe glanced at Hannah, who was mixing lard and salt with the flour to make biscuits. She looked up and grinned.

"We were just discussing that very thing, when you came in. I'm wondering if I can buy that nice army tent we slept in last night from you for a fair price. It won't be good for the cold weather, but it would do until then. Once Jones gets here, we'll build them a cabin, or could be his wife knows how to build a shelter. I don't know much about the fellow; where he lives when not working for the company. Baldwin seemed to think he's a hardy worker with animals. I'll sure be glad to have him with us."

"Well, let me think. I got several extra tents left so I can't see why I shouldn't let you have that one that Graham took from the pack." He looked closely at Joe, wondering how much the man could afford to pay. "How about twenty dollars for the tent and the poles and a loose tarpaulin set up for a porch? Lots of fellows swear it keeps the rain out better to have a front porch."

"Done, and a bargain at that." Joe stood up and took his leather coin holder from his pocket. He found a twenty dollar gold piece and handed it to Taylor. They shook hands, but Joe kept the other man's hand in his a mite longer than normal. "Now, it's not that I don't trust a person who's generous with his supplies like that, but I'd like a receipt. Don't want those fancy pants guys coming for a visit from the East and accusing me of stealing company property, you know." He released Taylor's hand and smiled.

Taylor broke out in a loud laugh. "Damn, Joe, but I wish

you were working for me. A smooth character like you would go a long way toward settling the disputes between the North and the South." He grinned and took out a small tablet from his wallet and a pencil from his pocket and wrote a receipt for one company tent, six poles and a tarpaulin. He surprised Joe by handing it to Hannah, who took it with her floured hand. "You hold on tight to that note, Mrs. Hadley, in case those fancy pants company men come when Joe ain't around. Thanks for the hearty breakfast, ma'am." He left the room, still chuckling under his breath.

Joe quickly put his hat on his head and followed him out. They stopped a few steps from the tent entrance. Taylor started laughing again, and then soberly looked to the far distant mountains. "Gonna be a long summer, I'm thinking, which is good for my business. We might have time to build that next station and one or two more, if I can keep those misfits from fighting all the time. If it holds clear to September, we might have the stage running from Mozier's place to Denver in time for the fall travel season. That'll please the authorities, but whether they can find good men to manage the stations is all up to them. I just build the houses and corrals. Now, Jackson, he's the engineer who's supervising the road gang, has decided to move the crew to another camp today. That'll cut down considerably on my strength in case of attack from marauders. I'll put two of my carpenters to work finishing the fence around this place, and I'll have to be on my way. If Jones doesn't come in today, you'll be on your own in a few days." He looked at Joe with apprehension in his eyes.

"Yes, I've thought of that. Baldwin assured me that his intelligence agents claim that there are no Indians on the war path this summer. They stay mostly along the major trails between St. Louis and Santa Fe. They haven't realized yet that the stage coaches bring settlers from the east. Those same settlers will be yearning to set up towns and homes. I suspect some bandits who were run out of Kansas and Nebraska might head this way, but if we all get frightened and run at the sign of trouble, the stage line'll never be built. Dempsey says it won't be many years before the moguls in the Eastern cities start talking about railroads. Civilization will be on the move soon. There's no stopping it, I'm thinking."

"Yeah, you're right. I've heard rumors that the bigwigs in Washington and New York are already mapping and surveying a route across the plains and mountains. Until civilization does get here, you watch your step. I'll roust out my crew and finish this job soon." He started to walk away.

"Wait, Mr. Taylor. I was thinking while I have a little time before Jones gets here, I'd do a little exploring around. It'll give me a better idea of what I'm up against if I know the lay of the land. Since your men have been here longer than me, I'd appreciate any advice on that score. If you'd keep an eye out for my wife while I'm gone, I'd be grateful. It won't be more than a few hours."

Taylor looked at Joe with speculation. He liked Joe. He liked him a lot. The man had a head on his shoulders. It was wise to take his tour of the area while there were men to protect the house and animals. He had several men watching the animals, which was not what they hired on to do, but he had persuaded them that it was important to their own mission to secure the animals against danger.

"Tell you what I'll do, Joe, I've got a man in my crew that knows this area mighty well. He grew up a few miles south of here. He's been valuable to both Jackson and me with the local terrain and wild critters. If you don't mind company on your sashay around the territory, I'll ask if he'd like a day off work."

Joe was in a quandary whether to take a stranger with him to the hidden box canyon, but before he could answer, Taylor looked toward the cook tent where his crew was beginning to emerge and take up their daily chores. He saw the man he wanted and called him over.

"Patterson, come here a minute." A large-boned man with dark hair and shaggy beard left his neighbors and walked toward the boss. He wore brown corduroy pants and a blue plaid shirt. A gun hung low on his hip, and he looked like a man who knew how to use it.

"Patterson, this is Joe Hadley, who has taken on the responsibility of running this station. Joe, Tom Patterson." The men shook hands and neither gave ground to the other. Although naturally suspicious of strangers, Joe decided he would take the man with him. He had to trust someone who knew the area, since he knew nothing about it. Taylor wouldn't have recommended him if he wasn't trustworthy. "Patterson, Joe has decided to explore the area a little and see what he's up against, in case the Indians or bandits decide to steal his animals and burn down that nice house we just finished for him. You reckon you can show him the area this morning?"

Thomas Patterson was surprised by the request. Or, was it a request? Maybe the boss was commanding him to guide the greenhorn. He looked more closely at Joe. He'd liked what he'd seen yesterday, and the gracious manner in which his wife had received the rowdy bunch of workers. He thought of the antics of Jupiter Smith and the dog. A trip around the area on a horse was better than working on the forest road.

"Well, Mr. Hadley, depends where you're planning to go, whether I want to ride along with you. Might be worth some smoking tobaccy to me." He had a quiet, lazy manner, but Joe wasn't deceived. He had known men like Patterson in his Army unit, pretending to be mild and humble, but deadly with a pistol or rifle in a fight. His brother James had been such a man. His instincts were telling him to take Patterson with him.

"Sure, you can have some tobacco when we get saddled up. My idea is to head a few miles northeast some distance west of where the South Platte River makes a sharp bend and then drops down toward the south. My map shows a clearing just before a stretch of deep water. I want to follow the ridge until it comes up to the base of that hill over there near Cherry Creek." He pointed toward a distant marker. "Have you ever been in that direction, or followed the creek to its source?"

"I been there." It was a simple statement, which Joe took to mean agreement with the route of the exploration that he had in mind.

"You got a horse of your own?"

"No, sir, I don't."

Joe turned to Taylor who was keeping up with the conversation, while at the same time watching his crew begin their work day. He could tell that the older man was anxious to get to his own business. "Taylor, if you'll loan me the use of your man for, say, three hours, I'll see that he's outfitted with horse, saddle and rifle. I'll pay for his time, if you think it necessary."

"No need to pay me for his time, Joe. You go on with your exploring. I'll keep an eye on the station for you."

Joe understood his intent, that he'd keep watch over Hannah while they were gone. The men shook hands and Taylor walked away toward his camp.

"Come along, Patterson, if you're willing, and we'll select a couple of horses from the stock in the corral." He didn't wait to see if the man followed. He walked with a brisk pace to the corral and dropped the bar into the circle of logs. He waved at the guards who knew him by sight since his visit the previous night. "Gonna select a couple of riding ponies, and take them up to the hills a ways, men." He turned to see Patterson a few steps back watching the guards with a wary eye. He walked among the horses until he saw a rangy bay stallion. He looked to be about four years old and accustomed to the saddle or team work. He turned and walked back to the gate.

Out of the corner of his eye, Joe saw that Patterson had

selected a sorrel mare, but he didn't try to approach the animal; he just looked at him with speculation in his glance. Joe walked over to his personal supply wagon, uncovered the top and lifted two saddles from the back of the vehicle. He dropped one on the ground, took out bridles and blankets, and placed one of each on top of the saddle. He marched back to the corral with his favorite saddle and blanket hitched over his shoulder. He noticed the two guards watching him closely.

Patterson finally moved from his position at the gate and went to the wagon. He picked up the extra saddle and followed Joe to the corral. Not a word was spoken as the men saddled their respective selections and led them to the back of the house, after carefully putting the log that served as a gate in its former position. Joe waved at the two guards, who still had their close attention on him. He tied his horse to the small tree that had been left near the corner of the house and went in the door. He crossed the threshold and took a metal container of tobacco from a crate of supplies on the floor. He scrounged in a box until he found his old army canteen and filled it with water.

Hannah stood near the stove, a tin of lard in her hand. She glanced up when her husband came in and listened carefully to what he had to say. Jack the pup gave a bark of welcome, then curled into a ball near the stove and watched with wary eyes.

"I've got a young man familiar with the area to travel with me. Name's Patterson. Taylor says he knows the country, so you don't need to fret while I'm gone. I won't be long if the map is correct. Maybe two to three hours should be long enough to find what I'm looking for." He came to stand beside her, but didn't touch her.

"That's fine. I've made some soda biscuits. They'll hold you over until supper, maybe." She uncovered a basket on the table, releasing the fragrance of freshly baked bread. Taking several large, puffy, tan-colored biscuits from the basket, she wrapped them in a cloth. Joe took the packet of biscuits and gave her a peck on the cheek. Jack had risen, watching the man carefully with his soft brown eyes. Joe waved to her from the door, and disappeared into the yard.

Hannah felt her heart turn over when she heard the sound of horses trotting away from the house. It was the first time since their marriage that Joe had been away from her side more than a few minutes, and already she was lonely. She felt her eyes sting with unshed tears. It was the beginning, she knew, of the long days and weeks when he would have to ride away from her. They had scarcely been at Sweetwater Station a full day and he'd gone to explore. If he found the box canyon and the mustangs that Dempsey had mentioned, she knew that he would return again and again to the place and leave her alone with Buck Jones and his wife. She dried her eyes and rose to continue the chore she had started, baking pies for her new acquaintances. If she kept herself busy, maybe the time would pass faster, but oh, how she wished he was back safely at the station.

Having finished the pies, she set them on the table to cool, while she washed the utensils and spoons she had used. She looked admiringly at the table which now held a basket of cold biscuits, two loaves of wheat bread, and three pies. It had been a busy morning, and her back ached from the stooping and lifting. She had made many trips to the box for firewood, and the supply was low. She dared not leave the house to get more. Earlier, as she was baking biscuits, she'd decided as a precaution to put the gun in her pocket after seeing one of the workers observing her actions, and now, alone in the house, with the small caliber pistol in her pocket, she was confident she was relatively safe. The men had finished their work, and the windows and doors were complete. There was no reason why any of the men should be about the house. Yet, if she went outside, she would be subject to the whims and stares of the men, and they might be goaded into unwise behaviors.

She poured a glass of water and sat down in a chair to rest. It was the first time she had really looked at the cabin built to serve the passengers of the Overland Stage Line. The front room was quite large, rectangular in shape, with a stone fireplace set in the back wall. This would be the Public Room, where the passengers would dine and relax while waiting for the horses to be switched. There was no furniture in the room except the table and chairs that Joe had removed from the tent early that morning for use in the kitchen. Hannah knew that one of the carpenters would bring a large table for the center of the room tomorrow.

The table would take up most of the space in the room, and be large enough to seat twelve people. Two more carpenters were working on the chairs and benches. She hoped one of the chairs was a rocking chair, but she had no say in the matter. She had been told by Rebecca Mozier that all the furnishings were provided for the stations, and made alike so there was no squabble over whether one station was better equipped than another. If they had only the standard equipment, maybe Joe could order a rocking chair from Denver and have it hauled by freight wagon with the supplies. Surely, the stage line authorities wouldn't balk at a rocking chair for the personal use of their managers, she thought.

On either side of the fireplace was a door leading to the bedrooms. The northern and southern walls were blank with twin windows on the left and right of an open space. She could picture a large painting there between the windows. Her fingers itched to get out her water colors and begin, but there were many other essentials needing her attention before she could start the decorations for the house. She decided to tour the other areas of the building. She closed the door on the dog so he couldn't follow her. The left hand door entered a long hallway, with doors on each side. She opened the first door. It was an empty bedroom with a few pegs to be used to hang clothing. The second door was the same. There was no furniture in the rooms.

There was a third door at the end of the hallway, and she opened it, expecting to find another bedroom, but it led into a small garden area. There were no flowers, but a high wall of rocks was in the center of the grounds. She moved to the wall and looked down into the dark depths, curious why the contractors would dig a well in the center of the house. She picked up a small pebble and threw it into the center of the space. She heard a splash and knew that the well wasn't deep. She circled around and looked at the symmetrical shape of the house and the setting of the doors. The inner windows were high off the ground with shutters to be closed when needed, she noticed.

At the far end of the garden, there were heavy double doors with a log used as security, with a chain and lock on each door. Casting her mind back to where she had begun her exploration, she decided the house was a u-shaped structure with the garden inside. She imagined the water from the well would be used in the case of an Indian siege. The animals could be brought into the garden to shelter them from harm until either rescuers arrived or the food ran out. It was a very clever arrangement, and she congratulated the contractor who had planned it. She wondered if Joe knew about the security measures built into the station house.

Hannah thoughtfully walked back down the hall and thence to the front room and kitchen. On the right hand side of the fireplace the configuration was the same except the two bedroom doors were on the right hand side of the hallway. The first bedroom held their bed and personal belongings that Joe had brought from the tent. She wondered why there was only one entrance into the garden. Perhaps it was not meant for the guests, and the manager was to keep the inside garden a secret from them? But, it couldn't be a secret with so many carpenters and builders about the place for weeks at the time of building. She was puzzled by it all.

She turned to the barrels and boxes that had been brought into the house and decided to explore the contents of those she hadn't already found. There were nails, tools, and pails. She found two large tubs for the washing of clothes or bathing. There were pitchers and bowls with pretty flower patterns, mirrors and combs, writing material and pencils, hand towels and soap. She held a bar to her nose and was astonished at the sweet fragrance of rose petals. Another smelled of lavender and honeysuckle. She knew they were for the female guests, to make them feel welcome and clean after their long journey from one place to another. She marveled as she found each item, carefully packed. She was lost in a nostalgic fog of home when she heard the sound of many horses' hooves stopping at the front of the house.

Hannah ran to the front door in a panic. No one had told her that a stage was arriving this morning. Her first coach, and her dress was wrinkled and soiled, her hair unkempt, and there was no food ready to serve her guests. Not even a chair for them to sit on, or dishes unpacked for their use awaited them. Oh, Joe, why did you leave me alone, she silently wailed. She opened the door with a smile of welcome on her face. The station's newly arriving visitors were not what she expected. It was a huge Conestoga wagon pulled by six mules, and a large man was descending from the driver's seat. Hannah stared and gulped at the sight. Jack ran out the open door and barked as though he were thrice his size. Running back and forth he tried his best to protect his mistress from harm.

Six

When Zedediah Harper Jones stood erect, he was six feet, four inches tall. He had large hands and feet, with broad shoulders and strong arms to match. His face was covered with a dark beard that was generously sprinkled with gray. His hair was long and captured in back with a ribbon of woolen cloth. He wore a buckskin suit that showed signs of sweat and grime from many days of unwashed travel. He glanced at the woman confronting him and saw the scar on her face, but didn't blink or stare at her. He walked the few steps to her. He looked down at the dog at his heels and scratched him on the head. He let the dog sniff his hand, and the puppy sat down on his tail.

"Hello, ma'am, I guess you didn't expect me so early in the day. Got a chance to buy this old wagon cheap, so me and the missus started out last night to travel by way of the Platte River. It almost drowned us in the bend, not knowing that it had rained in the far mountains a week ago. Took that long for the water to come down hill. If I'd known, we'd taken a different route. Best damn wagon I ever saw, though; she traveled light as a feather soon as I got her out of the mountains and into the open spaces."

Hannah's attention was caught by the sight of a heavy

Indian woman descending slowly from the wagon, with a bright-eyed boy watching from the seat. As soon as the woman was on the ground, she opened her arms and the boy jumped into them; then turned with a growl of displeasure that her husband had not helped them down. There were several words spoken by the pair in a language unknown to Hannah, while the boy waited, silently, his eyes going from one to the other. Hannah assumed that the family quarrel was not serious. She glanced out of the corner of her eye and saw the approach of Taylor, Graham and several of the other men. She welcomed their presence since she had no idea who this man was, but hoped he was the new animal handler, Buck Jones. She sighed. At least it was not a stage coach full of female guests to be entertained.

Taylor stopped just short of the giant and waited patiently for his quarrel to end. He was enthralled by the sight before him. He had come across some characters in his time in the western country, but this might be the strangest of them all. He looked at Hannah, standing as cool as a princess of England, with not a sign of fright or disgust. He admired her courage, especially as he and Graham had been witnesses to the casual greeting bestowed on her. He decided to take a turn in the conversation.

"Good day, sir. I suppose you're the famous Buck Jones for whom the Hadleys have been waiting. I'm Clifton Taylor, the supervisor in charge of the building crew. You'll shortly find that we're not yet prepared to welcome guests, but since you're an employee, not a guest, I think it'll be proper for you and your wife to withdraw into the house. Mrs. Hadley, I'll send the men up with the furniture already built, if I may be so bold as to act on your behalf." He stood ready to defend her or help her, whichever she needed at the moment.

Buck Jones gazed at him with suspicion in his eyes, but could tell by his dress and manner that he was a man to be reckoned with. He stood at attention, his backbone rigid, as a career soldier might in attending his superior officer. He turned as Hannah spoke.

"Why, thank you, Mr. Taylor, it would be most convenient to have more chairs, and if the table is complete, you may bring it, too. I have the pies ready for your crew if you want to pass them on to your cook for their supper. Things are in such turmoil, I was only able to make three, one for my own family. That will only give them a small taste, but I'll try to bake more when I have the supplies more ready to hand."

"Why, ma'am, I'm surprised you were able to find time enough to bake pies for even a few of my men. I'll see that the cook divides it among the most deserving, and the rest'll have to wait their turn. I see that Joe hasn't returned from his mission. If I can be of assistance in any way, just holler loud enough for one of the men to hear." He turned aside, and with the rest of the men stalked toward his camp, without receiving one word of acknowledgement from Buck Jones.

Hannah turned her attention to Buck, not at all sure what she should do under the circumstances, but determined to do something active.

"Please come in Mr. Jones, Mrs. Jones. You're welcome to some coffee, but I'm afraid my supplies haven't been unpacked, or my dishes or tableware. We only arrived ourselves yesterday, and the building crew was delayed a week by the weather." Hannah realized that she was defending the crew, who needed no defense from her, so quickly moved to the stove and began to build up the fire. Without a word, the Indian woman followed her and looked behind the stove for more wood. Finding the kindling and small logs, she gently pushed Hannah aside and fed the stove. Hannah turned and saw the child gazing hungrily at the pies on the table. The dog was sitting on the floor beside him, his tail thumping on the floor. Oh, dear, she thought, I've promised two of the pies to Mr. Taylor's crew. Joe, where are you? I need you.

"Where are these supplies you speak about, Mrs. Hadley? I'll bring them in for you." Buck had been eying the pies, and had heard the conversation with Taylor. "My wife's name is Prairie Flower, but I call her Rosie. The boy's called Sammie. I named him after my pa. They speak enough English to get along, but not what you would call fluent in the skill."

"Oh, thank you, Mr. Jones. I was wondering what to call them. It's good to know they can speak our language. Do you think Sammie would like a small piece of pie?" She received a nod of the head, and started looking for a knife to cut the pie. "Our personal supplies are in the wagon with the new brown paint, nearest to the house. The boxes and barrels are marked with bold lettering that will identify them as belonging to Sweetwater Station. The supplies in the other three wagons are provided by the stage coach line, but as you can see there's not enough room or shelves built for them yet."

As she spoke, she cut two pieces of pie, one smaller than the other. She looked around for a plate but there was none, so she lifted the pie and handed it to the boy. He opened his hands and received it. With a few quick bites it was gone. The dog barked and wagged his tail, but she would not give him any of her precious pie. She gave him a piece of biscuit instead. "Rosie, would you like some pie?" She asked Buck's wife politely, but the woman didn't respond to her question. She gazed out the front window at the two men who rode into the yard.

Hannah rushed to the window, knowing that the two riders were Joe and Patterson, back from their excursion into the unknown. She walked out to the step, leaving the woman and boy alone in the house. Jack ran down the step and toward the man, just climbing down from his saddle horse. The dog could not wag his tail fast enough; it swished back and forth in joy. Joe stooped and scooped the dog up into his arms.

"Hey there, Jack. Glad to see me, aren't you? Where's your mistress, and who the dickens came in that big wagon?" Just at that moment, Buck came from the wagon with a box in his enormous arms. The two men stood and gazed at each other for a second, each sizing the other up.

Patterson watched the scene unfold, then discreetly walked the horses to the corral where he unsaddled them and led them to water. He found a brush and stood brushing the first horse until his coat was dry and untangled.

"Jones?" Joe received a nod in reply to his question. Almost on the man's heels came four men carrying the largest table Joe had ever seen. It looked sturdy and smooth. They made a slow train across the yard and up the steps. Buck stopped to let the men pass him by, then continued walking toward the house, and Joe followed him.

The women and child backed into the corners of the room as the four men turned and twisted the table until it moved into the room. Hannah ran to remove the box in the center of the room, and the men set the table down. They sighed and rose from their labor, their eyes on the pies on the smaller table.

"Oh," said Hannah with a moan. Then she ran to Joe and hugged him with all her strength. He patted her shoulder while gesturing with the other hand for the four furniture movers to leave by the front door. Disappointed, they exited without a word. Buck dropped his box in the corner and signed to his wife and child to leave. The dog proceeded to sniff around the box.

"Wait, Jones." Joe released Hannah, who stood nearby as he talked. "The large tent in the yard is for you and your wife until we can get a cabin built. It should be fine until the cold weather sets in. The carpenters aren't obligated to build another cabin, so I bought the tent for you. I suppose that Conestoga is yours. You can park it next to the tent, if you want.

"There's a stage due in a couple of hours. Soon as I can, I'll be at the corral to select some horses for the return trip south. We don't have a regular route to the south yet, just whenever there's a need for it." He stepped forward and shook the man's hand. "Welcome to Sweetwater Station, and, to your wife and son, too. I'll meet you at the corral in a few minutes." He smiled at the woman and boy.

Jones nodded his acceptance of the dismissal and moved his family out the door. Joe took off his hat and wound Hannah back into his arms. He was aware that he'd left her in a bad situation, running off as he had to explore the area, but he had found what he was searching for and was satisfied. He hadn't expected Jones to come in his own vehicle. He wondered whether the northbound stage would arrive after all, since the passenger bound for Sweetwater wasn't on it. Well, he'd be ready if it came.

"My dear, I'm so sorry. You must be frazzled, me leaving you with all the strangers like that." He led her to one of the chairs, and she sat on his lap, while he stretched his long legs out in front of him. "I see you made the pies. Tell me about your day."

For the next few minutes, husband and wife got caught up on the news, while the dog slept peacefully at their feet. They were not left alone for long. As though a signal had gone from camp to camp, an exodus and entrance began to take place. The carpenters brought the new chairs, benches, beds and tables. One of the men picked up the two pies and took them to the camp cook. The smaller table and chairs were returned to the tent, for the use of Buck Jones and his family. The big house began to fill with furniture, first the large front room and then the bedrooms. Hannah was kept busy opening and closing doors. No one seemed to notice or didn't care about the one door that remained locked. The dog ran back and forth, barking and causing havoc until Hannah found a piece of heavy twine and tied him to the table.

Joe and Buck went to the corral and selected six stout horses to pull the coach Joe expected at any time. They hobbled them under a tree in the front yard in case of need. While they walked around the grounds, Joe pointed out the various improvements and his plans for the future, and Buck explained about the Conestoga and his reason for not coming in on the stage. With all the excitement and chaos, the subject of the box canyon was left for another day. Just before sunset, a loud, piercing shout was heard, and the rush of horses' hooves followed soon afterward.

There were two passengers on the stage, one a tall heavyweight man of indeterminate age, and one thinner, shorter and younger. They were both headed for Denver and looked to be miners. When told there was no stage to the west, they seemed to want to argue the point, but Buck volunteered to drive them in his Conestoga. It would be a matter of a week's time off from his work at the station, but Joe agreed it was the best solution. They were each given a bedroom with clean sheets and fresh water on the left side of the building.

The stage driver and his guard stayed long enough to change horses and eat a meal of beans, bacon and biscuits, and a slice of pie, then started for the return trip south.

At long last, darkness fell on the station. Taylor's crew were satisfied with their taste of apple pie and the promise of more soon. The dog made one last trip to his favorite tree. Hannah changed into her clean, white virginal gown and climbed into bed. Joe said he'd make one more round to check the animals and talk with the night guards. When he came in, he was brimming with desire and passion, but when he saw the exhausted Hannah sleeping so peacefully, he hadn't the heart to awaken her. He drifted off to sleep, his visit to the box canyon far from his mind.

The sun was peeping over the rim of the horizon when Buck, his stomach and those of his passengers filled with flapjacks and hot coffee, headed west toward Denver in the heavy wagon. They were given enough supplies for the three to four day trip. He left his wife and child behind. Rosie was up early and helped Hannah with the breakfast chores. The boy and dog romped cheerfully in the yard near the door where they could be seen by the women. The carpenters were busy in their tent shop finishing the furniture they had been contracted to do. Hannah timidly asked Taylor if one of the chairs could be made into a rocking chair, and he agreed if she would make some more pies. Joe milked the goats and Hannah made two custard pies, three apple pies and one raisin cake. It was enough for the men.

On the sixth day of Hannah's duty as the matron of Sweetwater Station, Taylor and his crew left the station via the forest road for their new camp fifteen miles northwest on the route to Denver, taking a nanny goat and a dozen chickens in wooden crates with them. They cheered as she stood on the steps of her home watching as they rode by. She waved her white handkerchief until they could be seen no more, then she went into the house, sat in her new rocking chair and wept.

With Buck still not back from Denver, Joe separated six mules in preparation for the next coach coming from the east, but it didn't come. Joe told Hannah he guessed there were no passengers to fill it. Likewise, there was no northbound coach that week. Joe spent this extra time with the animals in the mornings and making shelves for the large room in the evenings. As soon as three long shelves were built on the right side of the fireplace, he built three matching ones on the left. He started on enlarging the corrals and worked with the ax to build a substantial mountain of cut logs for the fireplace and stove.

Rosie gazed longingly out the windows watching for her man. Hannah put her to work emptying the boxes of books and placing them on the shelves. She showed her how to dust, sweep and mop the floors. At night, Hannah sat in the rocker, sewing curtains for the front windows. One night Rosie showed an interest in her chore, so Hannah patiently taught Rosie to sew. She gave her small lengths of cloth to make into napkins, not trusting her with a larger project. The stitches were uneven and larger than Hannah wanted, but she worked with enthusiasm. Likewise, she took out pencils and paper and began to teach Sammie how to write his name.

On the ninth day, Buck returned in the large, heavy wagon. He was immediately put to work on the corrals. He and Joe together completed one and started another, turning the six horses that Joe had selected for breeding into the new corral, and leaving them for nature to take its course. They were finished before the next stage from the east arrived.

The coach was high sprung, a faded brown color, and very dusty from its trek through the sandy country. The inside upholstery had a few tears in the seams. The mules appeared tired and damp.

There was a different driver and guard. Paul Ward was an extremely thin man, almost to the point of emaciation. He had dark hair and eyes and was clean-shaven. He normally drove the west-to-east route between North Platte and Julesburg, but Baldwin needed experienced men in Colorado Territory, so he had asked Ward to change his route. It was the first time he had driven this far west, he told Joe. "I plan to climb one of those tall mountain peaks someday."

His guard was called Manning.

"Just Manning, that's all," he proclaimed as he shook hands. "From Ohio." He was average in height and unassuming in manner, but Joe soon found he was deadly in action. He stepped off the stage with a quiet confidence. There was a shotgun in the crook of his left arm, a pistol slung low on his hip, and a knife in a leather scabbard at his back.

"Those trees are a welcome sight," Ward said as they walked with Joe to the edge of the spring. He sniffed the heady pine scent, clipped a small twig from a Ponderosa and picked up a cone from the ground. He stuffed them in his vest pocket with a sheepish grin on his face. "For luck," he said.

The passenger was a gray-haired gentleman from St. Louis named Franks. He wore a checked suit, a boiled collar and black string tie. The moment he descended from the coach, he was complaining about the two bandits who had rounded a bend in the trail and tried to hold them up. They were thwarted by Manning, however. Before the coach came to a complete stop, the first bandit was lying dead on the ground. The second bullet hit the other outlaw in the face and he crumpled like a marionette without a master.

Franks talked all through the evening meal that Hannah and Rosie prepared for the men. He was like a child; adding more details every time he went over the scene.

"That's enough, Franks. I don't want my wife upset, and the child doesn't need to hear about such violence."

Franks puffed up like a toad, his cheeks red and swollen; his eyes protruded from their sockets. Ward laid his spoon on the table very slowly, as though the sound of its dropping might wake the dead. Hannah, poised with the pot over Buck's coffee cup, stopped to listen.

"You can't tell me to what to do. You're nothing but a servant of the stage line. I paid my fare, and I'll say who can and can't talk." As he threatened Joe, he loosened his tie and collar, as though he were having trouble breathing. Manning stiffened and moved his arm off the table, but he was too slow. With a cold, flat voice, Joe brought his gun to bear straight at the stranger.

"Mister, you'd best finish your meal right now, or it'll be the last you down. This is my home, and I'll not have some dude from the East tell me who can talk in it. You've upset the ladies, and the child is too young to hear such talk."

Franks gulped and changed in an instant to a whining puppy. "Excuse me, ma'am, I didn't mean anything by my speech. Uh, excuse me." With that he left the table and the house, and emptied the food that he had recently consumed near the rear wall. When he sheepishly returned later, he didn't say a word about the attempted holdup.

The rest of the evening he sat in one of the chairs at the table, playing with a deck of cards. Joe wondered if he was in reality a gambler pretending to be an important businessman. He assigned him the bedroom on the right hallway, next door to his own, so he would hear if the man got up in the night, but there was no noise from the room.

Franks walked around the yard during the following day, watching the men at work, but there was no bluster or arrogance in his talk. He asked questions about the set up and the animals, but didn't wander far from the house. Around mid-afternoon, he went into his room and slept.

Ward and Manning shared a room. They rose early and prepared to return to the Mozier station. Buck had the mules ready and the coach clean and shiny, both inside and outside. Although flamboyant in manner and dress, Buck took pride in his work. Hannah fixed a large breakfast of biscuits and gravy, eggs and bacon. There were flapjacks and molasses for those who wanted them, and plenty of hot coffee. Rosie moved around the table, her coal black eyes watching, assessing.

With the coach gone, Joe and Buck returned to their hammering on the new corral. Both kept a careful eye on the gambler, and Rosie hovered over Hannah like a hawk. They cleared the table, stripped the beds, and prepared the tub for washing the clothes. Hannah built a fire in the dug pit at the side of the house, and the two women washed the bed clothes, then the garments of the household, and hung them on the cord that Joe had strung between a tree and a pole. They flapped and blew this way and that all day, causing the chickens to cluck and fly into the air.

The stage from the south arrived late in the day, just as the sun was dipping below the horizon. There were two passengers, named Hankins and Albertson. They almost immediately got involved in a poker game with Franks. With such a large crowd, Hannah decided to kill a couple of the chickens and open several jars of her precious vegetables. There were gravy and hot steaming corn bread and biscuits. She baked a spice cake. She hoped the supply train would arrive soon.

The driver of the northbound stage was Jim Owens, and the guard was Fizzure Rodriguez, a half breed from Arizona

Territory. It was rumored that he was Comanche, but he neither confirmed nor denied the fact. He was dark-skinned and slender. His hair was adorned with a red bandana and eagle feather. There were no incidents to cause alarm at the station, and Buck headed out the next morning in the Conestoga on the forest road to the next station with Franks and Hankins. The two men were responsible for obtaining their own transportation the rest of the way to Denver, as Buck couldn't be spared from the Sweetwater home base so long.

Owens and Rodriguez turned their mules toward the Mozier station carrying Albertson toward his eastern destination. Joe pulled the plow out of the wagon and spent a great deal of time at his sharpening stone honing it. He checked the other farming equipment and sharpened the hoes, the shovel, the sickle, and the scythe.

Late in the afternoon, Buck brought back information that Clifton Taylor and his men had almost completed the next station house and furniture. It would be called Buckboard Station after an old broken buckboard lying in the mud beside the river. There were indications that there had been a struggle with Indians at the site, but no bones of animals or humans were found. The road crew was working many miles to the northwest past the forest. Joe was mighty glad to see his partner back so soon, and pleased to hear from Taylor and Graham.

The next week was filled with activity, as the men completed the corral, and started on the barn. They sat at the table the first night for an hour looking over plans and a crude drawing of how it would look. Each had his own suggestions and criticisms to make, but finally settled on the plan of action. Jackson's road crew had left some logs, and Joe used a few for the foundation forms. The men went into the deep forest and hauled back several wagon loads of logs for the loft and corner beams. They made molds and dug the soil along the creek banks to fashion bricks. It was time consuming work, and they stopped early to care for the animals and check for any wild animals or human tracks leading to the station. They carried their rifles and pistols in their holsters at all times.

On the second morning after starting the brickmaking, Rosie came out and helped. She was fast and efficient, having learned the process from Mexican farmers. Joe and Buck left her to the task, while they went back into the forest for more logs and worked on other chores, such as cutting wood for the fireplace and stove. It would take many bricks to build a barn the size they planned. Hannah was relieved to have her kitchen to herself again. She took an inventory of her supplies and added saltpeter and paraffin to the list of things to order when the freight wagons arrived, as she was sure they would soon be driving through on their way to the new Buckboard station.

Halfway through the week, on a Thursday, Joe decided to plow a large area for the vegetable garden. It was late in the season, but certain vegetables would grow in the fall and winter, to be harvested in the early summer, like squash, cabbage, and turnips. He knew little about the higher altitude and the seasons in Colorado, but he and Hannah had brought seeds aplenty to experiment. He checked the bags of wheat, corn and oats to make sure no varmint had discovered them hidden in the wagon.

Friday, just after noon, saw the four inhabitants of Sweetwater Station at their separate tasks: Joe plowing in the open space that had once been the builders' encampment, Buck shoeing horses and tending to their cuts and bruises, Rosie making bricks, and Hannah busy in her kitchen, baking bread and roasting a ham for their supper. The child and the dog were playing in the field close to his mother.

Suddenly, the thin air was rent asunder with the loud sound of a brass trumpet. In a cloud of dust and creaking leather, and the thunder of mules' hooves, Rusty Backgammon pulled his team to a halt in front of the house. "Hallo, the house. Where the hell is everyone?"

All work stopped as the four station inhabitants came forth from their tasks to welcome the stage. Hannah was first to emerge from the house, her damp hair tumbled about her shoulders, her apron soiled with grease and flour. Rosie shuffled in her slow trot from the rows of wooden molds filled with bricks baking in the sun, followed closely by the wide eyed Sammie, and the dog, Jack.

Buck looked up from his temporary forge and continued shoeing the horse's hoof in his hands.

Joe raised his head, then unhitched the plow from the mules' yoke, and walked them toward the house. He wished he had more time to plow, but his duty was to welcome the guests and change the animals for fresh ones. He arrived in time to see a small, stylish lady descend from the coach. It was Rebecca Mozier and her two children, come to call. He tied the reins at the corral fence and walked forward. He was delighted to see Rusty and his partner Phineas Knell again, and he remembered he was to call him Scrappy. It had been three weeks since his and Hannah's arrival on the same coach. He gave it a critical look, and stepped forward to greet his guests.

Hannah was surprised and embarrassed to be caught in such a mess, her hair untidy and her hands full of drying sudsy water, for she had been washing the bowl in which she stirred the bread dough. She was caught out by Rebecca Mozier, whom she so wanted to impress with her skill as station matron. She smiled broadly and gave Rebecca a hug, and turned to greet the children. She heard a sound and turned to see another lady stepping daintily from the coach. She was taller than average and had blonde hair, covered by a lavender hat with netting over her face.

"Oh." Hannah was bewildered and chagrined. She turned to Rebecca, but her friend was scolding the children for some misdemeanor of minor importance. She said to the stranger, "Hello, ma'am, welcome to Sweetwater Station. I'm Hannah Hadley, your hostess." She got no further for a large, tall man descended from the coach. He had almost snow white hair, revealed when he raised his hat in salute. He had the most dashing smile and blue eyes.

Joe held out his hand in welcome. "Mrs. Mozier, how good to see you again." He turned to the woman and man, waiting for an introduction. He was slightly conscious of the three children and the dog making their own way with introductions among themselves. Jack was barking and wagging his tail in enthusiasm. The two Mozier children were running about and trying to catch him. Sammie stood as still as a prairie dog, afraid to move. Rosie gazed in awe at the women and the tall gentleman.

"Mr. Hadley, Hannah, I just had to come to see how you are getting along. This is Mr. Obediah Blessing and his wife Emily. They'll be taking over Buckboard Station as soon as it's finished. Mr. Baldwin has found a manager for the next station, so by the end of October all the stations will be ready for travel on the road to Denver, when it's finished. Oh, Hannah, darling, you look divine. I've missed you so much." Hannah was having trouble keeping up with the rumbling chatter of her only female acquaintance in the territory. She took each lady by the arm and turned them gently toward the station house.

"Do come in and have some tea. Mrs. Blessing, welcome to Sweetwater Station. I'm happy to have a new neighbor. I'm sure that our animal handler will welcome the news that a new station is opening up, for he's had the task of driving passengers in his Conestoga wagon up to now." She chuckled to herself. She was now chattering as much as Rebecca Mozier. It must come from being alone so much.

Hannah opened the door and ushered her guests into the Public Room of the station. After charging them to be seated, she went to the stove and looked for the water kettle. She filled it from the barrel, grateful that Rebecca was chattering with her neighbor, for she simply could not think of a word to say. She quickly tried to pin up her hair, but it was a shambles. She looked down at her apron and groaned. She straightened her shoulders, and thought to herself, "If they expected a fancy society matron, then they should have given me warning of their coming," then felt ashamed for thinking such negative thoughts.

She filled the kettle and took the tea tin from the shelf. She rarely drank tea herself, thinking to save it for her guests. She searched and found the nice tea pot and dishes that she and Joe had purchased for just this sort of occasion. She set out three cups on three saucers, and placed three silver spoons near the place settings. She was happy to see the eyes of the stranger open wide at the sight of pink flowers and green leaves painted on the china ware. Her heart beat so loudly and fast, Hannah was afraid that the other women would hear it.

"Rebecca, how are you getting along? Is your station as busy as ever? We've only had three passengers through in the last weeks." Hannah was hungry for news from the East.

"We're doing very well. Sam had to put down one of the horses that broke a leg. So unfortunate, to step in a gopher hole like that. Paul Ward told us that they had bandits try to hold them up on their route. Oh, but you know about that, since he was here before coming to us." She shuddered. "I would hate to meet Manning when he's angry. He's a cold character, although quite charming when not emboldened to guard the stage."

"Now, Rebecca, I do believe you have romantic notions in that head of yours. Tell me, Mrs. Blessing, have you been in the territory long?" Hannah poured the boiling water from the kettle into her tea pot, having already spooned in a portion of tea leaves. She would let it steep for a few moments and give the grounds time to settle. She drew the last of the cookies from the tin and placed them in three saucers. There were two for each of the ladies, if she took only one.

"Please call me Emily, if I might call you Hannah?" Hannah nodded her permission. "You are so kind. I feel right at home already. No, we've traveled all the way from New Hampshire on the coast. I do miss the ocean so. My husband read the advertisement in the Boston newspapers and decided to come west. He's a lawyer by trade, but felt the need for a change. You see, there are eleven children in his family, and he was swamped with responsibility to provide for them. He said one day, 'I'm tired of being the oldest son. Let Arthur take his turn at the wheel.' You see, Arthur is rather stiff-necked and brazen in his manner. He will see that the younger ones toe the mark." She laughed with remembrance of some conflict in the family. "So, here we are halfway across the continent from His Majesty, Arthur Blessing."

Hannah and Rebecca sat silently for a moment, trying to conjure the form and figure of Arthur Blessing with his younger siblings. Hannah poured the hot tea into three cups and offered sugar and goat's milk to the ladies. Rebecca took a delicate bite from a cookie and chewed thoughtfully.

"Emily, dear, surely you exaggerate the influence of your brother-in-law. I'm certain he didn't mean to be so rigid and critical of his peers." Rebecca was an only child, and couldn't grasp the significance of family quarrels. Hannah could visualize the scene very well. She had been the recipient of just such snobbery and dominance. She took a sip of tea, and hastened to soften the criticism of one she did not know well.

"You're here now, and you're very welcome. Isn't she, Rebecca? It'll be nice to have female neighbors on either side of us. You'll soon find, Emily, that we females are outnumbered in the territory, twenty to our one. I do so hope the stage line is successful, and more settlers can move along the road. Rebecca, tell me about the children. I have little Sammie the Indian boy to help care for, you know, and have no experience with small lads. I've begun to teach him his letters and to draw, but don't know such things as deportment and manners. I had only two female cousins in my family; no boys." Hannah was trying hard to overcome a sharp feeling of homesickness. She missed her cousins and her Aunt Ethel, although they had been cruel and unkind to her.

The conversation went on for several more minutes before Hannah asked if they were staying the night. Told that they were, she began to prepare the bedrooms for the guests and the drivers, helped by the two other women, all chattering like magpies on the loose. Fresh clean linens were placed on the unadorned beds, and hand towels and soap made available.

Emily picked up the lavender and honeysuckle scented soap and smelled it.

"Oh, Hannah, will we have these at our station, too? I do love the smell of lavender, don't you? It reminds me of my Boston grandmother; so eccentric and yet very kind. She was a real martinet if my sister or I did something to displease her, but then she would come into our bedroom at night and bring us a treat." Emily had a wistful look in her eyes.

"Oh, tell us, do. What kind of treat?" Rebecca was immature in some ways, and curious about other people's childhood memories, since she had been raised in a strict environment.

"I remember one night she brought us a small piece of marzipan wrapped in golden colored paper. Candy was forbidden, you see. Another night she brought my sister a beaded ring for her finger." Emily sighed. "She lived high on a hill in a great white house, with servants."

"She sounds like a marvelous woman." Hannah put the finishing touches on the room, smoothing the bed covers with her red, roughened hand. "Where is your sister, Emily? Is she still in New Hampshire?" She followed the ladies down the hallway toward the Public Room.

"No. She married a sea captain who was drowned when the ship was lost at sea. It was very sad; the whole town mourned the loss of the captain and crew of the vessel." The other ladies stood, stunned. Neither Hannah nor Rebecca had knowledge of ships and ocean voyages. Back in the kitchen,

Hannah put away the tea things and sat down with potatoes and turnips to peel for their dinner.

The other two ladies decided to take a stroll to the spring. Rebecca noticed some flowers in the meadow near the Jones' tent and picked them for the table. There weren't many flowers near the Mozier station. Nor, trees, for that matter.

Meanwhile, at the site of the unfinished barn, the men were discussing the merits of the animals, especially the goats. Hannah had for some time tried to make cheese from the milk but was unsuccessful. As for the donkeys, they were not cooperating in breeding with the horses, Joe lamented to the other men.

Buck Jones came up at that time and joined the conversation. It was enough domestic discussion for Rusty and Knell. They decided to head for the corrals and see about the animals selected for the trip east and the cleaning of the coach. The children and the dog continued to run and play in the yard, carefully watched by Rosie as she mixed soil and straw for bricks.

Dinner was a celebration. The roasted ham, cooked in a tart sauce of Hannah's own recipe, was accompanied by potatoes, turnips, corn fritters, and fresh bread. The men played a friendly game of poker. Joe was careful to keep the conversation away from the war and politics.

The ladies sat and drank their tea, and gossiped about the latest in Eastern fashions. The previous coach passengers had left newspapers and magazines at Mozier Station, and Rebecca brought several with her. It was rumored that the wide, many-petticoat style was coming to a close, and skirts would be slender and graceful. Pictures of the new style were displayed in one of the magazines, and the ladies were awed by the drastic change.

"Oh, look, Emily, can you imagine such a low bodice?" Rebecca gazed at the picture of a dress in awe.

"Well, at least it will save yards of cloth in the skirt,"

said Hannah in her droll way.

Both ladies joined her in laughter, and put aside the fashion magazine.

Emily talked of New Hampshire and her family living on a high point above the sea. She talked wistfully of sailing ships and of whalers and fishermen. The only discomfort between passengers, station managers, and drivers was the discreet withdrawal of Buck Jones, who took his wife and son and retired to the tent. With his exit, whether Rosie would be welcome in the parlor was quietly settled without bloodshed or argument.

Joe and Buck took their usual turn at night guard, but were relieved before daybreak by Rusty and Knell, who said they needed to be up and early on the road anyway. As the sun peeped over the horizon Buck hitched four horses to his Conestoga and took the Blessings to their new home. Rusty and Knell disappeared in a whirl of dust to the eastern station, carrying a jubilant Rebecca Mozier and her two sleepy children inside the vehicle.

Joe was left alone with the two women, Sammie and the dog, Jack. He wandered around for a few minutes after breakfast, undecided which job to tackle first. He finally decided to finish the plowing. While he made sharp clear rows of turned soil and weeds, Rosie made bricks, her son contentedly playing with the dog nearby.

Having fed the guests her bread, Hannah was forced to bake more loaves. While the oven was hot, she made a custard pie. She noticed the level of apples in the barrel had shrunk considerably since her arrival at Sweetwater Station. She had a small amount of dried apricots and peaches, and a tin of raisins. These would have to be used before they spoiled. She sat for a few moments while the bread baked, glancing at the new skirt styles, then with a sigh jumped up and strained the goat's milk and attempted to make cheese. This time it was tastier and of better texture.

As the afternoon shadows moved along the floorboards

of the cabin, she worked on her curtains. The warmth of the room, combined with the scent of fresh bread, the tangy smell of cinnamon and apples, and the remaining fragrance of the morning's coffee, made her sleepy. She laid her needlework in her lap, leaned her head back and was soon asleep.

Joe opened the door to the cabin, planning to get a drink of goat's milk to refresh him after his hot morning in the plowed field, and he saw his wife sitting in the rocking chair asleep. An almost overwhelming need for her arose in his mind and body. He stood a moment longer in indecision, and strolled across to her chair. He knelt at her feet.

"Hannah," he whispered. He kissed her on the cheek, the undamaged one. "Darling, wake up."

Hannah's eyes fluttered, and she looked up into the eyes of her husband. She was still in the grip of a pleasant dream. She raised her arms to his shoulders and drew him down to her level. She kissed him on the lips.

Needing no more invitation than that, Joe lifted her in his arms and carried her to the bedroom. He could hear the barking of a dog and the laughter of a child in the distance, but they were only a minor distraction. He stood Hannah on her feet and began to unbutton the pearl buttons at her neck. She reached behind and untied her apron strings and let it fall to the floor. She kicked off her house slippers and one went flying to the corner of the room, knocking a bowl off the table, but neither person noticed whether it broke as it hit the floor boards. While she finished undressing, he removed his own sweaty, dirty shirt and trousers. Completely naked, the couple fell on the bed in a passionate embrace. With gentle kisses and fingers of magic, Joe Hadley took his wife to heaven in the afternoon of a fine summer day.

Seven

Later, they awoke to the sound of many horses' hooves. Thinking it was Buck returning in the Conestoga, Joe rose and quickly dressed. Hannah scrambled to find her chemise and stockings. Joe ran to the door and opened it to the cool breeze of late afternoon. There before his disbelieving eyes was a freight train of maybe a dozen wagons; their drivers cursing and stopping the mules on the brink of disaster, as the first team balked at the sound of a barking dog. The chickens scattered in all directions. Jack ran back and forth like a deranged wolf, nipping at the feet of the animals. Joe darted from the house and pulled him into his long arms to save him from the sharp hooves. He yelled at Sammie to stand back, not knowing if the child heard his command. He apparently understood the message, if not the English words, for he ran to his mother, still making bricks in the lower meadow near the spring fed creek.

"Hell, man, I coulda killed the mutt, if'n you hadn't grabbed him. Never expected to see a dog at a relay station. For such a small critter, he sure makes a heap of noise, don't he? You Josiah Hadley?" The voice came from a heavily bearded stranger poised high in the box of the first wagon. He was large and aggressive, with a high beaver hat on his

94

head, and dressed in a dusty town suit.

Joe stepped forward after glancing at the other wagons and drivers. "Yes, I'm Joe Hadley. Welcome to Sweetwater Station."

"Welcome, hell. That was some reception, all righty. You keep that dog quiet, and I'll come down." Suiting words to actions, he began to descend. Behind him the other drivers tied their reins to their vehicles and climbed down from their wagons. About two dozen outriders now appeared behind them, leading a mob of horses, cattle and goats. One lone donkey and several sheep trailed slowly behind, guided by a large black dog and two Basque shepherds walking.

Good God, thought Joe. A menagerie. All that's missing are some camels and elephants.

The angry man spat some tobacco onto the ground at Joe's feet and stepped forward to shake his hand, wary of the dog in his arms.

"My name's White. Brody White, boss of this here freight train. We're headed to Buckboard Station, but Baldwin said to leave the first two wagon loads here with you, since you haven't received supplies in a while. Saw un Injun squaw on the way in, making bricks. That yore womun?" White sprayed another mouthful of spit toward Joe's boots and looked around him.

"No, she belongs to my animal handler, Buck Jones. You'd best not call her a squaw around here or you might find yourself buried under yon cottonwood tree." Joe glanced at the other men now surrounding him, but kept his attention focused on Brody White. He grasped the dog so tightly he began to squirm. Joe loosened his hold.

"That right? Well, now, what if I don't choose to take orders from no station manager out here in the back country?" He glanced over his shoulder, feeling confident with the other men to back him.

"Yes, that is right, Mr. White, and I would appreciate it if you would stop that disgusting spitting at my husband's boots."

Standing in front of the open door, White saw a woman of medium height, and wearing a gingham dress covered by an apron. In her arms, already cocked and ready was a rifle aimed at his head. The wagon team boss stared at the scar-faced woman in surprise.

"This is my wife, Hannah Hadley, Mr. White." Joe spoke with the pride of a man deeply in love with his chosen woman. At that moment the circle of men started to part, and a wrathful Rosie Jones came through, one hand holding that of her son, and the other holding a long, thin-bladed knife. She stopped beside Joe and turned toward the men, a menacing frown on her face.

There was a ripple of sound from the center of the men, as one man stood apart. He was large; not as big as Brody White, but nonetheless hard and commanding in his way.

"Stop this nonsense, White. I've had about enough of your bullying ways. I saw the woman, too, and it ain't no business of ours if a man has an Indian wife. You back down now, or I'll plant you myself under the tree." He gave White a fierce look of intimidation, his hand hovering close to the gun in the holster at his side. White spat once more and moved to the back of his wagon.

The new man stepped forward and shook hands with Joe. He glanced at Rosie and smiled. He looked up at Hannah. "My name's William Bowman. Mrs. Hadley, the men would enjoy it immensely if you'd lower that rifle a bit. We don't mean you folks any harm. We just came to deliver your supplies, and we'll be on our way west."

Hannah lowered the rifle, but she didn't move from her spot on the porch. Neither did Rosie; although she lowered her knife-wielding hand and turned to Joe for directions.

"Welcome to Sweetwater Station, Mr. Bowman. We've expected supplies for some days now. You men water your animals and rest under the trees. Light some fires and make coffee if you're thirsty." Joe signed to Rosie and spoke a few words in her own language, which he had picked up in the few weeks he had known her.

She nodded her understanding, taking the dog and walking into the house with Hannah, still holding the knife in her hand.

Hannah placed the rifle back in its holder near the fireplace, and hugged Rosie. She gave Sammie a sweet smile, and he began to play with the dog on the floor. They sat down to shell beans and scrape corn from the cob for corn fritters. The danger was past, but Hannah would feel better when the men were gone. She wondered how Brody White would treat Emily Blessing when he encountered her. She wished there was some way to warn her of his coming.

Outside the house, White sneaked a bottle from his pack and took a long swallow, his eyes darting from Bowman to Joe and the other men. He sat under a tree and continued drinking. The other men ignored him. They were used to his bluster and bullying ways.

Joe and Bowman walked to the animal herds and Joe asked about them.

"They're all destined for the Buckboard station," Bowman said, "except the donkey, which is to be left with you. There are no mules because the maps and Frederick Jackson's report on the progress of the road doesn't indicate any deep sand like that between the Mozier station and the Sweetwater. Since that station is closer to the Rocky foothills, Baldwin wants to experiment with sheep. The Basque shepherds will care for them. Once the last station is built, the sheep might be moved to the higher mountains. The cattle are for breeding and for food. If Blessing can raise the cattle while tending the station, then Baldwin might send some to the other stations.

"It'll be a matter of what works for each station and its manager. If things turn out like Baldwin hopes, and the stragglers and unsettled families in the states back East start heading west in great numbers, they'll need transportation.

It's bound to cut down on the wild game, with so many settlers building farms and homes. If the railroad does get built, the stage stations will have a chance at becoming the hub of the new west and maybe the start of towns, and cities. It's a big dream, and no one knows the outcome."

Joe thought he understood the picture. Baldwin was using the stations for experimenting towards the possibility of future growth in population. His own station was to provide horses and mules for the area. He could see the stations in future competition with the large ranches already in the southern and southeastern parts of the territory.

The subject of Brody White was breached. It was Bowman who mentioned him first. "Hadley, I can feel there'll soon be a showdown. White has antagonized several of the station managers, and the drivers and outriders are wary of him. He's kept his position of power through fear and intimidation. He's under a tree now, getting drunk. He can't be depended on and is lazy in the extreme. Once we've left the supplies at the next station, he won't have a reason to stay on with the freight wagons. I don't think the other drivers will allow him to take over driving their wagons. If we can just make it to the Buckboard station with all the wagons and animals, I'll see that he's on his way to Denver. The men will be heading back to St. Louis, I imagine. I plan to report him to the authorities as soon as I get to a telegraph office."

Joe didn't ask how he hoped to carry out his threat. He just hoped White would stay clear of his family.

It was the familiar bellow of Buck Jones and his Conestoga coming round the last curve and stopping at the front of the house that brought reality home to Joe. The man gave a great shout of anger, his face filled with consternation and surprise, and he came off the wagon seat in a bound.

Joe moved quickly to turn him away, but it was too late. Bowman moved as one with Joe, clearly at awe of the giant standing red-faced beside the heavy wagon.

"What's the meaning of this, Joe? Whur'd these wagons

come from? Whur's Rosie?" The tremor in Buck's voice said more than anything that he must have felt the presence of his wife would be a matter of contention between men of this type.

Joe had spent enough years in the Army to know when a battle was about to start. He hoped to calm things down before it came to that, but at that moment Brody White rose from his place under the tree, tossing the empty bottle aside, and yelling out curses in a rough and slurred speech.

Joe called in a loud voice, "Now, Buck, calm down. Rosie's in the house with Hannah. She's fine, and the boy, too. The supplies are for the Buckboard station, and as soon as our own goods are unloaded, they'll be on their way to the Blessing's place."

There was no stopping the conflagration from its course. White started forward, staggering and lurching as he came. He lit the fuse with his vile and defamatory words, stopping about ten feet in front of Buck.

"You that idjit what's got a squaw for a mistress? She tried to stick me with a knife."

Buck turned to Joe for confirmation of his charges. "No, Buck, Rosie lifted the knife to protect me, not herself. She's all right, I tell you. She's safe with Hannah."

"Why would she feel the need to protect you, Joe? You know she's as gentle as a lamb, but she's got fine Apache blood in her, too. There's something you're not telling me."

"I know, Buck. It was a mistake. This gentleman got angry because of the dog's barking at his animals and nipping at their legs. It was all settled an hour ago. Let's go in the house and you can see that Rosie's fine and dandy."

Buck was willing to be persuaded, but White suddenly jerked forward. Buck instinctively drew his gun. White had his weapon halfway from his holster when Buck's bullet hit him in the forehead. He collapsed like a giant redwood tree. Buck waved his gun at the gathering of startled men, and growled at them.

"Anyone else object to an Apache woman for a white man's wife? We was married proper like by the Catholic priest in Fort Laramie, in Wyoming. The whole kit and caboodle of the U.S. Army stood as our witness." Buck stood with his gun out and dared anyone to defy him.

The sound of the gunshot brought Hannah and Rosie from the cabin. Sammie stood beside his mother, his eyes big with fright. Buck yelled something in their language and they remained on the porch, as rigid as fence poles in winter.

"All right, Mr. Jones. We have no objections to your wife. Put your gun away. Please." It was Bowman, who stepped forward now. "We'll empty your supplies and be on our way, after we bury White. He was no good. We all know that. If you hadn't downed him, I'd have done it myself. We've had a belly full of his conduct. He's troubled us and bullied the drivers since we left St. Louis. We're well rid of him. We'll see to his burial."

Buck put his pistol back in the holster, went to his wife, and led her and his son to the tent. He left the Conestoga standing where it stood. He didn't say a word.

"All right, men, the excitement's over. Dick, you and Candy get some shovels and start digging a grave. Where you want him, Hadley?" Joe pointed to a slight incline a fair distance from the spring, among the pine trees, so as not to pollute the sweetness of the water. Two men picked up the body and carried him there, while the two named men searched in their supplies for shovels.

Eight

Hannah turned into the house. She felt sorry for Rosie and Buck.

Joe went to the Conestoga, and leaving the wagon where it was, he unhitched the team, took them to the corral and released them. He went into the half-built barn and brought a bucket of oats to the trough for the horses. They dipped their heads into the feed. He heard the sound of Bowman giving orders to his men, but his mind was not on the activity in the yard. The tragedy enacted before his eyes had started with an innocent dog's barking.

He watched the men on the slope digging the grave, bowed his head and shrugged his shoulders in frustration. Still, he let himself think, life goes on, in spite of it. He'd talk to Buck tonight, when the others were gone. He saw four men carrying supplies from the front freight wagon to the house. He was ashamed of himself. He had run and left Hannah with the task of putting the supplies in their place. He walked toward the house, but was stopped by one of the drovers. He wore a red plaid wool shirt and the gray trousers of a Southern Army veteran. He couldn't be more than twenty-three or twenty-four years old.

"Mr. Hadley, sir, what do you want we should do with

your donkey?" Joe wanted to howl with laughter; he wanted to cry; he wanted to beat his hands against the wall until they were bloody and cold.

"How old are you, soldier?" The man looked at Joe strangely.

"How old, sir?"

"Yes, that's what I asked. How old are you?"

"Why, I'm twenty-one, sir."

"Have you any family or friends back in the South?"

"No, sir. They were all killed or died of the cholera that swept through the town. I joined the Army because I didn't have any place else to go."

"Would you like to work for me?" Once again the man stared at him, with amazement on his face.

"Work here, at the stage station, sir? But, I work for Mr. White." He suddenly realized his mistake and glanced at the men on the hill with the body at their feet.

Joe watched him blush, his face turning fiery red. As the young man shuffled his feet, Joe could almost read his thoughts as he realized his job would end when the men arrived at Buckboard Station.

"Why, I'd think that was real generous of you to offer me something long-term, sir, but what would I do here?"

"Oh, take care of the animals. Help me plow and harvest the crops. Help me build a barn. Milk the goats, gather eggs. Protect my family from wild Indians, or bandits, if it comes to that." Joe watched the young man consider the different aspects of the job and then make up his mind.

"But, why me, sir? There's plenty men like me after the war. Why do you want me to work for you?"

"Because I need someone. Buck Jones will probably stay a while longer, but soon he'll go back to a place where his wife is welcome. We get all kinds of strangers here riding the stage west. The whole country is on the move. People will go to California, or Oregon or Santa Fe, a part of the migration west. I need someone who can handle animals, ride like the wind, dig in the soil and come up with potatoes. I need someone young and strong. Do you want the work?"

Jeremiah Fuller had never been needed before in his young life. He had been the youngest son in a family of four boys and a girl. His brothers had perished during the war. He had come home to a house owned by strangers; his sweetheart married to someone else while he was gone. He glanced around him at the green grass, the animals in the corral, at the far distant mountains that looked like clouds on the horizon. Hell, yes, he'd be a fool to turn down an offer from a man who had defied Brody White over a little dog; a man whose wife had fearlessly pointed a rifle and defended her husband and her home.

Jeremiah felt as tall as those mountains in the distance. He was certain he could lick a dozen Bengal tigers with one hand behind his back. Why, if he had to, Jeremiah could plant turnips and taters with the best of them, although he'd lived in town all his life. He reached out his hand and drawled in the most Southern Tennessee accent that he could muster.

"Why, yes, suh, I'll take that job yore handing out and I'll be as steady as a rock. You'll find me as cool as winter snow on the barn roof and as solid as yon cottonwood tree. I swear you'll never regret this day, suh."

Joe laughed out loud. It felt good to laugh. He noticed several men turned to look strangely at him, but he didn't care.

"What's your name? Tell me something about yourself." Joe started walking toward the house; his young employee by his side.

"My name's Jeremiah Fuller, sir. I came from a small town near Memphis, Tennessee. Before the war I was going to university to be a lawyer like my father. He was the justice of the peace in our county. I came home from college to find my father, mother, brother and baby sister dead from the cholera. Half of the town died of it that year. I had one brother who was killed at Shiloh; another died of an infection at Chattanooga, got his leg caught in a wolf trap, they told me. I got hired as a clerk in a warehouse; then as a stoker on a steamboat to St. Louis. I never rode a horse, or milked a cow, or planted taters, but I can learn. I learned to fire a rifle in the war, and I learned to speak only when the officer in charge gave me permission."

He sighed and hastened to keep up with the long strides of his new boss. "Last month, I got this post with Brody White, and I sure regret that decision." He shook his head and looked over his shoulder at the hastily dug grave on the hill. The men had finished filling the hole with soil.

"Well, Fuller, I'm glad, for now you work for me. Come in the house and meet my wife."

Joe stepped up on the porch and noticed Jeremiah's hesitation. He teased him a bit. "Don't guess I can call you Fuller from here on out if I'm introducing you to my wife. So, come on, Jeremiah, meet the missus. She won't bite. The dog maybe, but not my wife." He laughed and opened the door.

Jack ran to him and barked, wagging his tail vigorously. Joe picked him up and held him in his arms. Hannah was standing over a small barrel of apples and shaking her head. She looked up and smiled.

"I declare, Joe, I think my reputation has spread from here to Denver City and even to St. Louis. Look at this. They sent two barrels of apples, a box of dried apricots, one of peaches, and tins of prunes and raisins. Everyone from here to China wants a sample of my pies." She laughed, and looked at the young man standing with his hat in hand beside Joe.

"Hannah, my dear, it's my fault. I never should have told those men that you made the best pies in Indiana. You should have put salt in them instead of sugar, and made me out a liar. This young man's Mr. Jeremiah Fuller, from Tennessee. I took one look at his gray britches legs and decided he was a man with a future. He's going to spend that future with us.

He's agreed to work for us. I think I'll put him in charge of peeling apples. What do you think?"

"Why, Joe, darling, that's a splendid idea." She walked forward and took the man's hand in hers. "Welcome, Jeremiah Fuller. Don't be alarmed, young man. I only bake apple pies when there's a coach coming."

Jeremiah looked from one to the other. He didn't know what to make of this friendly kidding between his new employers. His family had always been serious and gloomy.

Joe leaned down and put the puppy on the floor. "Run along, you little trouble maker, before I cut your ears off. Hannah, I'm sorry for leaving you at the mercy of Bowman's men. Have you gotten everything you needed? If not, maybe I can buy some from Bowman before they leave."

"I've everything we need for now. They sent two boxes of empty glass jars and crockery pots and lids." She shook her head in amazement. "I think Mrs. Baldwin must have told her husband we would need them for canning the vegetables. And, I wouldn't think of depriving Emily Blessing of her supplies. You run along now, and I'll sort this lot out by myself. How are Buck and Rosie? Are they still in the tent?"

"Yes, still in the tent. They'll stay, I think, until the wagons are gone. I'll go and see what's holding them up. Come along, Jeremiah, I need to tell Bowman that you work for me." They started toward the freight wagons.

"Ah, sir? You never did tell me where to put the donkey."

Joe stopped in his tracks. Donkey? He had forgotten the donkey. "Put him in with the other donkeys, of course."

"But, there are horses in there, sir."

Joe laughed. "That's the reason why I want the donkey there, Jeremiah. So, if God wills it, we'll have more mules."

"More mules, sir?"

"Jeremiah, when you put a male horse with a female donkey, they produce a hinny. When you put a female horse with a male donkey, they produce a mule. Simple mathematics."

"Oh. Thank you, sir. I'll put the donkey with the horses, sir." And Jeremiah Fuller ran to do just that, his face almost burning with embarrassment, but how was he to know? He'd lived in town.

Joe continued walking to the tent of Buck Jones and his family. "Buck, you in there? It's Joe." He paused a few minutes. "Buck?"

"Yeah, I'm in here. Don't you come in. I already done enough damage today around here." Buck sounded despondent, as Joe expected.

"Buck, you did what you had to do. Hell, I'd a shot him myself if I'd had my gun on me. Or, Hannah might. Bowman said he was prepared to do it himself. The man was a skunk, stinking up the whole freight train. You got no call to feel guilty about getting rid of a skunk. Is Rosie all right? And Sammie?"

"Yeah, Joe. We're all right, I tell you. We're not coming out until those men are gone from here. Joe, will you take care of my horses for me? I don't like to leave animals hitched to a wagon for long."

"I've already taken care of them. Fed them an extra ration of oats, too. Don't take notice about the horses. Tell Sammie that the dog's fine. He's in the house with Hannah. Buck, there's one other thing. I hired a new hand, a young man named Jeremiah Fuller; an Army man, like us. Raised in town, but intelligent and strong. I thought with you working with the livestock, me and Jeremiah can get that barn built before winter. Maybe get you and Rosie a shelter built before the cold weather sets in."

"North or South?" The voice sounded resentful and gruff.

"South. He's still wet behind the ears, but he'll learn." Joe heard some cursing and some mumbling in the tent. "What's that, Buck? Did you say you didn't want to work with a Southern gentleman who was in the war? But, that's what you've been doing all along. I fought for the South, in Indiana, Tennessee, and Kentucky with General Morgan. I lost my brother James at Gettysburg, killed by a Rebel bullet in the head." Joe heard some rustling, and Buck was standing at the door of the tent.

"You fought in Tennessee and Kentucky? You never told me. Why didn't you tell me, Joe?" There was a frown on Buck's face. He was not his usual flamboyant self. He looked sick; his face pale and his eyes red.

"It didn't seem to matter. The war's been over for two years, and we were whipped, bad. But, the worse thing was the assassination of a fine man, Mr. Lincoln. There's no need to fight the battles over again between men of integrity and honor, is there? I have a lot of respect for you, Buck. You handle your problems the way you feel you ought. You're good with animals. That's why you were hired for this station. I was hired because I have an education and can plan ahead to the next step. When I signed up for this position, it was to put the past behind me, and live for the future. Can we do that, Buck? Put the war and the bad times behind us?"

Joe didn't realize it at the time, but Buck felt guilty about killing a civilian. Fighting in the U. S. Army was his calling; his life for over thirty years. Killing a civilian was not like killing an enemy in war. He stood as still as stone and watched the men of the freight caravan getting ready to pull out.

Joe held out his hand. "Buck?"

Without raising his head, Buck shook the hand of his station superior and ducked back inside the tent.

Joe turned away in sorrow. He tried to understand men like Buck, but he was puzzled. Maybe when the freighters were gone, they could have a long talk. He glanced at Bowman and started walking toward him. With his ability to absorb many things at one time, he observed Jeremiah take the donkey to the horse corral and set him free in the mix of horses and donkeys.

"Mr. Bowman, we need to talk, sir." Bowman was standing with several of the drovers. He turned at the sound of Joe's voice coming up behind him. The serious look on the man's face drew his attention, and he told the handler he'd talk to him later.

"Yes, Hadley, something on your mind?" Joe started toward the spring, heading away from the wagons and the house. Bowman followed. They stopped a few feet from the edge of the water, and Joe noticed the afternoon sun shining on the surface. The water was very deep at this spot; a good place for swimming, he thought.

"Bowman, first I want to thank you for bringing the supplies safely here and to the Blessings, when you get there. They're our lifeline to civilization and security. Without food and the necessary equipment, we wouldn't be able to run the stage line and help the line's paying passengers traveling across this vast land of ours. I regret the unfortunate loss of one of your company, but I don't blame Buck for standing up for his wife. It must be hard to live in a world where you're misguided but determined to live your own way. I've no condemnation for men like Buck. He chose his way, and I've chosen mine. If you feel it necessary to report this matter to the authorities, I can't stop you. But, remember this. I'll fight for him, or for any man's right to protect his family or his home. Brody White was a bully, as you've admitted yourself. He threatened me, and if it hadn't been for Buck showing up when he did, my wife and I might've been killed."

Joe paused and Bowman waited for him to go on before he said his own piece. When Bowman continued in silence, Joe picked up where he left off.

"Bowman, Buck feels bad about what happened today. He's a career soldier, spent over thirty years in the Army, before his body began to weaken and pain sapped his strength from him. He's earned the right to live out the rest of his days in peace with the woman of his choice, and with his child. Remember that when you talk to the authorities about what you and your men witnessed today. Now, to another matter, I've hired young Jeremiah Fuller to help me with the work here. The barn's not finished; the horses and mules need constant attention and Buck has his work to do. Young Fuller's just what I need to build the rest of the station for the future traffic along this route. I'll pay for any time left on his contract, if you'll release him from his obligations to your outfit."

Bowman looked around at the men who had come with him to Sweetwater Station. He turned and spoke from the heart. "Hadley, these are not the same men I camped with last night on the river. Today, they're free men. Yesterday, they were frightened cattle under the thumb of the bully Brody White. As soon as they arrive at Buckboard Station on the morrow there'll be no more reason to stay together. They've completed their contract. They'll scatter to the four winds, maybe go on to Denver or back to St. Louis, or to California or Santa Fe. I don't know Fuller; never met him, but I can see how a young man could build a life here with a man like you. I wish I could stay. It looks like a good place to live, but I have a family in Illinois and I want to get back safely to them."

"I can understand family and a good place for them. I've done the same. Hated to leave even when it was forced on me." Joe had, too, twice, once to a war he wished he'd never fought, and the second time to keep from fighting a war with his brother. "Worth it, though. Fuller says he has no home to go to. Maybe this is it."

"Joe Hadley, you're a good man who doesn't judge a person by his flaws but by his character. It's been my pleasure to have met you. I have my own responsibilities and ideas of what's right and wrong, and White stepped on them with his hard boots and gun violence. This wasn't the first time he chose to push a man until he squealed. He left a trail of sorrow all the way to St. Louis. I've no regrets over what happened today. I won't tell the authorities anything. If one of the other men chooses to talk to them, that's their affair. I fought in the war, too, in my own way. I was a school teacher and a scholar. I spent the years of the war at a college for young men, hoping to teach them to respect men like you. I'm a coward in many ways, but I gave money to the Union troops and supported them in their cause." He gazed at the distant mountains and then looked closely at the men under his care.

"You're wrong. There are no cowards on this land." Joe felt himself smile. "At least, none speaking to me now. Maybe a few under the land, but, we won't talk any more of those who can't speak back." He kept his eyes on the newly turned grave on the rise.

Bowman smiled at that. "I came on this trip because of a promise I made to my father, who died years ago in Illinois. He had a dream of connecting the cities of the East with the cities of the West. I've invested in this stage line, and I wanted to see for myself if my investments were worth the money. I talked to Ned Baldwin about you. He said if this stage line survives, it'll be because of men like you. I'm something of a fraud, you see. I'm not a wagon master, nor a horseman. The last few weeks have been hell, but I'm satisfied that the country is in good hands, in spite of our past differences. If you ever need anything that I can provide, don't hesitate to call on me."

"Thank you for being honest about your connection to the stage line. Not knowing about wagons or horses doesn't make a fraud of any man. It just means he hasn't learned it yet." He thought of himself arriving a few weeks ago, as unlearned as a turkey with down still covering his wings. "Tell Baldwin when you see him to keep the supplies coming. You might tell him to send some reading materials for the long winter months when it will be difficult for the coaches to come through, especially in the higher altitudes. Deal softly with Obediah and Emily Blessing when you get there. They've only been at the station a week. Good-bye." He shook the older man's hand and wished him well on his journey.

"Goodbye, Hadley." Bowman turned to his men and prepared to mount his wagon. He gave the signal and the wagons started to roll.

Joe turned and peered at Jeremiah still standing by the horse and donkey corral. He strolled over and laid a friendly hand on his shoulder.

"Well, Jeremiah, what do you think? This is your last chance to return to civilization. They're pulling out for the next station. I spoke to Bowman, and you're free of your contract."

"Oh, I think I'll stick around here for now, sir. I look forward to eating one of Mrs. Hadley's pies. They're famous, you know."

Joe strolled toward the house, laughing as he went.

Jeremiah remained by the corral and watched until the wagons and animals had passed from sight along the road to Buckboard Station. When the dust settled, he turned and walked toward the house. As he passed the tent of Buck Jones, he noticed that they too were watching the last of the wagons and animals disappear among the pine and spruce forest on the new road.

Nine

Joe was working near the uncompleted brick wall, turning the sharpening stone with his legs while he honed the plow. He was vaguely aware of Jeremiah working near the creek, lifting dried bricks into the wheelbarrow. He thought if he could get another couple of rows plowed before twilight, maybe he could finish with the field tomorrow. When he stopped a moment to ease his legs and back, he scanned the horizon and took note of heavy dark clouds building over the mountains, and he frowned. He'd welcome the cooling rain, but he was afraid the animals would be caught in the open if there was a storm. He put the plow aside and stood up, checking out the surroundings. He shivered as he felt a sharpening of the wind. His concern deepened as he scrutinized the smoke curling from the chimney, and the restlessness of the animals, standing in the corrals. The goats continued their browsing under the trees. Suddenly, he made up his mind, removed the harness from the mule he had been using that morning, and drove him to the corrals.

"Jeremiah, get a move on. We've a job to do." He raised his voice, and gestured for his hired hand to come quickly. Startled, Jeremiah pushed the wheelbarrow harder, and stopped breathlessly beside his employer.

"What's up, Joe?"

"There's a storm coming. Stack the bricks against the wall and put the wheelbarrow away. Run to the house and tell my wife we'll be late to supper tonight."

Puzzled, but quick to obey, Jeremiah hefted the bricks onto the ground, four at a time, and began stacking them against the wall.

Joe walked rapidly to the tent, where Buck and Rosie had been enjoying a leisurely Sunday afternoon. "Buck, I think we're going to have a storm, if not tonight, then tomorrow for sure. Come help me. We'll see if we can at least make some kind of shelter for the animals. There's several hours of daylight left."

Buck sauntered out of the tent, muttering under his breath, and squinted toward the mountains. His eyes took in the same signs of nature that Joe had noticed, but he saw no cause for alarm.

"Ah, Joe, there's plenty of time yet. It's Sunday, and I've earned my rest. Rosie's making me a new pair of moccasins. We'll come out when she's finished."

"Look at those animals, Buck. They're nervous and fidgety. They know the weather's changing. You better tell Rosie to go in the house with Hannah. Tell her to take whatever you need for the night. If a real blow comes, she and Sammie won't be safe in the tent. We need to get those logs over here quick and see what we can do about a shelter for the animals. Take the top off the Conestoga. We'll need it to haul the logs." He started to run toward the corral. He glanced back and saw Buck still standing in front of the tent. "Get a move on, man. It's for your family's safety."

By the time Buck had explained to Rosie to grab their possessions and go to the house, and Jeremiah was back from telling Hannah what was going on, Joe already had selected four good mules to pull the wagon. Hannah came out to see what the excitement was about.

"What's wrong, Joe?"

"I think we're in for a storm, the way the clouds are building over the mountains. Gather the eggs and take the chickens to the house. We'll need to put the goats in the garden for protection. Hurry, Sweetheart."

She grabbed a few chickens and corralled them toward the house. When Rosie and Sammie came out of the tent with a bundle wrapped in a bed sheet, Hannah called to her, "When you get the boy settled, I need your help!"

Rosie nodded with a bob of her head and hustled Sammie along to the house. She soon returned without the boy, a broom in her hand. Hannah was grateful for the help and laughed at the sight of the broom.

Rosie smiled broadly, and between the two women, all the eggs were gathered and the chickens in a huddle near the inner garden, Rosie threatening them with her broom if they were tempted to stray. She stayed with them while Hannah ran through the house to open the doors. She found the new locks on the garden doors smeared with grease, and it took precious minutes to clear them with her apron. She removed the lamps and objects that might be broken and tossed some old newspapers to Rosie. They spread the papers over everything in the selected bedroom near the garden door. The chickens flew about the room and onto the newspaper-covered bed, feathers flying like snow. "Keep them off the table!" She handed Rosie the flowered bowl in her hand. "Take this to the big room and bring a plain bowl with some crushed corn."

"You feed chicken in here?" Rosie looked shocked. "They make big mess, I think." She shuffled to the kitchen to do as she was bid, shaking her head. Sammie jumped up and grabbed at her skirts.

"Mama, what you know?" His eyes were big and round with signs of recent tears.

"You not worry, boy; Mama take care you." She flinched as he yanked on her braid, almost making her drop the precious bowl. "Sit, boy. Is good." The boy sat at the table and watched as his mother placed the flowered guest bowl out of his reach, and drew a smaller crockery bowl from the shelf and filled it halfway with corn. "Sit. I come back."

With the nervous fowl beginning to settle into their new quarters, Hannah shut the door, sighing in resignation at the mess they would be forced to clean when it was all over.

The women went through the house, making sure all the window shutters and doors were latched against the wind. It made the house dark and gloomy. She lighted the lamps and a few candles. Without being asked, Rosie stepped to the giant stove and began stoking the fire. Hannah breathed a sigh of relief and started preparations for supper's stew, including a peach pie.

Outside, the wind had strengthened, and the blowing dust was making it difficult to breath. The men tied cloths across their faces. Buck had hitched the mules to the wagon, and all three men rode to the pile of logs the road crew had left. They lifted a full load of logs into the wagon.

Joe turned to Buck, his voice muffled by the cloth. "You know we've got about three more loads of logs to move, and not much time. The logs belong to the Overland Stage Company, but I figure we need 'em more than they do right now." Buck muttered an answer and went for another log, Joe following him.

"Fasten them securely, especially that one on top. I don't want to lose any of them." Joe turned to Jeremiah.

"Rope?" The younger man gave him a blank look. "Oh!" Suddenly understanding, he ran to the front of the wagon to fetch more rope from under the seat. He handed it to Joe, grinning sheepishly. Not used to the hot, humid weather, he was sweating profusely.

When the wagon was loaded as heavily as they dared, Buck drove it to the markings they had made for the barn, which faced the west. If the storm came, it would be from the west or northwest.

Joe sent Jeremiah to the house for nails, saws and hammers. "Ask Hannah; she'll know where they are."

He and Buck took the logs off the wagon, and as soon as Jeremiah came back, went for more. It was a race against time and the elements. Joe kept gazing at the horizon, trying to judge how long they had to accomplish their mission. Once he thought he saw lightning flash, but it was so quick, he wasn't sure.

One hour passed, then another. They avoided unnecessary talk, while they hammered the logs into place, one at a time. An eerie orange-and-green glow came over the sky. Joe sent Jeremiah to the house for two lanterns, and by the last rays of the sun, they completed the first wall.

"Buck, we've got oil in the lanterns. What do you say we try for another wall?"

Buck scrutinized their surroundings. "We might not get it finished, but it's worth a try. I'd hate to lose the horses."

The sky was now overcast, and thunder rumbled in the distance. Lightning flashes threw a silvery warmth over the scene. The Conestoga was put to use once more, and this time, the last seven logs were hoisted onto the wagon and tied securely. Buck pulled around to the east side, and they unloaded the logs. He left the wagon where it was stopped and ran to take down his tent. Joe unhitched the mules and put them with the rest of the herd. With time at a premium, he and Jeremiah lifted logs and hammered them into place.

They were more than halfway up to the roof when the rain began to fall. They looked at each other in the dim light of the lantern, and worked frantically to complete the half-finished roof over the shell of the barn. The wind was fierce and strong. It blew leaves off the trees, and the chicken coop tumbled from its legs and lay on its side. The final logs were in place when the sky seemed to fall. Hail pounded their heads and shoulders. As Joe hammered the last nail into place, he grabbed for his hat, which flew off his head and went rolling through the yard.

"Jeremiah, get my hat!" Joe yelled to the man on the

ground.

Jeremiah ran for the hat and caught it. He waved it in the air, and Joe acknowledged his triumphant signal. The roof now finished, he and Buck climbed down, and Joe forced his hat securely onto his head while they ran to the corrals.

With all three men working side by side, they brought the frenzied animals into the temporary shelter. Those Joe had selected to breed with donkeys were kept at one end of the barn. The donkeys were placed nearby to keep them calm. They strung a heavy rope down the center to keep them separate from the others. Another rope was strung to keep the mules from the horses and the donkeys. They were restless and bumped against each other, stamping their hooves in rejection of the new situation. Joe began to imagine the disaster should they break free and be lost in a stampede.

Last to come inside were the goats. One billy goat tried to break away into the forest, but Jeremiah scrambled after him, while Buck and Joe kept the others restrained by their rope halters. They put them in the inner garden. They jostled each other and gave a loud protest to the tight fit. Another of the goats butted his horns against the well. He gave up in frustration and moved away. The nannies huddled together in a corner by themselves.

All the animals were now inside a shelter.

The men had to decide whether to go into the house and leave the animals to fend for themselves or to stay with them in the barn. Joe thought of the women and Sammie alone in the house, frightened and not knowing what was happening outside the house. He made a quick decision.

"Jeremiah, stay in the house with the women and keep them company. Help them with their chores. We'll stay with the animals in the barn, try to keep them calm. Tell Hannah to keep the chickens in the bedroom to protect them from hail. Take this lantern with you; it's almost out of oil."

Jeremiah was nearly swept from his feet by the wind, and a limb from a tree swished past him as he ran. Joe watched as the door was blown wide and the man entered the lighted building.

It was full dark. They could hear the hail falling on the roof, like sounds of the end of the world. Large claps of thunder rolled, and the sky rained both ice and water on the barn and house at Sweetwater Station. Joe wondered if the storm was also hitting the unfinished house at Buckboard Station and the camp of Bowman's freight wagons.

Buck began to sing in a soft monotone to the animals. The men moved among them, singing, touching them, calmly moving with precision from one end of the barn to another. In the distance, Joe heard the sound of a tree split in two and fall with a mighty thump to the ground. The wind howled through the uncaulked logs. He heard tree limbs and debris hit the side of the western wall. He watched with fascination the storm outside the open end of the shelter where they had not had time to build a wall. The light from the lanterns showed the size of the hail, now lying on the ground like snow.

One hour? Less than an hour? It was here and then it was gone. Joe heard the thunder drift more to the southeast and wondered about the Mozier's. Had they time to prepare for the storm? The rain began to fall in soft gentle sheets. The thunder stopped. The wind grew calm. They were safe for now. Joe sent Buck into the house to see about the women while he stayed with the animals. He crooned to them in a soft calming tone, and they stopped their restless stomping of hooves. Joe saw through the open end a giant ball of fire and wondered what it could be? A tree? It was too far to see the Mozier station, and it was the wrong direction. Oh, God, he thought, surely one of the coaches was not on the road to-night.

After half an hour, Buck returned and brought a plate of hot stew, four johnnycakes and coffee. The women and Sammie were good. The child had been sent to bed in one of the bedrooms. The women were sewing by the light of a

118

lamp. The chickens were beginning to roost for the night in the bedroom. Joe groaned to think of the stink and damage to clean in the morning. Buck said he would stay the night if Joe wanted to go to the house, but they both remained, singing to the animals, and talking softly to each other. The night was still, but rain continued to fall in a steady stream. In a few hours, the sky cleared and the stars came out. Joe walked out through the open end of the barn; the moon sent a dim light over the forest and plain. Joe strained his eyes but couldn't see any damage to the house or corrals. He sat against the wall at the entrance to their temporary shelter, bent his head and fell asleep.

It seemed like only minutes when Buck shook him and whispered that he would like some sleep himself. Joe quickly apologized and kept watch during the early morning hours while Buck slept. The animals again became restless and shuffled their hooves. Joe could see the dim light of dawn breaking. He walked past Buck and looked to the eastern sky. He could smell wood smoke and knew that Hannah was awake. He longed for a cup of coffee. He took care of nature against the side of the barn and went back into the three-sided room. He was tired but jubilant. They had survived, and the animals seemed in good shape, restless but safe. Once more he thought of his neighbors on the east and west. He waited until clear dawn before awakening Buck. The sky was a dark blue and streaked with crimson, gold and silver. The air smelled fresh and clean. It was going to be a good day.

Jeremiah came from the house with the coffee pot wrapped in cloth and two tin cups. He reported that Sammie was still asleep but the women were up and preparing breakfast. The aroma of fresh coffee permeated the barn, where before there was the smell of horseflesh, dust and ammonia. They emptied the pot and drove the animals back to the corrals, in the reverse order in which they had entered it. He tethered the billy goats under the trees so they could browse among the vines and shrubbery. He brought the nannies to the corral next to the barn. The ground was wet with standing puddles here and there. Joe saw that three big trees were lying on the ground near the spring. There was a start for Buck's cabin, he thought.

When the animals were all back in their proper places in the corrals, Joe walked the perimeter of his station and assessed the damage. It wasn't too bad, some fallen trees and limbs, a few shingles broken from the western side of the roof of the house, but not enough that they couldn't wait until he or Jeremiah could replace them. One shutter sagged at the window beneath the fallen shingles. He laughed as he straightened the chicken coop and a rooster scrambled from the wooden wreckage. He spread his wings and crowed his protest.

The men went into the house and sat at the long table while eating their breakfast. Hannah and Rosie had made porridge and flapjacks, with molasses, ham, goat milk, and hot coffee.

"Oh, Joe. It was terrible, with the wind blowing so fiercely and the hail on the roof." As Hannah came to stand beside him, the coffee pot in her hand, he could see that she had been terribly frightened. He gave her a pat on the arm.

"Joe, you should have seen the chickens flying around the bedroom." Jeremiah stuffed his mouth with a bit of flapjacks, his chuckles muffled by the food. Joe could see he had enjoyed the excitement of the hour.

Even little Sammie declared it a Big Storm, his black eyes as round as twin moons. Jack barked in agreement, his tail wagging swiftly.

After breakfast, the men set to work repairing the damage. Buck took over looking at the animals, tending to their needs. Joe and Jeremiah set the damaged coop against the wall of the house to be rebuilt later, and released the chickens into the yard. With Buck's grumbling approval, Joe drove the Conestoga to the fallen tree farthest from the spring. They sawed off a few larger limbs for lumber to rebuild the chicken coop and to fashion into shingles to repair the roof. Several smaller branches they chopped into firewood and tossed into the wagon. The trunk they left until another time. Jeremiah helped Joe tie the timber down and vaulted into the back of the vehicle. With a loud shout to the mules, Joe drove to the yard near the house and they unloaded the wagon. Jeremiah found a draw knife and began to strip off the twigs and bark, while Joe sawed the limbs into uniform lengths. With all the sawing and hammering and chopping, the men failed to hear the sound of wagons approaching from the west, their wheels covered in mud.

Joe looked up and saw the freight wagons from William Bowman's train with about twelve men on horseback. The cattle drovers, he thought. Bowman alighted from the first wagon and came to shake hands with Joe and Jeremiah, his eyes assessing the temporary log walls nailed to the barn and Buck in the corral. The men climbed down from the horses and sat or stood under the trees, smoking their pipes or cigars.

"Hello. I didn't expect you back this way. I thought you would go to Denver before you headed east, Mr. Bowman."

"We had a little trouble at Buckboard Station late yesterday afternoon. The house is finished, and the roof is on, so the things didn't get soaked, but some of the animals are lost. We had just emptied the wagons of the supplies when it hit. It was hard; a lot of hail damage to the wagons. The Blessings are well, but it'll take a while to get them back to where they were. A message came through early this morning that Frederick Jackson and his road crew were caught less than twenty miles from Denver. Most of their tents and equipment were destroyed."

He looked to the place where Buck Jones' tent had stood on his earlier trip. "Did Buck's tent blow down in the wind?"

"No. He put it in a bedroom. He had enough presence of mind to take it down before the storm hit." Joe gazed toward the forest road, a frown of concern on his face. "I hate to hear this about the road-building crew, Bowman. Was anybody hurt?"

"One man was killed and two injured by lightening or falling branches. There wasn't anything for Jackson to do but pack up and go to Denver until the things can be replaced. That's why we're headed back to St. Louis. If the weather holds and there's no trouble along the way, we can reach Baldwin's place by the end of next week and start a new crew and supplies to the station. It hasn't got a name yet. We'll stay long enough to eat and rest the horses, and be on our way. We hope to spend the night at the Mozier place."

"And the Blessings; are they staying at the station?"

"Yes, he's decided to stick it out. The woman's shook up, but she's a tough little gal, in spite of her size. Said she'd lived through a hurricane once; a little hail and wind don't scare her. They have food and shelter, but the outhouse blew over. I left some of my men to help round up the strayed animals, then go help Taylor, if they can. Terrible hail storm; I've not seen hail that large before. A few downed trees and limbs torn off. We brought you some fresh meat. Two of the cattle were down and one sheep. We figured we may as well slaughter them and dry or smoke them. We brought you one of the steers. Best have your women get to it right away before it spoils." With that message, he turned and told two of his men to carry the carcass to the house.

"Jeremiah," Joe called to his hired hand who had returned to stripping bark and small limbs from the downed tree trunk. "Go to the house and tell Hannah to put on a big pot of water and get out her knives. They've brought us some fresh meat."

Joe walked to the corral and asked Buck if he'd come and help him cut up the steer. Within the hour, the meat was cut and prepared for smoking. Hannah and Rosie spent the rest of the day taking care of the meat. It was a chore keeping Jack away from the women. He sniffed and barked and generally got in their way. They finally locked him in the inner garden area. It smelled of goat, and the dog was frantic until they put him in a bedroom.

Bowman's men ate roasted beef over their open fire. They rested their horses and with a last good-bye handshake were soon lost to sight along the muddy road to Mozier Station. The water in the creek was up to the hubs of the wheels, but they crossed without having to build a raft. Joe wondered how they made out at the sandy patch, but it was nothing he could do anything about. The day hadn't gone as he'd planned, but he couldn't complain. They had fresh meat, and lumber for a cabin for Buck and Rosie. The next day, when the ground was dry, they'd bring out the tent and set it up again. Night fell with a bright moon, and the stars seemed closer than usual.

After sunrise, wrapping a long chain around the logs, the men tore down the temporary roof and the east side of the barn, since it was the less vulnerable. They lined the logs back where the road builders had left them. Using the strength of a mule, the men pulled the second wall of logs down. It was backbreaking work, and Joe and Jeremiah went to bed early.

The bricks were still wet and needed at least another day to dry, so they spent the next day taking care of the animals. The chickens seemed to have recovered from their luxurious stay in the bedroom. Hannah and Rosie cleaned up the mess with only minor damage to the linens.

On the following day, they finished the partially built brick wall. All the while Rosie formed more bricks, building a stockpile for their future use, but it would be a few days before they were dry enough to use.

Mid-afternoon of the next day brought the coach from Mozier's Station, driven by Rusty Backgammon with a new guard, a young man named Grover Mayhew. He was a short, dumpy fellow with brown hair and eyes. He didn't have much to say, letting Rusty do the talking. Phineas Knell was sent east to replace a man with a broken leg, Rusty told them. The family at Sweetwater Station would miss Scrappy; he was a good man, although he was rough-hewn and dangerous when roused. In spite of Hannah's encouragement, the men wouldn't stay the night.

"We missed out on the storm, went a ways south of the station, but it was hard coming through the mud; the mules bogged down to their knees in a few places. The two male passengers got out and helped some." As soon as the animals were changed, and they finished their meal, he and Grover climbed aboard ready to start back to Mozier Station, with Grover driving.

"You're letting the new man drive?" Joe teased, surprised, because Rusty was a haughty man.

Rusty took a long puff on his stogy and shrugged his shoulders, not offended by the remark.

"The man needs experience; just came out from Virginia. Baldwin sent word he needs another driver somewhere along the line in a few months. We'll circle around the sand bogs if we can. See ya' next week."

"Keep a lookout for snakes that might have been run into the open by the storm."

Rusty shrugged and gave a toot of his horn in farewell as Grover yelled at the team. They strained at the harness, and the wheels began to roll forward, leaving ruts in the still moist ground.

Hannah welcomed her female passenger; a loud-mouthed, gray-haired matron, who reeked of cologne. She and her husband were on their way to Denver. The man was tall and slender and dressed like a salesman, with high starched collar and cuffs. The woman bragged during supper of the sights of New York City, which they had left in February. The merits of the tall buildings, the large window glass fronts and the restaurants were all discussed and debated. Since none of her listeners had been there, they couldn't contradict her descriptions. She left behind a feeling of relief that she stayed only one night.

The other passenger might have been a gambler. He was dressed in sober black with blackened boots with a yellow tassel on the top, which he wore outside his trouser legs. He sat at the end of the table and played with a deck of cards after a supper of roast beef and apple pie. Buck drove them to Buckboard Station the next morning.

The men had only finished about two layers of bricks on the second wall because of the disruption, so they started again early the next morning. They were half finished by the time the northbound stage came late in the afternoon. Once again Jim Owens was driving, with Fizzure Rodriguez acting as guard. One of the horses was limping, explaining the delay of a couple of hours, as they had to keep the animals at a walk part of the way. Joe discovered that a shoe had been thrown, so Buck worked on the animal, putting new shoes on him. Joe thought it was a good time to teach Jeremiah how to shoe horses and mules. Buck grumbled, but he wasn't the boss, so like a good soldier, he obeyed orders.

The only passenger, a man with startling gray eyes and a full beard, had dealt with the mishap with patience and sobriety. He even walked the last few miles so the horses didn't have as much weight to pull.

"My name's Chadwick. I'm on my way to St. Louis to meet my wife who is attending her mother's funeral. We'll bring her father back to Colorado Territory with us if he'll come. We came west before the war with a large freight caravan and small group of pioneer settlers on the road to Santa Fe. We got held up twice by bandits on the road. I've got a ranch down around Pueblo; run horses, and a few cattle. It's mostly scrub oaks and creosote bushes, but there's good grazing along the Arkansas River. The wife traveled east with a freight train of empty wagons. There's not as much travel on the old Santa Fe, now that other roads have been built through Texas. I've heard rumors that now the war's over, they'll be starting the old railroad through the area. It should cut the travel time between here and St. Louis in half."

He and Joe spent a pleasant hour discussing the merits of stage coach passenger service versus slow lumbering freight caravans. Joe was encouraged by his sentiments, but was somewhat disconcerted to hear about the railroad being built through the area so soon. It looked as if men such as him wouldn't have a livelihood for long. He'd let men like Dempsey and Baldwin worry about that end of the company; he'd make sure the passengers were provided food and shelter as long as the stage line lasted.

With no coaches expected for the next five days, work on the barn was more intense, and the final brick wall was underway. Joe taught Jeremiah how to frame windows and doors. There would be stalls for the horses and large double doors at both ends of the barn, so a wagon or team could be driven from one to the other in case of danger.

In the meantime, Joe found the time to harrow the garden area. He had no hope of bringing in a fall crop, but Hannah encouraged him to try. She studied a seed catalog she had brought west with her and planned to send for some fruit trees. With no mail service, it would be chancy at best, but she had hopes of someday having her own fruit in her yard.

Having grown up in town, Jeremiah had no farming interests. Instead, he began to think of studying for the law again. There were schools in Denver, surely. Or, he could apprentice himself to a law firm and study with an experienced man. He didn't discuss it with Joe or Buck, for it was just a notion in his head. He got along well with Sammie and taught him simple things such as reading and about nature. Buck was surprised when Jeremiah asked to take his son for a nature walk along the spring. He could see no harm in the exercise. The dog followed along with them. Jack had now grown almost to his adult size, which was not large. He wasn't partial to any member of the household, but trotted or ran between anyone who was outside. He spent most of his time with the boy.

The curtains were finished, and Joe hung them over the Public Room windows to Hannah's satisfaction. That same night she whispered in his ear that she was with child.

"What? Are you sure? Are you ill? Oh, this is good news. You don't mind do you? I hadn't thought much on the matter." Joe's words came out with a rush he couldn't seem to control. He was pleased. They had all been so busy with building the barn, that he was surprised that he hadn't noticed the change in her body. Hannah had wondered if he would want children and had been nervous for days, trying to gain the courage to tell him. They cuddled in the warm bed covers for a long time, before finally falling asleep in each other's arms.

Hannah awoke earlier than usual the next morning, feeling queasy. She silently stole from the bed and wrapped herself in her heavy woolen coat. Although the weather was warm, a fog hovered over the spring, giving a ghostly scene among the tall trees. She made her way to the outhouse. As she came back she noticed at first what seemed to be a large bundle of rags left at the corner of the house. Curious, she drew closer and saw that it was a man, fast asleep, lying next to the wall of the house. She entered the house, wondering where he had come from and why he was there. Since she was wide awake by now, she built the fire in the huge cook stove.

Should she awaken Joe? Putting off the question, she decided to start breakfast. She filled the coffee pot with water and coffee and put it on a burner. She sliced bacon from the larder and put out the ingredients for biscuits. As she rolled her dough, she pondered this unusual thing. She had heard no horse in the night; how did the man get here? While the coffee was brewing, she opened the door cautiously and walked out far enough to see if he was still there. He was! She quietly went inside. The pleasant aroma of coffee brewing woke Joe and he quickly dressed and came to the kitchen where

Hannah was cutting potatoes for their breakfast.

"Joe, there's a man asleep at the side of the house." She whispered, as he came behind her and took her in his arms for a morning snuggle.

"What? A man asleep outside the house? Where?" Joe's heart beat rapidly. He backed away from Hannah and looked at her closely to see if she was serious. She nodded her head and pointed toward the front door. He walked across the room and lifted his rifle from the place where it was kept high so Sammie couldn't reach it. Stepping to the front door, he gestured for her to stay back. He went outside and looked around the corner of the house. He spied what looked like a mission blanket and pile of rags. Walking closer he could see two moccasin-encased feet. Still closer, he poked the bundle with his rifle barrel. The man was instantly awake and on his feet. It was an elderly Indian with long gray braided hair and red-rimmed black eyes. His face was wrinkled and dry. He dropped the blanket and stood, blinking at Joe.

"What are you doing here? Can you speak the white man's language?" Joe watched closely, but he saw no weapon or act of aggression about the man. "Hungry?" There was no answer so Joe lowered the rifle and made motions to indicate hunger or thirst. He hadn't been around any Indians except Rosie and Sammie, so was unsure if the man understood him. He pointed to his mouth, and swallowed, then rubbed his belly, then pointed to his mouth again. The man seemed to understand and nodded yes. Joe held up his open hand and said, "Wait!" He gestured to the ground and the blanket. There was a puzzled look on the man's face, but he didn't move.

Joe went in the house and told Hannah the man seemed hungry but not aggressive. He went to the bucket and poured some water in a cup. He could see that the biscuits weren't done, but the bacon was ready, crisp and hot. He cut off a slice of yesterday's bread and the last of the apricot pie and took them on a plate to the man. Hannah poured a cup of coffee, but Joe said that he might not know the taste of coffee, so she opened the lid and poured it back in the pot.

Joe left his rifle inside on the table, although he was nervous about it. Hannah picked it up and followed him to the door. Joe carried the plate of food and the cup of water to the man. He was in the same spot, sitting once again; his blanket wrapped around his thin body. Joe offered the cup first. The man hesitated then took the cup and drank as one lost in the desert for days. Joe took the empty cup and handed him the plate, just remembering that he had brought no spoon or fork, but it wasn't necessary, for the man grabbed the food and woofed it down as though starving. Hannah stood on the porch with the rifle in her hands in a non-threatening manner but ready for trouble. The Indian ate the food and gave a loud burp of satisfaction. Joe knew it wasn't enough to fill his belly, but he would have to wait until Hannah finished cooking breakfast. He held his hand out again and pointed to the ground.

"Stay here!"

The man nodded and sat still.

Joe gave the plate and cup to Hannah, who took them and stood in the doorway, while holding the rifle in her other hand. Joe walked to the tent and yelled, "Buck, come out here, please. We've got company. An Indian. I fed him some water and a few bites of bacon and leftover pie. Tell Rosie to come with you. See if you can find out who he is and why he's here. I have to get back; I left Hannah with the man. Hurry, Buck!"

Buck, aroused from a deep sleep, at first didn't grasp what Joe was saying, but then he jumped up, muttering to Rosie in her language to get dressed. There was an Indian in the yard. They dressed quickly, leaving Sammie asleep, and ran to the house. The man was still sitting where he had lain during the night. By now, the dog had awakened and was barking aggressively at the stranger. Joe shushed him and told Hannah to take him inside. She stepped in the house, laid the rifle aside and returned to grab the dog and took him in. She saw Buck and Rosie come running, so she went back to cooking breakfast. She put on a pan of porridge and checked her biscuits.

Rosie looked closely at the man and said, "Arapahoe." Buck asked questions in the sign language of the western country. He interpreted for Joe: "Says he was lost in the storm and sheltered in a sort of cave, much thunder and hail; then started walking. He saw our buildings and came here. He was tired and hungry and laid down to sleep. He lived at his village northwest of here, but he don't know where. He's lost, Joe. He seems harmless." Buck talked to Rosie, and she turned and said something to the Indian. He answered her, and Rosie turned to Buck. "He's been turned out from his village because he's old and can't ride a horse in battle anymore. He has no sons or family to care for him, and he has no weapons or food. Guess we'll have to take him in until we find somebody else to do it, Joe."

Buck looked at Joe with a question in his eyes. Joe could tell this would be the ultimate decision that would turn Buck from him or keep him working at the station. "Tell Rosie to ask him what he can do, if he can't ride. Does he have any skills like taking care of horses and mules, or hunting deer or anything useful to us?"

Buck talked to Rosie, and Rosie talked to the Indian and then back to Buck. "He says he can tan hides and make moccasins or deerskin shirts; and he can work with horses and knows big medicine to cure their ailments. His name is Standing Tree."

Joe walked to the door and went inside. "Hannah, what do you think; should the Indian stay?"

"I think he'll have to, Joe. From the looks of him, he has nowhere else to go."

As he turned to go back out, Jeremiah came from his room in the back of the house, yawning and combing his hair with one hand. "What's all the noise this morning? Hannah, is breakfast almost ready? I'm starving."

Joe and Hannah both looked at him with odd expressions at his choice of words. The Indian might literally be starving, if he hadn't found the station. Joe sighed and went out.

Hannah filled the young man in. "There's an Indian in the yard. He was asleep beside the house when I went outside this morning."

She had no time to say more, for Jeremiah hastened to the door in time to hear Joe say that the Indian could stay. He could sleep in the barn for now, but he needed a bath. Joe was thinking of the lice or vermin on his person that might harm them.

"You tell him, Buck, no bath, no stay here. I'll give him a loan of my clothes, but you burn those he's got on, and burn the blanket, too. Tell him, Buck."

Buck translated the message to Rosie, and she to the Indian; and he nodded his understanding, his black eyes watching Joe closely. With the experience of an old warrior he dismissed Jeremiah, with no reaction at all to his gaping countenance.

"All right, if you don't mind, Buck, take him to the spring and get him washed up. I'll get some clothes and soap and towels, and a clean blanket. You show him what to do. Then see if you can make some kind of bed for him in the barn. Hannah has breakfast almost ready. Ask Rosie if he eats white man's food, although he sure ate that bacon and pie fast." Joe laughed and went in the house, followed by Jeremiah, who was full of questions.

As Joe searched for a pair of trousers, a shirt and clean socks in the trunk, Jeremiah stood in the doorway watching him.

"Where did he come from, Joe? How did he get here?"

"I don't know the answers, Jeremiah. He was asleep next to the outside wall when Hannah went to the outhouse early in the morning. It gives me pause to think a person can sneak up on the house like that. Buck and me've been watching over the animals at night, but we've been so busy building the barn lately, we've grown careless. We'll need to keep a sharper lookout; post a night guard every night. We'll take turns, I suppose." He found an old wool army blanket and a towel, soap and old comb, and took them out to Buck.

Jeremiah went into the bedroom and came back with a draw knife. He followed Joe cautiously, pulling his shirt and vest tighter to his chest. He started stripping the bark from branches they had brought up the previous day. Every few minutes, he turned his head and glanced at the Indian, a frown on his face, wondering why he had come to the station.

Buck tried talking to the Indian. Standing Tree didn't respond, but sat gazing in the distance with his clouded eyes. Rosie had gone to the tent to see if she could find a clean pair of moccasins for the man to wear. Joe gave Buck the items of clothing, gathered the eggs, and took them into the house for Hannah. A few minutes later, his holster on his hip, he came out and went to the corrals to check the horses and mules. The Indian's eyes watched him go. Buck gestured for Standing Tree to follow him. The old man got slowly to his feet and walked to the spring. Buck used the few words of Indian language and signs that he knew to explain what the man was to do with the soap and towel. At last, Standing Tree removed his clothing and plunged into the ice cold water. Buck handed him the soap and made gestures that he was to rub his skin with it, and then soak in the water. He gestured to his hair and rubbed his own. The man untied the leather string on his braids and soaped his hair. He emerged from the water, shaking and cold, but clean. He dried with the towel and donned the fresh clothes.

Buck handed him the blanket, and he wrapped it around his shoulders; then Buck picked up everything and made a bundle to be burned. They walked to the house, where the smell of bacon and coffee teased Buck's senses. He threw the soiled bundle and the old mission blanket into the fire pit and set it alight. He watched until the blanket was consumed by fire, and opened the door for the Indian.

The dog started barking at once and sniffed around the man's feet. Hannah called the dog, and he lay down in front of the fireplace, his eyes alert. Standing Tree didn't react, but his eyes searched and found Joe sitting at the table. Joe stood up and came forward, hand outstretched in welcome. The Indian hesitated a moment, then shook hands vigorously, pumping Joe's hand up and down for some time. Joe gestured for him to sit down.

All the residents were there, Jeremiah, Buck, Sammie, Joe, while Hannah spooned up the porridge, and Rosie poured coffee into cups. They sat down and began to eat. Standing Tree sat in his blanket, watching them. He inspected Sammie, who squirmed in his seat, his eyes frightened, until his mother muttered something in his ear. It was awkward at first, no one talking, everyone eating except Standing Tree.

"Jeremiah, I think we should finish the barn walls and caulk around the roof. There's no heat in the building, but at least the animals will be safe and sheltered from the wind."

"Sure, Boss, whatever you say." He answered dispiritedly. He had not recovered from the shock of an Indian appearing at their doorstep and Joe's calm reaction to him.

"Hadley, one of the horses needs shoeing, so if you don't mind I'll get to that as soon as the goats are milked."

"Fine, Buck. Hannah might try making some more cheese if she has the time." It was a joke because her first attempt had ended more like buttermilk.

Rosie whispered something to Sammie, and he grinned. The dog stood next to Hannah hoping for a piece of the bacon. Drool fell on the floor at his feet, leaving a tiny pool of saliva.

Suddenly, a deep male voice spoke, and everyone jumped, startled. "Standing Tree thank White Man for food. What your name, White Man?"

Joe looked the Indian in the eyes and replied, "Joe Hadley."

The man experimented with the sound and started mumbling in his own language.

"Yo Hadley. Is good name. Strong name. You good man, Yo Hadley. Take in Injun woman, and boy. Take in Standing Tree. Apache. Arapahoe. Is good. I eat now." He shook the blanket from his shoulders and passed his plate to Hannah, who put some biscuits and bacon on it and handed it back. He ate the bacon and took a few bites of the biscuit. Rosie spooned some porridge into his bowl. Hannah gestured to his coffee cup. He handed it to her, and she rose and poured the dark hot brew in it. He sniffed like Jack would have done, then tasted it.

"Is not good. Scarred Woman, your wife, Yo Hadley?" Standing Tree looked at Hannah, and she smiled at him, unembarrassed by his description of her.

"Yes. She is my wife. Her name is Hannah."

"Good woman, make fine babies. Scarred Woman up early; cook food for Standing Tree and Apache Woman and boy. Not afraid of Injun, I think." He spooned some porridge in his mouth, his eyes showing surprise at the taste.

Ten

"Hadley, don't know if it's something to be alarmed about, but I saw animal tracks in back of the barn." Buck held his utensil in one tight fist. He let his eyes rest on Rosie for a moment and returned to his food. He lifted a bite to his mouth and grimaced.

Jeremiah looked up from his plate, startled. He waited for a response from Joe. Sammie stopped chewing to listen to what was being said.

"Wolf or coyote?"

"I'm pretty sure wolf. Can't say how many just yet." Buck absently lowered his food-laden utensil back to his plate, the food forgotten for the moment.

"Why didn't you say something earlier?" Joe frowned and glanced at Hannah to see if she was paying attention. She was talking to Rosie, and seemed preoccupied. His glance moved on to the Indian, but the old man was busily eating.

"With the excitement of the Indian, guess I forgot."

Standing Tree's eyes darted from one man to the other, and that convinced Joe he could understand their language.

Buck sat back in his chair with a scraping sound of wood on wood. He reached for the last biscuit on the plate, and stuffed a piece in his mouth.

"I'll take a look after I finish eating." Joe finished off the last of the eggs on his plate with a morsel of biscuit and sipped his now lukewarm coffee. He frowned.

They ate in silence for a few minutes.

"Sammie, do you want to take a walk with me this morning?" Jeremiah pushed his empty plate back and prepared to rise from the table, clapping the small boy gently on the shoulder.

"You best not take the boy until I see about the tracks, Jeremiah. There may be a whole pack lying on the hill waiting to pounce on the animals. He should stay with his mama."

Sammie jumped down and started playing with Jack who barked and wagged his tail.

Once again, the others were startled when Standing Tree spoke. "What name for Apache boy?"

Using hand gestures, Rosie began to explain who they were and what they were doing at the station. Standing Tree looked from one person to another, rose, picked up his blanket, and with exaggerated dignity, walked out the door.

Hannah got up and started to clear the table. She laughed merrily. "Well, I guess we've passed inspection. Joe, find him something to do, or he'll think he's not wanted. It'll be better if he's busy with his hands."

"You're right as usual. What do you think, Buck? Horses or sharpening stone? His legs may be too weak for that. Making ropes out of the horsehair? Mending leather harnesses?"

It was Rosie who answered, surprising even Buck, who was watching the boy play with the dog. His head swung around. "Making bow and arrow. Arapahoe good hunters with bow. Good wood from trees. Tell Standing Tree make bow and arrows for hunt deer. He like that."

It was the longest speech Joe had ever heard Rosie say in English. He looked at Buck for an answer.

"Should do it, Joe. He'll be doing something he's familiar with and something useful in his mind. We could stand some venison occasionally. Don't know if he can track far, but there'll be deer coming to the spring for water when the weather gets cold. Early in the morning on a cold day they'll come, maybe antelope and other critters. He'd be a good lookout for the animals, see they don't get caught by a wolf or coyote. Something he could do easy, and shout out an alarm if bandits or renegade Indians come for the horses. That is, if he don't decide to rob us blind, himself."

"I don't think he will. That's fine then. You tell him to make a bow and arrows to guard the animals from wild creatures. Rosie, find out if you can where he came from, and we'll be warned if any of his friends come to call on us."

Joe rose and put his hat on his head. He gave Hannah a peck on her damaged cheek and walked out the door, Jeremiah following in his footsteps. The dog started forward, but looked back at the boy and hesitated. The boy's affection won the day. He stayed with Sammie.

Joe stood on the porch for a while, thinking what to do first. Standing Tree was at the corrals, and Joe walked to the enclosure and looked at the animals. Locating the horse Buck had mentioned needing new shoes, he grabbed a rope from the top rail and entered the corral to catch the animal. The other horses and mules were nervous and circled around. Joe caught the pony and brought him to the gate to examine his hoof. The horses ran to the opposite side of the enclosure.

He looked up to see Buck walking toward him. "Hold him steady while I look him over."

"No need to tell me. I know when a horse needs shoeing," Buck snorted.

"Alright, Buck, you take care of the horses, and I'll round up Jeremiah and get on with the wall building." He looked toward the house and saw Jeremiah. He raised his voice so he could be heard. "Jeremiah, come with me. I'll open the gate while you gather some wood for the forge. Light the fire and then join me at the creek. We'll see how far we can get on that wall today."

Jeremiah gave a wave and shout and hastened to gather wood from the huge pile by the barn.

Joe opened the gate and stood by while Buck led three horses from the corral and tied them to a post to be shod.

"I found two more that need shoeing, Joe. See that right front leg on the chestnut?"

Joe lifted the horse's leg and looked at the shoe carefully. "You're right. You're an observant man, Buck." All the while Standing Tree stood silently watching them. They ignored him.

"Joe, I was a mighty good tracker in my Army days, but it'll be good if the Injun learns we can trust him. How 'bout I get the Injun to look at those tracks I saw this morning?"

"Sounds good; see if you can find where they lead off to and what kind of tracks they are. I'll be down by the spring."

Later in the morning, Joe saw what he thought were wolf tracks while he was gathering bricks to put into the wheelbarrow, but he wasn't sure.

"Jeremiah, check that out. Does that look like a wolf's tracks?" He pointed them out, and they followed them for a few steps until they disappeared in a soft bed of pine needles.

"Don't know, Joe, maybe wolves; maybe bear prints. I grew up in the city." He shrugged.

Joe laughed. "So you did. I forgot. You take these bricks to the wall while I talk to Buck." He joined Buck and Standing Tree who were looking at the tracks by the barn.

The big man was trying in a halting way, with gestures and the few words he knew, to tell Standing Tree that he had seen some wild animal tracks, and he needed the man's advice.

"Thought you'd be out finding the den." Joe teased with Buck.

"Not through with the shoeing. We did find these." Buck pointed to the ground where two prints were in the soft dirt. He pressed his lips together, finally speaking with emphasis. "Standing Tree wants to head towards the butte, but I don't know. See anything fresh out there?"

Joe told them what he'd seen, and the three of them walked around the mouth of the spring and followed the tracks for several yards into the trees.

"Wolf?" Joe knew the two old-timers saw more than he did, although he was curious to know where the tracks led.

"Believe so." Buck pointed to the Indian, inquiring with hand signals and short words what he might think.

"Leaving you to it," Joe called, waving and heading back up the embankment.

"Don't expect we'll be out today, Joe. I'll be back to work with the horses in a bit."

"Your call, long as it gets done." Joe returned to Jeremiah, and they set up the bucket of mortar and began laying bricks for the last wall of the barn.

They worked at a steady rate, and Jeremiah returned for bricks, while Joe continued with the necessary work. He noticed from time to time the sound of Buck's hammer, telling him he was back at the forge. The neighing of horses, and the stomping of hooves, had him interested, but he was too busy to watch him.

The sun rose hot and yellow in the sky, and his back was damp with sweat by the time they had completed two full rows. Tired, he stopped to take a breather and get a sip of water. Joe gazed around and saw that Buck had finished with the horses but was still at the forge hammering on a horseshoe. The Indian wasn't visible, but he didn't worry about it.

"Jeremiah," he called to the young man. "Can't rest all day. Back to work."

The men took a break just past noon and went to the house. They were half finished with the wall. The forge had been silent for some time. Joe saw no sign of the Indian or Buck. He went into the house. Hannah was sitting in the rocking chair, sewing. Rosie was at the stove. Sammie was at the table trying to write out his name, and Jack was in his favorite spot beside the fireplace, asleep. He bounced up when he heard them come in. He ran to Joe, barking and growling a welcome.

"It seems quiet in here. Is everyone all right?" Joe hung his hat on the peg by the door; Jeremiah found his own peg beside Joe's.

Rosie turned from the stove. Sammie started to get up, and she muttered to him. He sat back down. Hannah came forward. "You must be tired, my dear. Come and sit down. You, too, Jeremiah. We'll have something for you to eat in a minute."

"Where are the Indian and Buck?" Joe took the vacated rocking chair, and Jeremiah sat at the table next to Sammie and tousled his hair. The boy grinned and showed him his letters. Jeremiah quietly complimented him and took the pencil and wrote something on the tablet.

Hannah frowned. "I thought they were outside with you."

"No, I haven't seen them since early morning. Buck was shoeing horses, and Standing Tree was looking at wild animal tracks by the spring."

"Standing Tree go look for wolves." Rosie put a pot of beans on the table. "Husband say many wolves try steal horses."

"Wolves? So, that *was* what the tracks indicated. We were looking at them this morning. Where did they go to search?" Joe rose from the chair and crossed the room.

Hannah carried some hot fried potatoes with soft bacon bits and onions and placed them on the table before Joe and Jeremiah. There were fresh fried peach pies. Sammie gave them special notice. He loved beans and potatoes, but the sweet treat was his favorite meal.

Jack wanted a sample, but Rosie kicked at him gently, and he went back to the fireplace, his tongue and mouth drooling saliva onto the floor. With his tail silent and his eyes focused on the food, he sat quietly until someone indicated he was welcome.

"Husband say wolves go forest; he go far; see wolves." Rosie poured some cool water in the glasses for the men and Sammie. "Maybe take one, two days, Husband say."

"One or two days? Why didn't he come tell me?" Joe was perturbed. It wasn't like Buck to go off like that on his own without consulting him first. What did they have up their sleeves?

"You busy, too much. Work hard on barn. He say I tell when you come house. I tell." Satisfied that she had done her duty, Rosie filled Sammie's plate and her own, sat down and began to eat.

Joe looked at Hannah as she ladled some beans onto his plate, and then on Jeremiah's, hoping for a more detailed explanation. She just shook her head. A secret look passed between them. He smiled and turned his attention to his beans and potatoes. Jeremiah reached for a slice of bread.

"I'll betcha they went after those wolves to kill them before they come back for the horses. Back in Tennessee the farmers would have gotten out their hunting dogs and tracked the varmints. Do you think Jack would be a good tracker, Joe, if you let him go after the wolves' scent?" Jeremiah was laughing.

Joe could see that Jeremiah was teasing him. The young man didn't realize the seriousness of the situation, having grown up in town. If they lost some of the horses or mules, they would have to be replaced by the stage line. Still, he didn't rebuke the man, and he went along with the joke.

"He'd track them down and wag his tail at them. They'd give up and run into the mountains to escape him." Jeremiah roared with laughter, and even Hannah chuckled at the sight of the small bundle of fur running after the wolf pack. Rosie took the suggestion literally, her black eyes shooting daggers at the others and their laughter.

"Yack no hunt dogs! You no kill Yack." She put her spoon on the table and gave Joe a poke in the shoulder from across the table.

"No, Rosie. Jack won't be hunting the wolves. We were joking about it." Joe watched as Rosie tried to understand the white man's way of talking. A strange expression crossed her face.

"What this yoking, Hannah?" She turned to the other woman, who might explain the odd ways of men.

"It means telling a funny story, like your men do when they sit around the fire and talk of the raids on other tribes or when they go to find wild horses in the grass." Hannah wasn't sure she had helped the woman, but she couldn't explain the source of their laughter any better. She frowned at her husband and Jeremiah.

"Yack not go hunting, Hannah?" Rosie reached across and wiped some bean juice off Sammie's shirt. He darted back from her reach and leveled another spoonful in his mouth.

"No, Jack will not go hunting the wolves." This seemed to pacify Rosie better than Joe's attempt to calm her fears. He wished he had Buck around to explain to the woman.

The rest of the meal passed as they ate in silence, each with their own thoughts. Joe chafed at the thought of the men being gone all night; Hannah worried about Joe, and Jeremiah thought about the bricks. He was sure there weren't enough bricks made to finish today. His methodical mind was counting and assessing how many were required for each row and how many were still needed.

"Joe, we're going to need more bricks for that wall. There aren't enough molded. I figure we'll need at least three dozen more of them." He blurted his thoughts out loud.

Joe wasn't thinking about bricks; he was still thinking about wolves and horses. "What, Jeremiah? More bricks? What makes you think we need more bricks?" Joe spooned some peach pie in his mouth and chewed.

"When I made the last trip to the molds, I saw that they were dwindling fast. It takes a couple of days for them to dry hard enough to use. I figure we'll need more, and if they're made today, then it'll be a couple of days before we can finish the wall." He wiped his mouth with his cloth napkin. He didn't notice that the stitches were crooked and unevenly stitched. They were using Rosie's napkins for everyday use in the family, saving the better ones for the guests.

"Rosie, do you think you can make us some more bricks today? Hannah, do you need her help with something? Lordy, I hope it doesn't rain and make this business slower. It seems to take forever to build a barn," Joe declared in frustration.

Rosie agreed to make more bricks, and Hannah promised to take care of the boy and the dog, so they wouldn't distract her. The subject of wolves was set aside for the moment. The men went back to the wall. Rosie went to her wooden molds and clay. Hannah washed the dishes and started a raisin cake for supper.

The day remained warm and dry, with nary a cloud in sight, except some white puffy ones high in the sky. Jeremiah was right. They had to stop, two rows short of their goal. Joe decided to caulk the area between the bricks and the wooden beams of the roof. He went inside and saw a few cracks where the mortar wasn't thickened enough to keep out the wind and rain. He told Jeremiah to caulk in the places where he pointed out the cracks. The sun was low on the horizon and the shadows long and dark before they finished, but at least three walls were snug and tight for the animals.

Rosie had long since stopped her chores and gone to the tent to put Sammie to bed. She left behind dozens of molds filled with clay soil to dry in the sun. Jeremiah counted them and hoped they would be enough.

As he washed the clay and grime from his face, arms and hands, Joe spoke his fears aloud about the men, still missing from the house.

"Hannah, it concerns me that Buck and Standing Tree might be out all night. Both are experienced trackers and hunters, but I can't help thinking they might run into some white marauders or a tribe of hostile Indians. Standing Tree's thin and frail. Buck might leave him behind in his enthusiasm."

"Is that why you've been so quiet?" She pulled a flannel cloth from the laundry basket and handed it to him.

He dried himself and sat at the table, his shoulders slumped. Hannah gave him an understanding pat on the arm and poured his coffee.

"Drink your coffee, dear, you'll feel better after you eat."

The food drew his attention, and he ate his supper in a solemn mood, hardly noticing the people around him and their nightly chatter.

The men hadn't returned when the families went to bed, and even Hannah voiced her worry over the Indian out in the damp air. Joe reassured her as much as he honestly could, but told Jeremiah out of her hearing to keep a sharp look-out, in case they returned.

With thoughts of wolves, bandits, and hostile Indians on his mind, his sleep was restless. It wasn't surprising that he had one of his nightmares about the war. He awoke in a cold sweat and hoped he hadn't screamed aloud; his dreams had been so vivid. Hannah slept peacefully beside him.

He crept out of bed and put on his clothes in the faint light, carrying his boots to the front room to pull them on without waking her. Stirring the coals in the stove, he watched them flare up, building quickly when he put some small pieces of shredded wood into the firebox. He gazed at the colorful flames as though mesmerized, then shut the door with a clang.

Once the round, metal lid on top of the stove was sufficiently warm, he filled the coffee pot with water. Jeremiah would be cold and hungry when he came in. He went to the rocking chair to pull on his boots, and when he'd finished, laid his head against the chair back and rocked silently in the gloom of night.

It felt good to rock back and forth and ponder his dreams. He cast his thoughts back to men he'd known and died in the war, including his brother James. In the beginning of the hostilities, he and his family had argued over which side was in the right. It had been a difficult decision for Joe to oppose his family and fight for General Morgan. He sighed and kept his eyes closed. A tear fell on his cheek, and he wiped it away.

He'd received no word from his family in the five months since he'd left Indiana, but he hadn't expected to get a letter. The older folks were consumed with their own sorrows and regrets, and he doubted if Luther would ever write to him. He heaved a long sigh and rose to make the coffee. When he'd taken a few quick, hot sips, he felt better. He set out a cup and spoon for Jeremiah, who liked sugar in his coffee, reached for a few biscuits, put them in his pocket, strapped on his pistol holster, grabbed his rifle, and left for night guard duty.

Jeremiah was surprised that Joe appeared so soon; he'd expected at least two more hours in the cool, moist air. He was pleased, nevertheless, and went to the house for food and sleep. All was quiet around the corrals. The horses and donkeys were calm and stood or lay on the ground untroubled by thoughts of past battles or lost families. The mules nickered and pawed the earth but weren't alarmed when Joe moved among them. They were used to his smell and voice, as he crooned a slow mournful song to soothe them back to slumber. Joe peered up at the moon; it looked to be just past midnight. He found a place away from the animals where he could observe any unusual movement or hear sounds of danger. He leaned against a tree, pulled his coat collar tightly against his neck for warmth, and nibbled on a biscuit.

About an hour later, he moved among the herds, more to keep awake, than to calm the animals, but it accomplished both tasks. He watched as the sky grew light in the eastern sky, and welcomed the approaching dawn. Later, he saw a light in the Public Room windows and knew that Hannah was awake. A slim trace of dark smoke curled from the kitchen stovepipe, and he pictured breakfast being made. He visualized Hannah's skillful hands moving back and forth, eggs cracking; bacon sizzling in the large skillet. He smiled at the thought and wished he had spent the night in her arms.

He watched Rosie walk toward the house, with Sammie at her side. She paused at the outhouse, then after a few minutes, she and the boy went into the house. It was a peaceful scene this morning; his stage station. There were two more days before he might expect a coach from the east if there were passengers on it. It didn't come without them. He wondered how long it would be before the last station, the unnamed station, would be built, since the plans were ruined with the storm. Then the route to Denver would be complete, and they should see more travelers headed to the mountains. He felt a thrill of anticipation at the thought.

Eleven

Joe made one more sashay through the animals and walked to the house. When he opened the door the pleasing aroma of coffee and fresh bread drifted into his nostrils. The rustic scene spread before him, and he tried to imagine it in the eyes of a visitor: the scrubbed table topped with plates, glasses, cups and flatware. The embroidered curtains at the windows reminded him of comfortable living. The rocking chair sat near the fireplace, which had still not been laid, since it was late summer. There was a comfortable feeling of cheerfulness and warmth spread by the presence of the women and a child. It was home.

Joe took off his hat and placed it on the peg next to Jeremiah's. He put the rifle away and unbuckled his gun holster and laid them on a high shelf.

"Good morning, ladies, Sammie. I trust you slept well."

Hannah brought him a cup and poured a cup of fragrant coffee. She leaned in to kiss his cheek, which was cold and damp from the early morning air.

Rosie muttered a greeting and took a plate of food to Jack, sitting in the corner. Joe could swear the puppy had a smile on his face as he lowered his head and ate. There was a bowl of water beside it, and he dipped his whiskers in it and smacked his lips. He lay on the floor and closed his eyes.

"Now that," Joe said, "is the way to live; no responsibilities, no troubles." He sat in the chair at the head of the table. Hannah filled his plate with flapjacks. He dug into the butter, took a spoonful of molasses from the tin and spread it onto the mound, and began to eat. It didn't occur to him to wait for the ladies, because he had work to do with Buck gone.

"Jeremiah still asleep?" Hannah nodded yes. He finished his breakfast and coffee and smiled at Hannah, who smiled back. "Thanks, Sweetheart." He rose and walked to the hallway that led to the young man's room. He knocked on the door.

"Jeremiah, best be getting up now. Time to do the chores. Buck's not back, so we'll have to do it ourselves. Coffee's hot." Joe walked back to the Public Room, grabbed his hat and rifle and left for the chicken coop. He gathered the eggs in a basket and scattered some corn for the chickens in the grassy yard. He went to the house, and Jeremiah, sleepy-eyed, was still eating his flapjacks.

"It's going to be a long day, if the men don't get back. I think we'll need to chop some more firewood from that big tree that blew over in the wind storm. Maybe make some lumber to start a shelter for Buck and Rosie. Winter will be coming soon, and that tent won't keep them warm. Maybe haul some rocks from the river banks if we can find them for the fireplace. Do you think we have enough bricks, or does Rosie need to make more today?"

Jeremiah talked around the flapjacks in his mouth. "I think there's enough bricks already made, but I can't tell for certain until we get started on the wall. It'll take another day for these to dry out, if the weather stays mild. Joe, you might think about using bricks to make the chimney for Buck's cabin instead of river rocks, since we already have the molds made."

Joe looked at him in surprise. He hadn't considered that possibility. It made good sense.

"And, Joe, if you think we have time this afternoon, I might take the boy down to the creek and see if there's any fish in it. It'll make a good change in diet, begging your pardon, ma'am, but a good string of fish sounds good to me."

Hannah nodded and smiled, not offended by his mild criticism of her monotonous staples. She cooked what she had on hand, which was supplied by the stage line.

"That's a fine idea, isn't it, Joe? I'd like to have some fish myself. My father liked to fish, but my aunt bought them at the market. It would be good to teach Sammie some fishing skills." She picked up the batter bowl and turned, as if remembering something. "Do you think there are trout in the spring?"

"I'd be surprised if there's anything in it. The spring feeds the creek, you know. Jeremiah, I'd cast my hooks in the river farther south instead. It comes down from the mountains, high up from the snow melt. That's where the fish will be, I think."

Joe put on his hat and left to milk the nanny. Jeremiah quickly jumped from the chair and joined him at the door. He hated to milk goats, but since Buck wasn't there, he guessed it had to be done. They were each seated beside a nanny, drawing milk from the teats, when Jeremiah broached the subject most on his mind.

"Joe, I've been thinking. Do you think I might write to Denver and maybe get some law books and start my studies again? I'll keep working for you, but I think enough time has passed since the war that I need to look to my future again. If I can study in my free time, I might be able to find a judge or experienced lawyer to let me read the law with him." He cleared his throat. "It's not that I don't appreciate what you've done for me and all, but this farming isn't my idea of a career."

Joe scooted his stool away from his goat and regarded Jeremiah's announcement. He had done enough that he thought the nanny wouldn't suffer from not having finished his business. He rose and took the bucket of warm milk to the gate and set it down on the other side, covering it with the cloth he had put in his pocket. He came back and watched Jeremiah pull long streams of milk into his bucket.

"How long have you been thinking this way, son? You never gave any indication before that you were interested in finishing your studying of the law."

Jeremiah squirmed on his stool, embarrassment making his ears warm. He continued milking the nanny. He was afraid to look at Joe.

"I've thought about it all along, but I never had the money before. If I'd never come west with that freight outfit, I'd probably be in some stuffy building adding up numbers for some wealthy merchant. There's not much money in that type work. I got a good wage, working for Brody White, in spite of his nasty ways and bad character. I saved it. I have enough to buy some books and paper and ink to start studying again, if you don't object to it." He rose from the stool, and holding the bucket of milk in his hand, pleaded with his eyes for Joe to agree to his plan.

"Why, I've no objection to your idea, if that's what you have in mind to do." Joe took his hat from his head and rubbed his hand over his eyes. He was tired from his restless night, but there was too much to do to quit and get some sleep. He settled his hat on his head, pulling it low over his ears, and started walking to the gate.

Jeremiah followed him out, his pail in his hand. At the gate, he picked up Joe's bucket, walking briskly to keep up with his employer's long stride. He held his breath for his answer.

"You might write a letter to the mayor or the county officials in Denver and see what you can do about getting started. I'm sorry, Jeremiah, I don't know about such things. I was raised on a farm. You think some more on it, and we'll see what can be done. Right now though, take these buckets of milk to Hannah, and I'll get started chopping some more firewood."

It was a very sober young man who carried the pails to Hannah. He'd thought that Joe would object to his plans. He wondered now why he'd imagined it. He'd never planned to work here at this out-of-the-way station for long. He had enough money to go to Denver to study, but something about Joe had kept him here. Compared to White as boss, Joe was kind and understanding. He liked working for him. But, he didn't want to do it forever. The law was in his blood.

Joe went to check on the horses and donkeys in their corrals, then selected six mules for tomorrow's stage coach if it came in. He put them in the separate holding pen and made sure their mouths and tongues weren't sore. He examined them for any harness burns or cankered ears. He probed their hooves for stones or cracked shoes. Satisfied that they were well, he gave them a portion of dried grass and headed for the edge of the forest road where the trees had fallen during the storm. He selected a strong tree trunk with many branches and limbs and began to saw them off the trunk. He worked for a long time, thinking about what Jeremiah had said to him this morning. He finished the limbs and left them in a pile to be picked up later.

He glimpsed Jeremiah working around the barn, and was later surprised to find that he'd honed the felling axes and the blades on the station's hand planes, while Joe had worked on the tree limbs. The two hitched up the wagon and went for the felled limbs. He had almost a wagon full of wood to be cut into firewood. Jeremiah volunteered to cut the wood and kindling. Joe left the horses hitched to the wagon and walked back to the log. He discovered another fallen tree about fifty yards away and began to work on it. He left some thick branches for making lumber and shingles. Having done all he could without assistance, he yelled for Jeremiah to help him lift the limbs into the wagon. By early afternoon, they had a huge stack of unprocessed lumber and a mountain of firewood for the stove. It was time to stop for some food and rest.

After a quick supper of sliced beef and stewed peaches, Joe took a nap. His almost all-nighter and the hard work of the day finally caught up with him. He could hear in the background Jeremiah busily chopping the smaller limbs into firewood and a couple of female voices droning in the kitchen. A mighty shout awakened him, and he jumped out of bed before coming totally awake, thinking he was back in the Army. He raced for the door, but fortunately common sense returned before he opened it. He put on his britches and shirt, and in his socks, went out into the Public Room. He didn't take the time to pull on his boots.

He looked at Hannah, but it was Rosie who drew his attention. She had a big smile on her face, and she was on her way out the door. Joe and Hannah, holding Sammie's hand, followed more sedately. Jack scrambled out the door ahead of them, barking at Buck and Standing Tree, just dismounting from their horses. They had a pack horse with them. Joe observed these things in a quick glance, while his mind churned with the fact they had taken three horses from the station's stock. Jeremiah came from the barn, where he had been sharpening his ax after an hour cutting wood.

"We got 'em, the mangy varmints. Followed them all the way to the ridge about two miles from Buckboard Station. Five of the critters. All good clean skins and yellowed teeth."

Standing Tree walked stiffly to the pack horse, and lifted down a bundle of wolf skins. It was hard for Jeremiah to look at them. He knew that wolves were predators and would have killed or injured their animals, but he hated indiscriminate killing of any kind. He turned away. He decided it would be a good time to go fishing. He'd noticed a fine strong limb earlier that he liked and pulled it from the pile. He squatted in the dirt, and using his pen knife, trimmed the small nodules. Then he skinned the bark off, making it smooth and slender. He set it aside, saddled a horse and without glancing at the men by the wolf skins, picked up his pole and mounted, yelling, "I'm going fishing, Joe."

Joe, distracted by the sight of Standing Tree rolling out the sheet of canvas to display the wolf skins, waved at Jeremiah. They had talked of fishing this morning, he recalled, but wasn't focused on its importance. He heard Sammie fussing, but Hannah had a grip of iron on his small hand and prevented the boy from going with Jeremiah. She held the dog, Jack, in her arms. As soon as she saw what the excitement was about, she returned to the house with her two charges. Standing Tree was excitedly talking about the killing of the wolves in his own language, but Joe couldn't understand him. Joe could see the glowing eyes and the hand gestures, and thought this must have been how the old man had been in his youth and vigor. He watched for a while, before returning to the bedroom to pull on his boots.

It wasn't until later, when the skins were laid out on some bushes near the river bank several yards away to dry that Buck explained how they had tracked the wolves and caught them feasting on a fawn they had killed. It had been easy to pick the wolves off one by one. It was a gory tale, and one that Joe wished Hannah hadn't heard. He knew what Buck planned. He would take the skins to a trading post and sell them and collect the bounty money. He wondered if Buck planned to share the proceeds of their kill with Standing Tree, but he wouldn't question him about it. He did plan to discuss the matter of taking off without asking for permission and using three of the horses when he did it. But, not today. There had been enough excitement. Standing Tree ate some of the food that Hannah had prepared, then took his blanket and slept in the forest. Joe suspected he was watching over the wolf skins.

Jeremiah returned, and alongside his saddle, he carried seven nice-sized trout hanging on a string. He was quiet and subdued, and simply handed the scaled and gutted fish to Hannah for cooking. He ate hearty of his catch and turned in early, after telling Joe he would stand the early morning watch.

Joe was exhausted, both physically and mentally. He asked Buck to stand the first watch, knowing he'd get a negative answer. As he expected, Buck was too keyed up and excited. Joe dragged his coat out of the storage trunk, took his rifle, and stood guard over his animals.

He was glad of the coat when a fine mist started to fall. He imagined the wolf skins drying on the bushes and the old man sleeping in the forest, cold and damp. He was vexed at the thought of the bricks getting wet, delaying the finishing of the wall, and about Jeremiah going off to Denver to study law. He was almost certain Buck would leave with the wolf skins. He and Hannah would be alone to do all the work, if he and Jeremiah both left. At last, almost stumbling with cold and exhaustion, he went to the house, aroused Jeremiah, and fell into the bed, instantly asleep.

Hannah rose early the next morning as was her custom, but she let Joe sleep. He'd earned it; doing the work of two men, responsible for so many animals and buildings. There was a slight mist falling, and she pulled her heavy wool coat about her ears as she went to the outhouse. As she exited, she looked to the corrals but she didn't see Jeremiah. There was no light in the tent. Everyone except her was still asleep. She opened the firebox, stirred the coals in the stove, adding only a few pieces of wood to start a middling fire. She took some kindling and logs and made a fire in the fireplace to take the chill off the morning. She stood for a moment with her back to the fire, holding her hands out so they would get warm. It was late August, but already there was a feeling of autumn in the air.

She took out the ingredients for biscuits, but changed her mind and decided to make sweet rolls, instead. It was the same thing, really. She would put in a beaten egg, some brown sugar and cream, and dribble some molasses on top to make a frosting. She needed some more eggs, but hesitated to go to the hen house to fetch them. One of the men usually did that for her. She had a half dozen, but that wouldn't be enough with so many mouths to feed. She'd have to wait until someone woke up to gather the eggs.

The dough was in the oven and the ham frying nicely in the skillet when Joe strolled into the room, his eyes red with sleep. He came to her and kissed her cheek.

"Morning, Sweetheart. Is it still raining?"

"Yes, a slight mist; like a heavy fog. Joe, could you get some eggs? I'm almost out. Wasn't that awful, Buck's story about the wolves? What will he do with those skins?" Hannah moved the skillet from the burner. She poured coffee for both of them and sat warming her hands on the cup. She liked their early morning time together best, when it was just the two of them in the kitchen.

"He'll probably take them to some trading post and sell them for the bounty money. That's why he was so excited, I suppose. Wolves are predators, and the government pays for proof of a kill. For Standing Tree, it was the thrill of the hunt at his age. I doubt if Buck will share the money with him."

"That's not fair, Joe. Standing Tree should get some reward for tracking and helping Buck." Hannah had a gleam of anger in her eyes. She blew on the coffee to cool it; then took a small sip.

"It's the way of the world. Most men are prejudiced in some way. It wouldn't occur to men like Buck, even those married to an Indian woman, to share his bounty with an Indian. Forget it. It's not our business if Buck makes a little money on the side, as long as he does the work the stage line pays him to do. Besides, what would the old man do with the white man's money? Paper and silver coins mean nothing to him." He took his coat from the peg and put it on his strong shoulders, opened the door and disappeared into the rain.

Hannah pondered that for a long time. Buck hadn't done his work for a day and a half. It'd been left for Joe and Jeremiah to do. She could understand better now why Joe asked Jeremiah to work with him. He'd known that Buck wasn't reliable. He might have been a good soldier, she didn't know, but now he was shiftless and lazy when he thought he could get away with it. Oh, Joe. So many dreams and hopes for the future, yet weighed down with responsibility. Maybe it would be better when the barn was finished, and some of the animals enclosed inside. She smiled as she took her sweet rolls from the oven. They were perfect, fat and brown and ready for the hungry mouths that would taste them.

Joe returned with six eggs. They needed more, but six would have to do until the hens laid again. Hannah put a bit of lard in the skillet along with the ham grease, and fried two for Joe. He drank his coffee and ate one of the sweet rolls. His eyes rolled with joy at the taste. It was the first time that Hannah had cooked them, and they were delicious, better than biscuits and honey. She brought the coffee pot to fill his cup, but he pulled her into his lap and kissed her. It was at that moment that Jeremiah chose to walk into the Public Room from the hallway that led to his bedroom.

"Ho ho, should I go back and wait a few minutes?" Jeremiah looked much more cheerful this morning. It was the day for the westbound stage, and he always enjoyed that arrival, especially if Rusty Backgammon was driving.

Hannah jumped out of Joe's lap and poured his coffee. His eyes still shined with an inner glee; to be caught kissing his wife was exciting. She brought another cup and poured coffee for Jeremiah. She turned to the skillet to cook Jeremiah's eggs.

"What's on the schedule today, Boss? It's still raining, so we can't build the wall, and we have enough kindling to feed that monster of a stove until December. You can't get any plowing done or race the horses in the mud." He tore a small piece of sweet roll off the whole and chewed it slowly, his eyes reflecting his pleasure at the taste.

"I wouldn't race the horses even if it wasn't muddy. I thought we might make a start on the shed for supplies. Right now they're in that back bedroom, but we'll need the room

156

for guests when business picks up some. Have you counted how many pieces of lumber are ready for building? I counted fifty-four, which should be enough for one or two walls, any-way, if we saw them in half." Joe watched as Jeremiah ate his eggs and sweet roll. He'd sure like another one, but knew he should leave a few for the women and child, who had a hankering for sweets.

"Ah, Boss, you mean we'll not be using bricks? Just when I learned a new trade, you take it from me."

Jeremiah had a mournful expression on his face, but Joe wasn't fooled. He hated laying bricks. In fact, Jeremiah didn't like any of the hard work, but he didn't shrink from it like Buck did. Maybe it was for the best for the young man to become a lawyer, but at least he would have skilled experience in another occupation to fall back on if the law business didn't work out for him.

"No, it'll take too long to build the shed with bricks. It was probably a mistake in the first place, but I wanted a good strong barn that wouldn't burn to the ground." He reached for his cup and found it almost empty. He held it up to catch Hannah's attention. "I'm thinking about what you said about the brick chimney for Buck's cabin. It might be the better way rather than collecting river rocks."

"You like my idea? Really?" Jeremiah grinned, pleased.

"You thought I wouldn't consider it?" Hannah was fill-ing his cup, and he held her arm, keeping her from walking away from the table. "Our friend says he wants to be a law-yer, yet he doesn't know when he's won his case." He re-leased her, and she went to the stove. "I like the idea of a brick chimney, but it means Rosie will have to work outside. Can you spare her, dear?"

"We'll manage." She threw a few pieces of kindling in the firebox and closed the door.

Keeping his eyes on his wife, Joe continued, tapping the table with his finger for emphasis. "We need to get that shed up in two days at the most. I wish some of Taylor's carpenters had stayed behind, but they had the other stations to build. I understood that when I signed on here. John Dempsey made it crystal clear that the carpenters and road builders would make a start but it's up to us managers to finish the remains of whatever projects were left undone. I agreed to it, so that's what I'll do long as I'm able."

Joe looked up when Buck, Rosie and Sammie walked in the door, together with the dog. Jack had become such a pet for Sammie they had agreed that he could sleep with him in the tent last night. Joe didn't think that Buck liked the notion, but he did like to please his son. The dog ran to Hannah and sat gazing at her, hoping for some food.

Rosie went to the stove, lifted the pot of coffee and poured a cup for Buck. She looked chagrined. "Sorry. Late. Not help with meal." She took over the skillet and cooked Buck's eggs, three of them. Afterward, the excess grease was poured into an empty lard tin that was meant for used grease, and the last of the eggs were scrambled for the women and Sammie.

Rosie looked at the sweet rolls in surprise, but Buck knew what they were. He took two, and with a large bowl of porridge, ate more than his share. Food and board were part of his wages, and he took advantage of the fact. Rosie put some porridge in a small bowl for Sammie and poured milk in it. She gave him a cup of the milk to drink. He made a face, showing everyone he didn't like the taste.

"Buck, Jeremiah and I will start on the supply shed today. Looks like the rain may let up by the time the stage gets here. It'll take another day or two for the last of the bricks to dry. If the rain keeps falling we'll make a start on the inside of the barn where it's dry. I've already selected the mules for the eastbound stage, but check them again before the stage gets here. They're in the holding pen. Then as soon as that coach leaves, get the six horses for the southbound ready. You might need to drive some of the passengers over to Buckboard Station, so it wouldn't hurt if you clean up the

Conestoga. We've used it to haul timber. I hope you don't mind. It's larger than the farm wagon and can hold more large logs."

Buck did mind, but he only mumbled something as his mouth was full of sweet roll. Before he could swallow and speak, Standing Tree walked in and crossed to the table and sat down. The eggs were gone and only one sweet roll remained, so the man was left only porridge, the roll and ham. He frowned at the coffee, but it was hot, and he tasted it and put the cup down. Hannah gave him a glass of water.

"Much wet. Skins no dry out. Sun come out by and by, Yo Hadley. Scarred Woman make fine biscuit." That was the extent of his conversation for the morning.

"I've already gathered the eggs, Buck. There might be some more later on. Milk the goats before you start with the mules. It's going to be a fine day when the sun comes out."

Joe put on his hat, grabbed his rifle, and he and Jeremiah walked from the room. He didn't wait to see if Buck did as he asked him. They went to the stack of lumber and selected several pieces longer than the others. He then selected some for the four corners and set them aside. He asked Jeremiah's opinion on where the shed should be placed, and they decided on a spot near the house. They carried the lumber they had selected and picked up the saws, hammers and nails in the farm wagon beside the sharpening stone.

Joe noticed that Buck went to the holding pen and checked the mules before heading into the forest to check his wolf hides. He seemed to have had an argument with Standing Tree, but Joe figured it didn't concern him. However, the goats did and decided he would see about them in a while.

He and Jeremiah had the four corner posts buried deep in the soil for strength when the sun came out. It didn't take long to heat up the atmosphere, and he began to sweat. He told Jeremiah about mid-morning that he needed a break. He wanted to check if the goats had been milked. Buck and Standing Tree were not in the yard when he crossed to the goat pen. Their bags were light and soft, so Buck must have milked them, and he was reassured. He went to the house after answering nature's call. Hannah had saved him a sweet roll. He ate it with some cool milk.

"Is that a new project?" He stopped on his way outside to ask.

Hannah was stitching a cloth for the long table, the drab gray material stretched across her lap. "Yes. As soon as I have the hem finished, I have a pattern in mind for some flowers and green leaves at each corner. It won't match the curtains, but it might brighten the room." She smiled. He leaned over and kissed the top of her head.

Rosie and Sammie were not in the room, and Joe assumed they must be in the tent with Buck. Jack lay in his favorite spot by the fireplace asleep. It was pleasant to have the room to themselves for a while, with no one around. They chatted about who the passengers might be on the coach. Hannah hoped there would be a woman, so she could talk of the latest fashions and news from the East.

There was a large roast beef in the oven, and she had made a cake and a peach cobbler for dessert. The vegetables would be cooked later so they would be hot and fresh. She had her usual pot of beans simmering on the stove in case there was a need for more food. Three loaves of bread cooled on the table, each covered with one of Rosie's attempts at stitchery. She had tacked a couple of Sammie's better drawings on the wall next to the front door.

With a sigh, Joe decided he should get back to work. By the time they heard the sound of Rusty Backgammon's brass trumpet, Joe and Jeremiah had completed a fourth of the small shed. It would take maybe three more work days. They walked over toward the house to see who was on the stage. Buck came from the direction of the holding pen. Standing Tree appeared at the side of the house with his blanket wrapped on his shoulders. Rosie and Sammie came from the tent. Joe had time to wonder what they had been doing in there all day, when she usually was in the kitchen with Hannah, and the boy playing with the dog.

Twelve

"Hello, Rusty. Who have you got for us today?"

"Got a surprise for you, Joe. Came all the way from Indiana, I hear." Rusty dropped from his driver's seat, and the new man, Grover Mayhew, climbed down from his side of the coach. Rusty went to the door and opened it wide. Out stepped a nicely dressed older couple, and Joe almost burst into tears.

"Mama, Papa, why are you here?" Joe hugged them both and didn't notice anyone else in the yard, not Jeremiah standing near the unfinished shed, nor Buck coming to unhitch the team of mules. He studied his father's gray eyes and wrinkled face to see if he had been drinking, but he was stone cold sober.

He saw his mother's kindly, pale face. As they moved a little to the side, a very large woman stepped down. She was at least six feet tall and weighed close to two hundred pounds. Joe had never seen so large a woman. She was dressed in the latest style and wore on her head a blue hat with a white feather in the brim. Joe stepped back and gently moved his mother to the side so he could welcome the other passenger.

"Welcome to Sweetwater Station, ma'am." He smiled

and held out his hand; and she took it in a firm, strong grip. "Come into the house out of the sun."

Jack jumped from his place by the fireplace and set up an awful racket, barking and wagging his tail at the strangers. Joe went over and picked him up in his arms. Hannah was busy at the stove, but when she saw Joe's mother and father, she ran forward with a glad cry.

"Mr. and Mrs. Hadley? Oh, this is a wonderful surprise. Welcome to our home." She glanced at the other woman and stepped back in surprise. She stood almost tall enough to reach the ceiling, and there was something about her manner that was rigid and unyielding. "Ma'am, welcome. Come in and refresh yourself. Please sit down." Hannah spoke in her most pleasant voice.

The woman stared rudely at the scar on Hannah's face.

"I guess you might wonder why your parents have come here, Mr. Hadley. And, why I came with them." Priscilla St. John could not keep quiet a moment longer. She was used to getting attention, and she spoke in a loud aggressive voice that went with her height and weight. She started rolling off her long blue gloves, all the while standing like a soldier at attention.

Ruth Hadley gladly took the seat that Hannah offered and sighed. She took off her hat, ready to relax after the tiring journey. Her hungry eyes searched her son's face, seeing for the first time the maturity and strength in him.

"My name, young man, is Priscilla St. John from Indianapolis. Since I was making the trip anyway, your brother, Luther, paid me to bring them here. Said it was time for you to take responsibility for your folks. What with you going off to war and all, leaving him with the obligation for three years. Then traipsing off to the wilderness with no thought to their care was a very selfish and unkindly act. He told me I was to bring them here and go on to Denver where I have good friends to entertain me."

Jack growled at the stranger, and Joe calmed him by

rubbing the top of his head.

Miss St. John glanced at the people who had followed them into the house. She clearly showed her displeasure at their appearance. Rosie and Sammie were standing at the table, eyes wide open in awe.

Standing Tree went to the fireplace, his dark brown face stoic and unsmiling, and sat down with his blanket. He kept a wary eye on the odd white woman who looked as much like a man as a woman.

Lastly, the driver Rusty and his guard Grover came in and stood by the door as if poised to withdraw in a hurry if need be. They had already put up with the woman's bullying for several hours and were curious to see how Joe would handle her. It was like a circus side show to them.

"Well, ma'am, my parents are very welcome in my home." Joe smiled at her look of surprise. "It's true that I went to war, but so did hundreds of other young soldiers fighting for their cause. Please, let's put the war behind us. You're welcome. Hannah has a nice meal planned and a fine room for you to spend the night. Buck'll take you to the next station in the morning." Joe smiled again, a warm, charming smile, but from the look on her face, she was having none of it. He could see she was on a rant and determined to have her say.

"Young man, don't try to fool me with your charm and deceitful face. I've met men like you before in Indianapolis. Selfish to the core. Uncaring of your parents and your brother—"

"Now, just a goddamned minute Miss St. John. I've put up with your cruel ways all these miles, because the missus and I know nothing of ships or trains or stage coach schedules. But, I by god will not stand for your abuse of my son. Who do you think you are anyway? Why, you're a paid servant. You just admitted it. My older son paid you to see that we arrived safely at my son's home, and now you shut your mouth. He'll take care of us now. Catch your coach tomorrow and be on your way. We don't need you anymore. That's what I say." The elder Hadley's words were enough. The audience remained silent for several minutes, and then it seemed they all spoke at once.

Hannah asked Miss St. John if she would like to go to her room and freshen up before supper, to which suggestion the woman was glad to agree.

"Thank you, Mrs. Hadley. I do feel a little tired and hungry. Maybe if I can rest a few minutes I can eat. What time is dinner, did you say?" Her neck bore a red flush of anger, and Hannah felt no sympathy for her as she led her down the hallway and to the bedroom.

"In an hour at the most, ma'am. Would you like a cup of soothing tea while you wait?"

"Yes, please. I'm parched from the hot sun and dust." Her words were clipped, and she sat down stiffly on the chair with a sigh.

Hannah quickly went to the kitchen and brewed a pot of tea, and brought a cup in her pretty flowered china ware to her guest. She curtseyed, and with a smile of welcome, left the woman alone.

Miss St. John spent the next hour in silent contemplation of the docile old man's sudden change in manner. She had had no trouble keeping them under her thumb until today. She was shocked and a little intimidated, if the truth were known. She finished her tea, a frown on her face, set the cup on the table and rose to remove her hat.

She could find no fault with the furnishings, although simple and functional. She pulled back the quilt covering and felt of the mattress. Goose feathers, if she was any judge of bedding. And, clean white linen sheets covered the mattress. The small table contained a lamp and a flowered pitcher and bowl. She looked in the pitcher and found clean water. Only one chair, but then she only needed one at a time. Yes, Josiah Hadley was a fine host, in spite of what his brother's poisonous words had led her to believe. But, his wife, what a pity her face was marred by that hideous scar.

Joe went down the hallway and put the dog in the inner garden so he wouldn't bother the strange woman. He'd think about that scene later when he had time. He came back and told Rusty and Grover that they would be in the same room as before. They knew where he meant and took their satchels with them. Grover combed his hair, and they washed their hands and faces. They discussed the old man who had set the fine lady in her place. It would be something to remember for a long time. Rusty had seen many strange people in his years as a driver, but this was the oddest woman he had encountered.

Joe led his mother to the room next to his and Hannah's on the opposite hallway from Miss St. John, where they would sleep for the night. Hannah might decide later to put them in another one, as they had not expected permanent guests.

Rosie helped Hannah finish the vegetables. She was puzzled by the conversation and was trying to decipher what it all meant. She had been in the tent all day packing their possessions, for Buck had decided to leave tomorrow, taking the passenger to Buckboard Station and not returning to his work. He told her to keep it a secret. He was afraid someone would take his wolf skins. She wanted to stay, but she must follow her husband.

Buck finished unhitching the team and stood near the corral quietly, his face dark and moody. He was deep in thought. He didn't want to call attention to himself tonight. He planned to pull out in his wagon tomorrow and continue on to the first trading post he found. He had already slipped the wolf skins into the wagon and hidden them in an old barrel. He figured he might even go as far as Fort Laramie, where the older soldiers knew him and Prairie Flower. There were a few of her tribe there, but they mostly lived further south. He'd have money once he sold the skins, and he could decide later where he would go. He hated to give up the good situation, but Joe had Jeremiah; and now his father had shown up unexpectedly. He wouldn't miss Buck. Besides, he didn't like the way Joe made free with his Conestoga, as though he could use it any time he pleased. Yes sir, it was time for him to move along, and to hell with the stage coach business.

Peter Hadley was left alone with his thoughts. He sat in the rocking chair and pretended to watch the women cooking, but his mind was troubled. Ordinarily a mild-mannered man, he'd exploded with temper when he'd heard the abusive words hurled by that strange woman that Luther had put in charge of them. He'd let Luther get too powerful, that's what had happened. He should've spoken up sooner. It was too late now. Luther had it all, which is what Peter suspected he wanted all along. It'd been so subtle and slow in arriving that he hadn't recognized that it was Luther who was the dominant, selfish one.

The woman was wrong there. She didn't know his son as he did.

Joe had never asked for what he didn't earn, nor had he said an unkind word to anyone, not since he was a small lad. James had been a wild one, gambling and womanizing, but he'd not been selfish or grasping as Luther had been. Yes, he could see it now when it was too late. He'd let his drinking become too pleasant and costly. He'd grieved for James as had Ruth, each in their own way. Joe had been grieving, too.

He understood better now, and they hadn't helped him. They should have recognized what Luther was becoming. He had what he wanted now, the farm, the land, the house, the tools and animals. He had it all. Peter had signed the papers, and it was gone from his hands. He'd been so drunk he hadn't realized what he was signing until the fancy lawyer had explained it to him. God bless him. Peter hoped Luther would be happy and content now that they were gone.

Peter was thinking so hard that he didn't see Hannah approach him. She tapped him gently on the shoulder.

"Mr. Hadley, would you like a cup of coffee, or maybe some goat's milk? Supper's almost ready, but I'm sure you must be tired and thirsty."

"Yes, thank you, Hannah, I would like a cup of coffee." Peter scanned the perimeter of the large room and found only the Indian sitting at the fireplace, and the woman and boy by the table. "Where's everyone gone?"

"Most have gone to their rooms in the back of the house. Joe and Buck are looking at the coach and the mules that pulled it from Mozier Station. They always look for sores or bruises or stones in their hooves after each trip before they release them in the pen with the others. If they don't do it first they might forget which mules just came in and send them out with something wrong with them. Oh. I'm talking too much and you wanted some coffee." Hannah moved with grace to the stove and poured a cup of coffee for her father-in-law.

"Thank you, Hannah. This is a pleasant room. Are all the stations built like this? This one seems different from the Mozier station and the one east of it."

"Mostly. They're built to a certain standard, but the con-tractors can add rooms or use logs or river stones or bricks. This one is built in the shape of a 'u'. There's a nice garden spot in the center of the building with a well. You'll see it later. We haven't been here long enough to plant flowers or bushes."

Rosie called to her and she excused herself to go to the kitchen. She smiled at Standing Tree. Peter sat and slowly sipped his coffee. He gazed at the Indian sitting on the floor near the fireplace and was surprised to find him scrutinizing him just as intently.

"You Big Father from beyond mighty river? You be Yo Hadley papa? You like Scarred Woman fine?"

It took Peter a while to understand what the man was asking. He had never talked with an Indian before.

"Yes, I'm Joe Hadley's father from Indiana. Farming

country, we grow corn and wheat and oats. Are you a farmer? Scarred Woman? Do you mean Hannah Hadley?"

"I not farmer. I hunter of big game, deer, antelope, elk. What this Indna, you say? Scarred Woman my friend. Make good cook. No like coffee. Like tobacco. Yo Hadley no smoke. Shame. Smoke good."

"I see. You're not a farmer. You're a hunter of big game animals. Indiana is the name of my village beyond the mighty river. I like Scarred Woman. Her name's Hannah. She's Joe Hadley's wife. I like to smoke, too." He took out a box of slim fragrant cigars from a pocket. He offered one to Standing Tree. The man put it in his mouth, and Peter struck a match. The Indian drew back when it flashed brightly. Peter calmly put his cigar in his mouth and lit it, then offered the match to Standing Tree, who accepted it once he understood its usage.

The two men smoked for a while in silence. Peter flinched when Standing Tree spoke in his deep, solemn tone.

"Big Father good friend. He like smoke good tobacco. Yo Hadley no smoke. Why you no teach Yo Hadley smoke?"

Peter didn't know how to answer the question. He spoke in the same way that the Indian did.

"Joe Hadley no like smoke. Bad for lungs." He pointed to his chest and coughed. Standing Tree understood perfectly. He roared with laughter.

And that was when Joe walked in the door, followed by Buck. Joe was startled to hear Standing Tree laughing. The sound seemed to come from somewhere deep in his chest cavity. He was smoking with his father like twin chimney stacks. He put his hat on the peg and his rifle in its place and looked at the table.

It seemed to be the signal for everyone to gather for supper. Rusty and Grover came from their room. Buck sat in his usual place as far from Joe as he could get. Hannah went to get Ruth and Miss St. John, while Rosie seated Sammie and started bringing food to the table. Ruth took a seat beside her husband, who had found a saucer and put out his cigar. Standing Tree copied his every move and threw his blanket on the floor and sat next to Buck. Miss St. John came in, followed by Hannah, who went to the stove and started filling coffee cups or glasses with water.

Priscilla St. John took one look at Standing Tree and refused to sit beside him. Hannah tried to defuse the situation by filling her plate and suggesting she might enjoy the comfort of the rocking chair beside the fireplace. Miss St. John accepted the compromise and sat alone across the room.

Ruth Hadley didn't mind sitting at the same table as Standing Tree. She had been born and reared in Boston, and in spite of being timid, shy and easily frightened, she left the comfort and luxury of her family's splendid home and followed her husband to the farming country of Indiana as a bride. Today, she found herself even further away in the wilds of Colorado Territory, sitting across from Indians.

The room was pleasant and the food delicious, she had to admit, in spite of her misgivings before she left Indiana. She might learn to love this place her son had chosen for his home. She smiled at Joe and took his large hand in her own. He looked surprised; but he smiled at her, and she was satisfied. Joe was the best of her sons, she was only now discovering. James had been wild, and Luther cold and demanding, but Josiah was kind and gentle, yet strong and brave. She let the conversation drift by her as she wallowed in this new sensation of love and acceptance.

Hannah was glad that she had cooked the beans, for there might not have been enough food without them. The beef roast was tender and juicy, the beans tasty, and the beets, turnips and potatoes were well seasoned. She was surprised that it had all turned out so well, what with the activity going on around her this afternoon, and being interrupted so many times. This was the way she had dreamed it would be. The table cloth was not finished and her matching candle sticks still unpacked, but the two lamps let off a soft mellow glow, and the warmth from the stove lent a homey touch. When she estimated that everyone was ready for dessert, she set out fresh plates from the set for twenty that she and Joe had bought in Indiana, and served peach cobbler and spice cake. A fresh pot of coffee was brought by Rosie and cups replenished.

As always when he spoke, Standing Tree received everyone's attention.

"What say now, Big Father? Fine cook, Scarred Woman. Yo Hadley fine fellow. He no smoke but good friend." He waited a few minutes, then got up and picked up his blanket from the floor by the fireplace. He strutted by Miss St. John sitting in Hannah's chair and spoke to her.

"Tall Woman no belong. She no friend of Yo Hadley and Scarred Woman. You go." Priscilla St. John watched in fascination as Standing Tree wrapped his blanket around him and swept out the door.

That started an exodus from the room. Rusty and Grover left for their room for an early start east in the morning. Buck and Rosie, holding Sammie's hand, went to their tent. Sammie cried because Jack was not with them, but Rosie soothed him. Sammie would have to learn to live without the dog.

Jeremiah went out after telling Joe he'd take the first watch and sleep in the barn. He took his rifle with him. Miss St. John, her manner somewhat subdued, left the Public Room. She felt lonely and embarrassed. Her host and hostess had treated her well, and she couldn't deny that of the two brothers, she preferred this one. Luther Hadley had deceived her, and she was ashamed of the way she had attacked Joe.

Left alone with his wife and parents, Joe relaxed and moved to the fireplace area, bringing a chair with him. He told his father to sit in the rocker. Hannah got up to wash dishes, wondering why Rosie hadn't stayed to help her. Maybe she was shy in front of Joe's parents, or perhaps she was being tactful, leaving them alone. She sighed and tied her apron. Ruth got up to help her.

"If you'll give me an apron, Scarred Woman, I'll help you with the cleaning up." She laughed, and after a surprised gasp, Hannah laughed with her. She found a clean apron and helped her mother-in-law tie it around her waist. "Who is that Indian, anyway? Obviously, he lives here. What tribe is he? He seems to have an education of some kind." While the women washed up and put the extra food away, Hannah explained how each of the residents of Sweetwater Station happened to arrive there.

The men sat at the other end of the room quietly talking. Peter lighted his half-smoked cigar, noting that supplies would be limited in this distant place, and he shouldn't be wasteful.

The next morning the Hadleys got a sample of how a way station on the Overland Stage Line route was run. Hannah was up early, as usual, and started the stove to burning brightly. She filled the coffee pot with water. She stepped out for a moment. It looked to be a fine morning and a warm sunny day. There was no fog over the spring. She found Standing Tree gazing toward the spot where the Conestoga was normally parked. It was gone. And the tent. She didn't know if it was true, but from the Indian's puzzled expression, Buck and Rosie were gone.

Just then, Joe came from the direction of the corrals. He was striding like an angry man, and she couldn't blame him. Standing Tree caught up with him, but didn't speak.

"They're gone, Hannah. They left about an hour ago. He didn't even have the decency to tell me he was resigning from his duties. He took the tent with him and two extra horses. I suppose he took the table, chairs and bed, too. Damnation. I should have known from the way Rosie was acting yesterday. She wouldn't let Sammie play with Jack, and kept a close eye on him. Today's the day I need an extra hand, too." He blew out his cheeks and looked toward the barn.

She didn't see anything that made this day different except that his parents had arrived. Was that what he meant? Before she could ask, he continued, his eyes bright with anger.

"I was over on the other side of the corrals. It looks like one of the horses is sick, but, I'll have to find out what's wrong later. I heard some noises but wasn't expecting this to happen. I heard him drive away, but couldn't leave the damn horse. It wouldn't have mattered anyway, if he was determined to go."

"How can I help?" She looked at him expectantly.

"Go in the house. I've got to wake up Jeremiah and get back to the sick horse. I sure would appreciate a cup of hot coffee to warm my bones."

Hannah went to grind the coffee beans and start breakfast. Standing Tree followed her and sat in his normal spot by the fireplace, his face sober and his black eyes watching her.

Joe walked straight to the barn where Jeremiah was sleeping. He lit the lantern, and banged on a bucket.

"Jeremiah, wake up. We've got work to do. Buck's gone and taken the tent and two horses with him. Wake up, please." He left the lantern for Jeremiah and strode to the house, his long legs stretched out in his haste.

He walked through the Public Room and stopped at the middle door in the left hallway. He knocked. "Rusty, Grover, wake up! Buck's gone with the Conestoga and the tent. He took two of the stage horses, too, damn him."

The door opened. Rusty stood there, already up and dressed, his suspenders drawn tightly over his slight paunch, his bald head shiny and his beard scraggly from tossing and turning in the bed. Grover, his face unshaven, stood behind him. He had his shaving mug in one hand and his brush in the other. He gaped at Joe in surprise.

"Did you say Buck took off with two horses that belong to the stage company, and the tent? Hell, I thought he was a good worker. What does this mean, Joe?"

"It means the man's a damn thief and a quitter. He

signed on as animal handler for a year. He's only been here a few months. I thought something like this would happen after he killed Brody White."

"What's going on, Joe? Did you say Buck's gone in the Conestoga?" It was a sleepy-eyed Jeremiah, stuffing his shirt tail in his trousers' waist, his breath swift and shallow with his run from the barn. "He was supposed to take Miss St. John to Buckboard Station."

"Damn, Jeremiah, I know that. Lordy, I hope we're not stuck with that woman until I can find a way to get her to the next station."

"What killin' are you talking about, old son? We never heard over at the Mozier station 'bout no killin' that Buck done. Grover only came a few weeks ago; he don't know nothing." The old-timer squinted at Joe through red-rimmed eyes. "Now that I think on it; there was a rumor at Fort Laramie 'bout a stolen horse, but it couldn't be proved. Ya think ol Buck's a horse thief?"

"I'm sorry, Rusty. I don't have time to tell the story now. It happened when the freight wagons were here; the ones that took the supplies and animals to Buckboard Station for Obediah and Emily Blessing, before the big storm. Jeremiah can explain; he came in on that train. I've got a sick horse on my hands and a crazy woman on the way to Denver."

As they were talking the men had been going down the hallway toward the kitchen, Joe and Jeremiah together with Rusty and Grover trailing behind. When they got in the kitchen, Hannah looked up, a worried look on her face.

"Sit down, please, Joe. The coffee will be ready in a minute, and I'll start some porridge. If Jeremiah will bring in some eggs, we can eat before the others get up."

"We're already up." Peter walked into the room, followed by Ruth. "We heard voices. What's happening?" No one noticed Jeremiah quietly slip from the room. Standing Tree came over to sit at the table. He could follow only half of the conversation, but he understood something bad had happened, and it had to do with the man with the Apache wife.

"I'm sorry, Papa, I didn't mean to wake you and Mama. Did you sleep well?"

"We slept fine. Now, get on with your tale of woe."

As he spoke, Ruth moved over to the stove and started to help Hannah. She didn't know anything about running a station, but she knew how to cook breakfast for hungry men. She had raised three boys. Hannah helped her with an apron and whispered that she could help her by pouring the coffee. She pointed to the cups and the spoons.

"Papa, Buck Jones, my animal handler has driven off in his wagon, leaving Miss St. John stranded without a ride to Buckboard Station, the next station to the west. He took two of the company horses and my tent, and probably a table, chairs and a bed. Besides that, I have a horse with the colic or something that I need to get back to right away."

"Where's that sick horse? I know something about sick animals. I can take care of that problem for you, Son." Peter thought it only fair that he do something to help his son after treating him like he had.

"Here's the eggs. Joe, we have the farm wagon. If you'll tell me how to get to the next station, I can take Miss St. John there for you." Jeremiah's breathing was rapid, having run from the chicken coop. His eyes were bright and excited.

Ruth reached for the basket of eggs and moved back to the stove, unnoticed by the men.

"Thanks, Jeremiah, but you've no experience with driving passengers, and you've never been west of here. Why don't you show my father where the corrals are located? The sick horse is in the small pen behind the donkeys. Papa, wear my coat. It's cool out in the mornings."

Jeremiah and Peter moved to see about the sick horse. That took care of one of the problems.

"Did the young man say that you have a farm wagon, Joe? Is it well sprung and fairly comfortable? Clean? If

Rusty'll take the stage alone back to Mozier's place, I can drive Miss St. John to the next station, if you'll give me a map or directions where I'm to go. I drove the stage to Mozier, and I can manage a farm wagon." The men didn't consider how Grover Mayhew would get back to Mozier from Buckboard Station.

"That's wonderful, Grover. I sure appreciate your willingness to help. Hannah, how long until breakfast is ready?"

"It's ready now, if you gentlemen will tell me how you like your eggs cooked." Ruth was well pleased with her new position as cook's helper. That had been her recent problem, she thought, that she was no longer needed by her sons. Luther had a cook and housekeeper, who didn't like for Ruth to putter in her territory. For someone used to taking care of a large family, that was bad.

The men sat down, and the ladies spooned porridge, flapjacks and fried eggs, with hot coffee as soon as the men could eat it and swallow. In between bites, Joe drew a crude map on a sheet of tablet paper for Grover to follow. He explained that really it was a matter of following the new road west along the river. It was a rough, up-hill journey, through huge boulders, thick forest and deep gullies.

They left the room and headed to the corrals, where a team of mules was brought out for the stage coach and a team of horses for the farm wagon. The wagon had to be unloaded for it had been used as a storage facility for the last few weeks. It was swept out and dusted off.

Within minutes, Rusty was ready to go. Joe had written a short note to be sent to Ned Baldwin, the field supervisor, to explain how Buck Jones had deserted his post and taken two horses with him. He didn't mention the tent and furniture, because technically the tent belonged personally to Joe, since he bought it from Taylor, the building contractor. In his note, he asked Baldwin to send him another animal handler.

"Grover," asked Rusty, his horn in his hand, "How ya gonna get back to Mozier Station?" He stuffed Joe's letter in his shirt pocket.

"I'll bring the wagon back here and borrow a saddle horse from Joe to ride the rest of the way. I should be back tomorrow or the next day for sure, if there are no stops on the way."

With that settled to his satisfaction, Rusty said his farewells to the ladies, played a tune on his brass trumpet and he was away in a great cloud of dust.

"Oh, damn, I forgot to milk the goats." Joe moaned, as he watched the stage disappear in the distance.

Grover laughed. "You milk goats?"

"Sure, I milk goats when I have to. Where did you think that milk came from you had in your coffee this morning?" Joe sounded a little testy; his frustration and anger were beginning to come to the surface. "That was one of Buck's jobs. Damn him. I guess we best see if Miss St. John's ready to go." The men left the farm wagon and its team of two horses parked in the yard, under the watchful eyes of Standing Tree and Jack, who was sniffing the ground where the tent once stood. One of the chickens squawked and flew into the air when the dog got too close.

"Yo Hadley. You want I track that Apache squaw?" Standing Tree had followed him.

"No, no track. Let him go. He ain't worth the effort." He shook his head and muttered under his breath. He regretted that Buck had gotten away with two of the company horses under his care. And he might lose a third if his father couldn't cure him of his illness. The six mules pulling the Conestoga didn't count as a loss to the company since Buck had arrived with six of his own. Standing Tree, disappointed, went over to a tree and sat down to await the next development in the life of Joe Hadley. Jack lay down beside him, and soon both were fast asleep.

When the men stepped into the Public Room, Miss St. John was sitting at the table drinking hot tea and eating a bowl of porridge. Hannah had told her about Buck going off in the Conestoga. Joe sat across from her and explained that Grover had volunteered to drive her in the farm wagon to the next stage station, where she would be guided on her next step to Denver by Obediah Blessing and his gracious wife, Emily. The woman was most unhappy, but resigned to her fate.

Leaving her in the hands of the ladies and Grover, Joe went to milk the goats, with Jack trailing along, stopping to sniff at the place where the tent had been. He seemed to sense that the boy was gone, for he stayed close to Joe in the barn. Joe returned from the barn, buckets in his hands, in time to see Grover and Miss St. John riding away in the farm wagon. He breathed a sigh of relief. Jack looked up at him as if to ask why he was troubled.

He left the buckets of milk with Hannah and inquired of his mother. She said Ruth was changing the sheets on the bed.

"Don't let her overtax herself, Hannah. She's been ill."

"I'll watch over her, Joe. You do what you have to out-side," Hannah promised. She took a clean cloth from a shelf and began to strain the milk. The dog sat at her feet, watching her closely.

Joe sought out Jeremiah who was in the corral with Peter and the sick horse. He suspected Jeremiah was hiding from Miss St. John. He told him to go and have his breakfast, and if they could manage it, he wanted to get some more work done on the shed. He asked his father what he thought about the horse. They discussed several remedies, and Joe told him to go eat his meal and he would sit with the horse.

When Peter was returning from the house, he got his first good look at the station as a whole. He scanned the hori-zon—to the north, south, east, and west—and liked the scene. There was a comfortable house with several rooms for guests and the inner garden which he had yet to visit. He admired the beginnings of a plowed field and intended to ask Joe about it. There was a large, substantial barn, forests and three sources of water, according to Hannah, one never ending: the natural spring flowing from an underground reservoir, the second the manually-dug well in the inner garden, and the third the fast-moving river a few miles away whose source was the snow melt in the far distant mountains. The stage line planners had chosen well. He was grateful that Joe had been assigned such a permanent setting. Peter could visualize a city standing near this site someday.

Jeremiah left the house in a more leisurely manner, picking his teeth with a straw he had found in the house. He had no great desire to work on the shed today. He had enjoyed the hour shared with Mr. Hadley. Just as he thought, when he arrived, Joe left the horse and they began the work on building the shed. They finished except for the roof, at which time Joe called a halt for supper. Joe went to see about his horse, and Jeremiah headed to the house and food. He had had no midday meal, as Joe was so determined to finish the shed.

The second night of the Hadley's visit was much different from the previous night. There was no driver or guard, no temperamental passenger, no unscrupulous animal handler and his wife and child. Hannah missed Sammie. She had grown quite fond of the boy. Jack wandered around sniffing the ground, and Hannah decided he was searching for the child. Ruth made her potato pancakes, and they ate the last of the beans. There was enough roast beef left to make a stew with potatoes, onions and carrots. The carrots were precious for their rarity. The supplies they received didn't include a large number of carrots or beets, two vegetables that Hannah planned to grow in her garden. Standing Tree made no loud pronouncements. He ate his meal and left the table.

Peter went out soon after, and the two men sat under the tree, smoking in silence. The night sky was clear, and a million stars shone in the blackness of space. A sliver of a moon was just above the horizon, and Peter gazed at it with wonder. He took a deep breath of the cool fresh air. The Indian began to talk of past triumphs, and Peter listened politely but

179

didn't understand a word of the old man's language. He put out his cigar and went to bed, contented and pleased with his new life.

Thirteen

As the weather remained mild and pleasant, so did the affairs of the Hadley family at Sweetwater Station. The ill sorrel stallion rose the next morning to his feet and began to walk. A day later, Peter declared him well again and ready to assume his work load.

Joe and Jeremiah finished the shed and the remaining supplies were sorted and moved out of the living quarters into it. Hannah cleaned the room; it had been Jeremiah's until now when not needed by passengers. He appreciated the additional space where he could spread his books and papers.

Ruth and Peter took over the work of gathering the eggs and milking the goats. She was an expert at making cheese. Peter went to examine the field and came back for the plow. Three more feet were added to the end of Joe's rows, and ten feet to his width for the kitchen garden. An additional field of two acres was plowed for wheat, oats and corn. The plots were small, but their hopes were high. A row of fall vegetables was planted and only awaited the time for harvesting.

Standing Tree made a bow and several arrows out of a sapling near the spring. Both Standing Tree and Peter were older men, and although miles apart in culture and background, found much in common: fishing, hunting, and smoking. The cool evenings found them sitting under a tree near the barn, dreaming of past adventures or simply enjoying the night breeze. The dog slept peacefully near them.

As the contents of the barrels and boxes brought from Indiana were unpacked and put away, Hannah found the lamp that she and Joe had purchased. It was no ordinary lamp, but one with painted pink and blue flowers and green leaves with a golden crest. She proudly displayed it on a small table near the rocking chair. From their own baggage, Ruth brought forth the Hadley family Bible and carefully printed the names of Hannah's parents and grandparents, their birth dates and date of marriage and death dates. She placed it near the pretty lamp, and it added a homey touch. She commenced to knit a scarf for the table.

While Joe and Jeremiah took care of the needs of the animals, Peter roused Ruth, and together, they took Hannah into the inner garden.

"What?" Hannah laughed. "I have a meal to prepare, you can't forget. What do we want in here?"

"My dear, we need a private respite, one that is for the family's use alone. Mother and I thought this would be just the spot, away from the animals and noise. Flowers and trees; maybe a bench over there." Peter pointed to the wall against the main building.

"Mother Hadley?" Hannah questioned her, finding the idea of a secret place enticing, but she hesitated.

"Yes, dear, I agree with Peter." Ruth took his arm and smiled into his twinkling eyes.

"But, where would we put the animals in case of an attack?" She was thinking of the hailstorm and the goats and chickens. They moved back into the Public Room and approached Joe about the idea.

"Why is it necessary now, with the large barn built? I think the builders meant it for the use of the station family. What do you think, son? There may not be another storm for years."

Amused at his parents' plan, Joe shrugged and said, "It would be a waste to leave the space unused. Maybe we can build a shelter for the goats later."

With the question of the small space settled, the family proceeded to fashion the inner garden into a place of beauty and relaxation. Weeds were hoed, pulled and burned. Seed packets were brought out of the boxes, examined and discussed. Peter found a few saplings near the river banks that caught his eye and he dug them up and replanted them near the well. It didn't look like much now, but his eye was on the future.

Five days passed in splendid harmony and then the peace was rent by the discordant sound of Rusty Backgammon's trumpet. The western bound stage had arrived and slid to a stop in the muddy tracks left by an early morning rain. On it were a minister of the gospel named Ezra Conway in sober black suit and stiff collar; his wife, Clotilda, heavyset and gray-haired, dressed in a pale green frock which became the envy of Hannah and Ruth; and their sixteen-year-old daughter, Jenny. The married couple was given Jeremiah's room and the daughter the room previously occupied by Miss Priscilla St. John, whom the family fervently hoped was well ensconced with her friends in Denver City.

Mrs. Conway, in complete contrast to her sober husband, condescended to share the latest fashion news out of St. Louis with the women. She was very friendly, chattering on about her life in the ministry.

During the evening meal, when all were seated, the preacher demanded a long prayer, and young Jenny cast amorous eyes toward Jeremiah while her father's watchful eyes were closed. Even the mother suggested Jeremiah might wish to give the young lady a tour of the station.

"I'm certain it's charming in the moonlight." She winked and chuckled.

Hannah's mouth was agape with amazement at her boldness. Ruth touched her husband's hand and breathed deeply.

Joe paused, a piece of bread halfway to his mouth, and watched as Jeremiah gulped and laid his spoon gently on the table.

"Ah, Joe, I'll take the first watch and sleep in the barn." He rushed from the room with his supper half eaten, went to his room, grabbed a pillow and two blankets and escaped through the garden door, leaving it securely locked behind him.

Conway noticed the tableau and insisted on a Bible scripture reading and a long-winded prayer, making a point to include a specific admonition against youthful lusts of the flesh. Mrs. Conway preened and overlooked his disapproval, while the daughter lowered her head in embarrassment.

Once finished, Conway gave several scowls in the direction of Standing Tree, but that wise old man ignored him, wrapped his blanket around himself and left the house with the dignity of the Prime Minister of England, had he but known it. Poor Jack was once more sent into exile in the inner garden until the family had retired for the night, the scent of goats now mostly gone.

With the coach's arrival came a long letter from Baldwin. A shorter note was sent from Dempsey in Indiana. A third note was sent from Samuel Mozier warning of a renegade band of Indians that had been sighted about thirty miles north of Mozier Station traveling in a southwestern direction. He was keeping a sharp lookout for trouble and advised Joe to do the same. Joe later questioned Rusty and Grover about the problem and found that they were not as concerned as Mozier, although they promised they would keep a sharp-eyed look out on the way east.

Joe read Dempsey's note second. It confirmed that he had received the information on Buck Jones and a tracer was sent out to Fort Laramie with a warrant for his arrest on the charge of horse theft. The Eastern authorities held little hope that he would be found.

Baldwin's letter also acknowledged receipt of the charges against Jones, but the regional supervisor deemed it not as important as the information that the road into Denver was complete and Frederick Jackson's road crew were even now surveying a road north between Denver and Cheyenne in Wyoming, and south from Denver to Pueblo.

Clifton Taylor had completed the construction of the way station nearest Denver that had been interrupted by the hail storm, and named it Rockland Station for the huge boulders in the area. A manager for the station had been interviewed and would soon arrive with his family. Likewise, a freight caravan was on its way for all the stations to the west. Two new stage coaches and several relief drivers were in preparation for the trek west; and one would be stationed at Sweetwater if Joe could give them the appropriate accommodations. Extra supplies, as usual, would be sent for their comfort.

He asked if Joe had found the box canyon and mustangs. As for the new animal handler, he was working on the problem, but his first priority was to open up the new Rockland station, and Joe should be patient and wait his turn. In closing, Joe might be interested in a box of books and old magazines that he was sending with his supplies, and a subscription to the Denver newspaper had been arranged in his name. On a personal note, the children and the wife were well and his wife sent her regards to his dear wife, Hannah. It was signed: Your obedient servant, Ned Baldwin.

Joe gave out a loud whoop of joy. Everyone turned toward him with puzzlement. For Josiah Hadley, the last news was the best. More books to read during the long winter months were on their way, and a subscription to a local newspaper would be well received by those hungry for news from the outside world. He explained the situation to the passengers and they nodded in acknowledgement of the good news. Rusty and Grover assumed that the Mozier station would receive the same consideration so were not overly thrilled for Joe and his family.

As the evening wore down, Joe invited his father, Rusty and Grover to join him in a nightly walk. Grover volunteered to drive the farm wagon and team of horses to Buckboard Station with the current load of passengers, since the first trip had been successfully completed. The horse he had ridden from Sweetwater to Mozier was enjoying the oats of that station, but Grover promised that he would eventually find his way back to Joe. He never told how he got along with Miss St. John on that trip; and no one dared ask him about it.

The men discussed the warning of hostile Indians in the area, and Grover volunteered to act as night guard for a few hours, since he was restless and wouldn't sleep now anyway. Peter decided to take the next duty, leaving Joe to take the early morning shift. They walked the perimeter of the corrals and said goodnight to Standing Tree, sitting under his favorite tree near the barn, smoking one of Peter's cigars.

Joe was on early morning guard duty, and so rousted Jeremiah out of the barn, where he alone of the men had spent a full night of slumber, thanks to Grover's help. They had the team of mules hitched to the coach and the team of horses ready for the farm wagon by the time the other men were awake. A light was burning in the Public Room, so Joe knew that Hannah and his mother were awake and preparing breakfast for the early risers. He noticed Ruth come out to gather the eggs, carrying a lantern in her hand. He left Jeremiah and Standing Tree to watch the vehicles and joined her in the gathering. He went inside with her for a bracing cup of hot coffee and his first meal of the day. He was half finished when his father rose to milk the goats.

When he had finished and taken the buckets to Hannah, Peter relieved Standing Tree and Jeremiah to eat their eggs and biscuits. The sun was still a faint glow below the horizon, when Peter took his first smoke of the day. He hoped the supply wagon brought tobacco, for he hadn't planned to share his precious cigars with another man and his supply was running low. He enjoyed this time of day at the station.

With all the liquor out of his system, he felt a new vitality and strength. He took a deep breath and gazed toward the far distant mountain range, hidden by the darkness of the forest. Damn him, he thought. Let Luther enjoy the fruits of his labor in Indiana. Colorado was much better. This short time he had spent with his son had given him a portrait of a mature man, not the laughing, boisterous boy of his memory. They hadn't yet spoken of the war years and the sorrow over the loss of James, but he was certain a day would come when each would share the joys and grief together. He heard the stomp of a horse's hoof and the whinny of another. He dropped his smoke on the ground and smashed it with his boot heel.

Suddenly from the house, a flurry of noise and laughter interrupted his private musings as Joe and Jeremiah walked to the team of mules, followed by Rusty, Grover and Standing Tree.

The drivers made a final check of the harnesses and coach, including the axles. They looked at the hooves and mouths of each animal and Rusty swung into the box. He pressed his trumpet to his lips and tooted a few joyful notes as he let loose the reins and the sensitive animals responded with a burst of speed. Grover and Standing Tree watched wistfully until the mud settled. Peter walked to the Indian and offered him an early morning smoke, which he accepted with a grunt. Peter knew the old man was too proud to beg. He went inside to eat his own meal.

Joe and Jeremiah didn't spend their time watching the coach depart. They were used to such events. They turned to the horses selected to pull the farm wagon. They hitched the pair to the wagon, and Joe examined them carefully.

Jeremiah took a cloth from his pocket and dusted the leather seats. He had spent an hour last evening in contemplation of women in general and Jenny Conway in particular. He had to admit she was a pretty little female, but he wasn't ready to settle down and start a family. He wanted his education and a position as lawyer in a progressive law firm. He walked to the barn, and kicking in frustration at clumps of hardened dirt on the floor, he came upon two harnesses, already inspected and cleaned, but set aside because of broken straps. To distract him from thoughts of Jenny Conway, he pulled them out and set to repairing them.

Joe watched him go and wondered what ailed the young man, but quickly turned to Grover and discussed the upcoming trip to the next station. He had written two letters before climbing into bed last night. He now pulled them from his pocket and handed them to the driver to see that they were passed on by Obediah Blessing to someone connected to the stage line traveling to Denver. He had thought to give them to the minister, but decided that might not be a good idea. They would be better sent through the official stage route.

One letter was addressed to his brother, Luther Hadley in Indiana, informing him of the safe arrival of their parents at the Colorado station. It was short and direct, and he expected no answer. The other longer letter was sent to Ned Baldwin, thanking him in advance for the supplies and reading material. He gave him a short description of the current events and activities of the station, including the news of a child expected in the spring. He asked for information on how his young hired hand could finish his education as he had a great desire to become an attorney. Any books, pamphlets or scholarly journals on the matter would be greatly appreciated. It was signed: With gratitude, Josiah Hadley, Sweetwater Station, Colorado Territory.

Joe went into the house where Conway was waiting for his wife and daughter to finish their preparations for departure. They chatted for a few moments on the route and the weather, and the identity of the next station manager and his wife. Mrs. Conway and Jenny came into the room in a flurry of skirts and petticoats, hats and gloves. The young girl appeared delightful in a peach-orange-red colored dress. Mrs. Conway was fashionably dressed in deep purple. Her hat was perched high on her head, and mounted above it was a stuffed bird of some sort. Hannah thought it most becoming; Ruth thought it ostentatious; and Joe had no thoughts on the hat at all. He guided the family down the steps and over to the wagon, where he politely handed the women to their seats and wished them a pleasant journey. Hannah and Ruth waved their handkerchiefs from the porch. Grover climbed into the driver's seat, released the brake and drove away.

Standing Tree stood like his namesake, happily puffing on his cigar. He turned to Joe. "Where woman kill bird on hat? She mighty hunter of sky animals?"

"She's not a hunter, Standing Tree. That's a stuffed bird, full of straw. It's not real." Joe had learned to speak in simple sentences that the Indian could understand.

"Not real? Why woman wear stuffed bird on hat?"

"It's a woman's fancy, like beads on an Indian's moccasin." He pointed to Standing Tree's feet. His moccasins had dozens of colorful beads sewn on them.

Standing Tree grunted and moved to the barn where he watched Jeremiah mending the harnesses. Joe observed curls of smoke encircle his head as the Indian squatted in the dirt.

After the departure of the guests, life settled down to its previous routine. Jeremiah finished with the harnesses, stitching in new leather to replace the old with an awl and thick cording. Joe gave him a friendly clap on the shoulder, and they chopped more wood for the fireplace and stove. Peter sat at the table drawing plans for the gardens and field. The women washed the bed clothes and dishes. Jack chased after imaginary creatures or slept beside Standing Tree under the shade of the tree. After the noon meal, Jeremiah and the Indian mounted horses and went fishing. They returned with a string of trout. While they were gone, Joe and Hannah spent some quiet time in their bedroom. Ruth napped in her bed. They had all earned a day of rest.

Joe didn't get to rest long. What sounded like a herd of buffalo stampeding through the station yard awakened him.

He moved into the Public Room, leaving Hannah behind to put on her clothes.

Alert and troubled, Joe grabbed his rifle and went to the front door. The dog rushed out before him and barked as loudly as his voice could manage. Joe picked him up and held him tightly. He gasped in wonder at the sight of maybe a dozen freight wagons drawing to a halt under the trees along the creek bank. Their dust was drifting toward the bed clothes hanging on the line near the house, and he knew his wife would be displeased.

Peter and Jeremiah also heard the sound and ran from wherever they had secreted themselves in the last hour, their rifles in their hands, pointed at the ground, watching the strangers closely. They must have had the same startling thoughts as him. Standing Tree stood tall and straight as was his manner day in and day out, under his favorite tree.

A short dumpy gray-bearded man dropped from the seat of the first wagon and walked toward Joe. Several burly teamsters and drovers followed the first man, and Joe met them on the ground in front of the house. Joe took a quick inventory of men and wagons; his sharp eyes noting they had come a far distance.

"Hello. Name's Stumpy MacGregor. I'm the boss of this train. Are you Joe Hadley?" The man spat a trail of tobacco on the ground, but he was careful to avoid Joe's boots. Jack growled and barked, and Joe quieted him with his hand.

"Yes, I'm Hadley. Are you from Baldwin?"

MacGregor reached out his hand and stepped forward. "Yep. We've come all the way from St. Louis on a mission to bring sustenance and stimulation to the wilderness. In other words, we've brought your supplies. We left Mozier's place early this morning." He turned around and gestured for three men to step forward. One was a tall, slender man with dark hair and eyes; the second wore the garb of a farmer and had the appearance of a horse trader; while the third was of average height and build but blessed with strong shoulders and slender hips, dressed in sober black. "This here string-bean of a fellow is your new animal handler, but it looks like you got all the help you need already." He looked hard at Peter and Jeremiah, and suddenly seemed to notice the Indian under the tree. His eyes blinked rapidly. He spat again.

Distracted, Joe's observant eyes noticed a covered carriage in the line of wagons, driven by a black-skinned man in gold and red livery. He watched, amazed, when a petite woman emerged from the vehicle, and began to walk forward, followed by a tall, slender maidservant, her head covered by a dark blue bandanna that matched her dress. As the women came closer, Joe could better observe the wide crinoline-fashioned skirts of the women. The lady's dress was a red and green tartan, half hidden by a black cape of the finest silk with a white collar and cuffs. She had a black wide-brimmed hat on her blonde curls decorated with a white fluffy feather along the outside edge, and carried an open parasol.

Joe swallowed and turned back to his male guests. He watched as the man dressed in black met the women and drew them forward. They stopped a few feet from him and the maid looked closely at Joe, then her dark eyes darted toward Peter and Jeremiah, dismissed them handily, and passed on to the Indian, who stood perfectly still and observed the scene.

MacGregor introduced the other two man and each shook hands in his turn. The man dressed like a farmer who looked like a horse trader was named Perkins, the new animal handler for Buckboard Station; and the other was Usamah Jones, the new manager of Rockland Station.

Jones introduced his wife, Clorinda, and the maid as Cissy. He had a gruff, deep bass voice that matched his somber demeanor. Joe took the hand of the white-gloved lady, and she smiled graciously and curtsied, her skirts billowing around her. He shook the maid's hand, and she gazed at him in bewilderment. He smiled as he saw the frown on Jones' face.

The slender man stepped forward with a grin on his face. "Good day, Mr. Hadley, I'm Matthew Grimshaw, but mostly I'm called Slim. I answer to both names. Baldwin said you were in a mighty big hurry for an animal helper. I'm also a doctor; a veterinarian, an animal doctor. He said you were the one picked to bring in more horses and mules for the line. I'd like to help you in your endeavor to achieve that result, if I may."

Joe was impressed. The man clearly had an education of the highest caliber, but what did he think of Indians? He'd wait a while to render judgment on whether he earned the right to remain. He turned to Standing Tree, and gestured for him to come near. His father and Jeremiah walked to his side, their rifles held in their arms.

"These are my crew and my friends: Peter Hadley, my father, who is in charge of the gardens and fields; Jeremiah Fuller, carpenter and fisherman; and Standing Tree, my special friend of the Arapahoe tribe, hunter of big game and wolf killer. This little fellow is Jack, my wife's pet."

He held the dog up for all to see. Jack barked, and everyone laughed. He glanced around him, but Hannah hadn't come to the door.

Joe threw out his hand. "Welcome. Welcome all to Sweetwater Station. Those of you who would like, come in and have a cup of coffee and meet the women folks."

Inside, Hannah was standing by the stove, her hand on the handle of a skillet. Ruth was at the table, making biscuits. They both looked up in surprise when an army of people filtered into the room. Hannah dropped the skillet with a clunking sound on the stove top and came forward. She smiled in the general direction of the men, but her attention was centered on the lady in the tartan dress, and her companion.

Joe walked to her and held her around the waist. "Gentlemen, this is my wife, Hannah. And, that lovely woman is my mother, Ruth Hadley. Please find a seat."

There was a loud scraping of chairs and benches as the men scurried to obey him. Clorinda Jones spoke to her companion and the woman stayed near the door. Jones seated his wife and took the place beside her. Hannah poured the hot, fragrant coffee, then gently issued the maidservant to the rocking chair and took her a cup of coffee.

Joe watched the doctor's reaction to Standing Tree, taking a prominent seat at the table. It didn't seem to disturb him. As the coffee was poured and drunk, except for Standing Tree, who always requested water, the conversation dwelt on the trip from St. Louis and the news from the East. One of the men mentioned rumors of the sighting of renegade Indians north of Mozier Station. Joe considered that normal, since they had just come from the place. He watched Perkins and Jones who remained mostly silent. MacGregor did most of the talking, aided by another man seated at the end of the table away from Joe, who hadn't been introduced. He assumed he must be one of the muleskinners, but later found he was the new animal handler for the Rockland station, named Hatton. As he had done before, Standing Tree spoke his mind when he finished his water.

"Yo Hadley good man. Big Father good man. Scarred Woman my friend. I go now." He rose, left the table and walked out the door, his blanket trailing on the floor. There was a moment of complete silence, and then the man at the end of the table started to laugh, but he stopped when he encountered the fierce look from Joe's eyes. The silence was broken by Slim Grimshaw.

"I understand, Hadley, that there's a band of rogue horses running wild in the area. Baldwin said you were considering catching some of them and training them to pull the heavy coaches. Is that correct?"

"Yes, there are feral horses in the area. I saw a large herd when I first arrived, but haven't had time to pursue the matter. We've been too busy building the corrals and barn. Jeremiah, there, is a first class stonemason."

193

Jeremiah must have heard his name mentioned because he stopped what he was doing and looked at Joe, pointing to himself and shaking his head. He made a face and continued his conversation with Peter.

Joe smiled as he finished his explanation to the guests. "The animals keep us busy. We have two stages a week when there are passengers. The route from Mozier to Buckboard is the most traveled with people going to Denver. The one from the south doesn't come as often, but we have to be ready when it shows. I don't know how much they told you, Mac-Gregor, at Mozier, but I guess you came across the deep sand on the way. We use mules on that route, and horses on the other one. We hope to have a coach here soon for the route west. Right now, we're using my farm wagon, but it's not a good solution. Baldwin wrote that he had two coaches ready to roll. Have you recent information on when they'll arrive?"

"They should be here any day. They were about five days behind us starting out in St. Louis. Taking into account the surface of the road, the weather and other obstacles, it won't be much longer. Baldwin said one would use this station as its base and the other housed at Denver. The problem has been finding experienced drivers. It's not easy driving a heavy coach carrying passengers. It's not like the freight wagons. If you turn over, you lose the contents, but not human lives."

MacGregor was right. Human lives were lost if a coach was robbed, turned over, or went missing in a snow storm, Joe knew that. He took new account of the risk that men like Rusty, Jim Owens, and Paul Ward took every time they left the stations for the next one on the route.

"All right men, time to gets those supplies settled." MacGregor roared out his orders, and the men jumped to attention. The three animal handlers, Grimshaw, Perkins and Hatton, not having anything to do with supplies, went to the corrals to see the animals. Jones kept himself apart from the others, which puzzled Joe, and he put Peter and Jeremiah to directing the men to the shed or to the house with their barrels, boxes and bundles, wherever the articles were best kept, while he followed the men.

The two women remained in the house with Hannah.

"Look at that, Slim. He's got goats. Been a long time since I had some real goat cheese. You milk them goats, Hadley?" Perkins was as excited as a school boy. He ignored the horses and mules and stood in fascination, watching the small herd of goats.

"Yes, I've milked them a few times, but my mother or father does it on a regular basis. It's better than having a cow, although I wouldn't mind one of those, of course. The milk is heavy and thick; makes great cheese. I'll have my wife slice you off a piece, if you remind me when we get back to the house." All four of the men regarded Joe with speculation. It was beginning to soak in what Baldwin meant when he said "animals" as he told them what their duties would entail. They had thought in terms of horses or mules, or maybe even donkeys, not goats or chickens or cattle.

Joe drew Slim Grimshaw a little aside while the other men were walking through the corrals. "We had a little trouble a while back with a sorrel stallion. Colic, I think. It seemed to come on him in an instant. One moment he was walking around, the next he was down on the ground. My father pulled him out of it. Since you're a doctor, I'd like for you to see him." He took the man's arm and guided him toward a group of horses standing near the rear fence. The sorrel was pointed out, and the doctor looked at his mouth and felt of his flanks and neck muscles.

"He seems to be well, now, Hadley. Did you say it came on him suddenly?"

"Yes, I was on guard duty that night . . ." Joe noticed the man looking sharply at him. "I post a guard every night. We take turns. We can never tell when renegade Indians or white horse thieves might strike. It would be easy enough to come out of those trees and attack before we could get our trousers on." Joe thought of himself just an hour ago, lying beside Hannah. It didn't have to be night when men came on the station without warning. He wasn't inclined to admit to a stranger to having intimate relations with his wife in the middle of the day. He pushed the thought out of his mind.

"I'd have to see the horse during the illness to make a full diagnosis, but there are certain weeds and bushes that might bring that reaction. We'll have to look around the area, see what we can find." Slim was thinking about talking to the father about it; he seemed to know more about sick horses than the son. "Did you say it was just the one horse?"

Joe glanced at the tall, thin man beside him. He hadn't considered that the whole herd might have eaten something to make them sick. It was a scary thought.

The other men joined them, and there was a general agreement that he had a fine mob of animals. They moved back toward the house, where there was a beehive of activity going on. Men were carrying crates and boxes, moving to and fro, under the direction of Peter and Jeremiah.

"There's a rumor in St. Louis that the telegraph will soon be strung along this route if it's successful." Jones had kept quiet while the others did most of the talking. "That will sure save a lot of time and eventually money, don't you think, Hadley?"

"It sure would. Have you heard anything about a railroad from the East to the West Coast? A guy came through a few weeks ago speculating on that. He was sure that the stages wouldn't last long. If they put through the telegraph, then the railroad's bound to follow to my way of thinking."

The men continued their talk of railroads and stage coaches as they approached the house. As soon as they entered, the dog started nipping at their ankles and barking. Joe stooped and picked him up, but he continued to growl. "Shush, little one, these are our friends."

"Oh, Joe, come and see what they've brought." Ruth's eyes were big and bright. She looked at the other men, but her focus was on her son. "Look, son, oranges and lemons. Have you ever seen such a beautiful sight?"

Joe dutifully admired the citrus fruit, but what made him happy was to see his mother's excitement and joy. When he came home from the war, she was wan and weak, almost a shadow of her former self. He sent a prayer to heaven in gratitude; then another one for Miss St. John who had brought them to him. In spite of her officious and arrogant ways, the woman had done him a great service.

He noticed that the lady, Clorinda Jones, was now leisurely seated in the rocking chair, her wide skirts bouncing with the movement of the runners, and the maid was helping Hannah peel onions and potatoes. They were talking in quiet voices together.

The men soon had the supplies emptied from the wagons and stored in the shed. They made ready to get underway to the next station. MacGregor drew Joe to one of the last wagons where some two dozen horses stood chewing on the grass. A couple of drovers sat under the trees smoking their cigars.

"Hadley, Baldwin said for me to replace those two horses that were stolen from you. I don't know much about your situation except what I've seen today and learned at the other stations along the line, but Dempsey told me about your mission to find those wild horses and train them to pull the coaches. I said to myself, you don't need more wagon or coach-trained horses; what you need are some good saddle mounts. I picked these out for you. I rode them myself to check their stamina and strength. If you keep it under your hat, nobody will know that I didn't give you just two more mangy critters for the stage coach line. They're your horses. I wish I was going on that hunt with you."

He pointed to a rangy well-fed mare and a recently curried chestnut stallion and had them brought from the rest of the herd. Joe looked them over and approved of them. They had shiny coats and thick manes and tails.

"Thank you for your generosity, MacGregor. I'll take good care of them. Have you told Slim Grimshaw? He'll know the difference." Joe wanted to get his saddle on one of the horses and ride like the wind, but had to restrain himself.

"Naw, haven't told a soul, except that drover that brought them over here. He's been caring for them like they're his own babies. It'd be best to keep them separated, or they won't be no use to you if the mare gets in the family way too soon." He drew a paper from his pocket and gave it to Joe. "You'll want to keep this. It has to do with the horses."

Joe slipped it into his pocket to read later. "I appreciate the horses. We'll make good use of them. Thank you again. This is a wonderful thing you've done. I'll try my best to bring in a string of fine horses for the stage line."

The men shook hands, and MacGregor yelled at his men to get off their lazy butts and get the train to rolling. He wanted to be at Buckboard Station before the darkness of night if possible.

Clorinda Jones and her maid entered the carriage with a swish of skirts, and Jones climbed in behind them and closed the door. The manservant mounted the high seat and the carriage wheels began to roll.

Within the hour, the lady, the men, wagons and animals were only a memory. Standing Tree came to look at the two new horses. He examined them closely and looked at Joe with awe. He knew good saddle horses when he saw them.

"Yo Hadley lucky fellow. Strong horses, clear eyes, good teeth; ride like wind."

Joe smiled and took them into the barn and tied one at one end and one at the other until he could get stalls built for them. He named the chestnut stallion Mack after his previous owner; the mare he would call Prissy, to remind him of Priscilla St. John.

It wasn't until supper that Joe thought to take the paper from his pocket and read it. It was a signed bill of sale for the animals in his name. The man had been more than generous. He'd bought them himself as a gift. They didn't belong to the stage line.

As the group was finishing supper Joe explained what MacGregor had done. The men trooped down to the barn to admire and examine the new horses. If luck held they would have strong healthy colts. Bred with mustangs, they would provide a generation or two of sturdy bloodlines for the stage line. Slim was especially impressed and promised to care for them himself.

Fourteen

In the next two weeks, Slim found out what his responsibilities entailed. He was required to be up before the dawn and down at the corrals. Several mornings he walked with Joe and Peter through the animals and led the horses into the barn. Two mares in the corral with the donkeys were pregnant, and would be the first of a fine herd of mules. Another mare with the stage horses was pregnant and would bequeath her offspring to the stage company. Joe had named her Eve for she would be the mother of the first horse born on the station under his care. With three births on the way, Slim realized he would have his hands full in the spring.

"You've met the goats, I suppose?" On one morning, Joe opened the conversation with the unusual question while striding towards the goat pen. It was a cool morning, and the air was especially fresh.

Slim smiled. "Of course. We learned something about a goat's anatomy at medical school." He kicked a stone in his path, wondering where his employer was going with his question.

"How about milking goats? Have you tried that?" Joe let a grin loose, glancing at the new handler as they stopped outside the goat pen.

"Yes, sir. I mean, no sir. I've never milked a goat before but I'm game to anything once." Slim saw the grin but didn't know what to make of it, whether it was a joke or a test. He wanted to object, but didn't dare since he had only recently taken the new position as animal handler.

Joe pointed to the two nannies, calmly browsing under the trees in the pen, the walls built high to keep them from escaping. "It was Buck Jones' job before he up and left us and Baldwin sent you as his replacement. You think you'll have time to help my parents with the chore?"

Slim was dismayed at the suggestion; he hadn't counted on milking goats as part of his job.

Joe continued, "It's like this. My mother is getting on a bit, and her hands pain her when doing certain things. If you could relieve her of the duty occasionally, I'd find it helpful. Besides, it'll give you a chance to study their anatomy up close." He laughed at the expression on Slim's face.

"Do they kick or bite?"

"Naw, hardly ever. Come on, I want to look at the new horses. Maybe saddle them and take a ride. Would you like that?"

The subject of goats was closed and Slim followed Joe into the barn. They saddled the horses and rode over the range for some time. Joe was well pleased with his new stallion and told Slim so; and Slim told him the new mare, Prissy, was spirited and well trained. They cooled the horses down and stabled them in the barn. Joe spent an hour inspecting the harnesses, and set one aside for repair.

Slim milked his first nanny the next day, relieving Ruth of the duty for a few days. That first morning, she didn't laugh at his clumsiness, and he felt an immediate bond with the woman. From then on, they shared the care of the goats and chickens with Peter.

The West Bound came in later than expected that week. They had bogged down in the deep sand and had to dig their way out of it. Rusty was blowing angry curses as he drew up to the door of the station. He swore it was the fierce wind-storm that had thrown him off the main road. The force of the blowing wind had almost toppled them over. Grover tossed Joe's borrowed saddle over the side, stirring the dust at Joe's feet, and Joe leapt backwards, letting out a curse of irritation, although not one as virulent as Rusty's blustery incantations.

"Sorry, Joe." Grover almost looked contrite. "Thought you needed this back. I couldn't get the horse on top of the coach. It'll come in the next trip."

Joe laughed, calling to Jeremiah to move the saddle out of the way and into the barn with the others.

The first passenger to step out of the coach was a merchant, wanting to start a trading post or general merchandise store near Denver. He had come alone to explore and buy a property if he could find one to his liking that would sustain a family in the future. He had left his wife and children with his parents. He was dressed soberly in a green plaid wool shirt and black corduroy trousers. His boots were brown and well worn. He reeked of horse. It had been his strength and powerful arms that had helped get the coach out of the sand.

Next to descend from the coach and into the house was Betty Tisdale, in pale blue, with a hat of silk, her husband Wallace and their two children: Mariah and Jefferson, whom they called Jeff, who slowly followed her. Tisdale was the new agent for the western division in Denver. He was average in height and weight and dressed like a dandy with slicked back hair and a handlebar mustache, and a stick tiepin that could cause the sun to blush, it shined so brightly in the light of the lamps. He wore a brown suit, finished off with a striped shirt and brown shoes. Just about the time that Joe was deciding that he would never make a good agent, he burst out laughing.

"Now, don't get any notions, Joe Hadley, that I think myself better than you station managers. I dressed this way to impress the other passengers on the way. We've come from Grayson County Virginia and have ridden on steamboat, train, stage and horseback. I thought if the people of the East see us in our fancy rigging, they'll feel safe enough to travel on the Overland Stage Line. I talked it up big, all the way. People back East are eager to come west to escape the horror of war. We've talked to people of a dozen states zealous for a change. Farmers, merchants, lawyers, doctors, even a few horse thieves and killers, probably. We lost our farm to a bunch of carpetbaggers, who took it when we couldn't pay the taxes, but I won't dwell in the past. We'll make a new start in this high country and see what we can do to make a better world."

Joe showed them to their rooms, which meant that Jeremiah and Slim would have to sleep in the barn while they remained at the station. He asked Jeremiah to draw water from the inner garden for baths for the guests. It kept him busy for a few hours, and Hannah and Ruth tried to entertain the children, while Betty relaxed in her room.

Joe went to help Slim unhitch the mule team. Slim said to leave one of them separate. He wanted to examine him more closely later when he had time. In a matter of minutes, Wallace Tisdale joined them, his clothing now plain and well worn. Joe and Peter showed him the inner garden and Peter pointed out his plans for the space. They walked to the edge of the field, and Peter discussed irrigation and crop rotation, and elaborated on how the fresh vegetables and fields would be of benefit to the passengers and family. Later, when they had a few moments alone, Tisdale told Joe of his plans for the future of the stations and equipment under his care.

All the chairs and benches were occupied that night at supper, and all the rooms filled with guests. Betty Tisdale was a pleasant woman, eager to learn about the station and its furnishings. She spoke with a soft Southern accent. Hannah showed her the rooms and talked of future plans. Betty, full of dreams for her own house, was impressed with the curtains and knitted scarfs. She admitted that she was blessed to be living in Denver. They would be able to take trips and explore the city. She hoped they would be able to find a good teacher to continue the children's education. The children, of course, became acquainted with Jack and ran through the Public Room with abandon until their father sent them outside to play. Jeremiah volunteered to watch over them.

After supper, as the sun made its slow descent, and the forest became dark and mysterious, Slim, Joe and Rusty checked on the mule that had concerned Slim earlier. He decided to keep him in the barn for a few days and watch him. Joe asked if there was any news of the renegade Indians, but Rusty had none.

Standing Tree, Tisdale and Peter enjoyed a congenial smoke together, since the freighters had brought a fresh supply of tobacco products for the guests and workers. Peter pounced on a box of smoking pipes and gave one to Standing Tree. The Indian had no gift to give in return, but promised to make Big Father a pair of fine moccasins.

The next morning, Slim and Peter were hitching the team of mules to the coach when Joe ventured out into the cool morning. There was the smell of rain in the air, and a hint of the winter to come. He watched some birds flying high in the early morning light, and wondered if they were ducks or geese headed south for the winter. He checked the axles for grease and the inside for dust, and went around the wheels looking for signs of damage to the coach in the sand dunes. He caught a glimpse of Ruth on her way to the hen house, carrying the lantern and a basket, and waved at her. Standing Tree came to watch them and Peter handed him a small bag of tobacco for his new pipe. They turned to the house when Tisdale, dressed as they had first seen him, came toward them. They went around the coach and team once more to explain their actions.

Rusty came from the house, a straw clutched between his teeth. He asked about the mule from last night, but Slim hadn't taken the time to see him yet. He shook hands all around, climbed into the box, picked up his trumpet and with a cheerful tune and a cloud of dust, he was gone.

Slim walked briskly to the holding pen and brought out the horses for the farm wagon. Joe helped him hitch them to the wagon and repeated the process of examination with the wagon that they'd done with the coach, keeping Tisdale beside them, explaining that he made sure the axles were greased himself, not leaving it to an underling. It was one of the major problems with breakdowns. They turned when the dog burst from the door and Jeremiah came down the steps with the two children to romp for a few minutes before their long journey to the next station.

The men went into the house for their breakfast, leaving Slim to watch the children and wagon. Standing Tree was sitting in his usual place on the floor in front of the fireplace, wrapped in his blanket, but his eyes watched everything with curiosity. The women were spooning up porridge, ham and eggs. Hannah smiled at Joe, and brought the skillet forward, while Ruth finished with her tasks. His wife looked beautiful this morning, Joe thought.

He watched his mother. She was blooming with health. Her cheeks were rosy and slightly damp from the hot stove, and her hair neatly combed in her favorite style. She dipped in her pot and gave him a generous portion. He looked up and thanked her with his most charming smile. He was certain she blushed. Her neck and ears turned red. He looked to see if his father caught the sight but Peter was busy with his spoon.

Joe poured a bit of milk into his bowl and took a bite. Hmmm. It was delicious. He reached for a biscuit and tore it into two parts. He wished the people would leave so he and Hannah could have the place to themselves for a few hours, but of course, that was impossible, and he sighed. Two matching eggs on a plate with a large slice of ham appeared before him, and he looked up into Hannah's lovely eyes. He winked and continued eating.

When Joe looked to Jeremiah, he realized the man had

seen the look between him and Hannah. Feeling a flush of warmth, he said, "Jeremiah, as soon as you've finished, start gathering some lumber. I think it's time we built the stalls in the barn before Slim has it so full of critters, we won't have room to move about in there."

"Yes, Sir, Boss Man. You know how much I love it when I get to hold a hammer in my hand." There was a shocked moment of silence before everyone caught the joke and laughed.

"Well, sonny boy, if you'll work extra hard this morning, I'll give you the afternoon off to go fishing." Joe teased back, the look from Hannah and now the young man's joke making the morning light. "I have a deep hankering for some trout for my supper. What do you say, Papa? You feel like fishing today?"

Peter thought it a splendid idea, and as soon as the passengers were on the road with Grover driving the farm wagon, the three of them, Joe, Jeremiah, and Peter, were in the barn, building stalls for the animals, with the help of Slim, who kept the animals out of their way. Standing Tree took off toward the forest with his bow and arrows. Joe watched him go, but wasn't concerned. The Indian was a hunter, more familiar with the outdoors than himself.

They had two stalls completed and a third started when Joe felt the pangs of hunger and decided to stop for a time. After a simple meal of beans and corn fritters, the men left the women to clean up. Soon, a string of sheets and clothing hung on the line. Slim worked with the ailing mule, while Joe finished the stall in the barn. He decided he would leave the rest of the room open in case they needed to board the animals in another storm. Jeremiah and Peter rode off to the river, with poles in their hands, and string and hooks in their pockets. Peter carried a bucket for the fish. They were still gone when Joe heard the sound of hooves and wagon wheels.

He and Slim went out to see who had arrived. Coming to a stop in front of the station were two magnificent Concord stage coaches, one freshly painted black with gold trim, the other a rusty red with black trim, pulled by mule teams. The dust of the sand dunes covered them, but Joe could see they were sturdy vehicles. Ten outriders encircled the coaches, hard-looking men, with rifles in their arms, and pistols strapped at their hips. Two more men were perched on the seats beside the drivers, with shotguns in their laps. All began to dismount and stretch their legs and swing their arms, or bend over to get the kinks out of their backs.

The horses were hobbled to keep them from straying. Joe suggested the riders move closer to the trees where there was plenty of grass. Two guards were dispatched to watch for predators. One man of average height and lanky build said something to the men, and came forward. The coach drivers and the guards walked respectfully behind him.

"Mr. Hadley?" The speaker was clean shaven, young and wore the garb of a westerner: brown plaid shirt, denim pants, worn boots with spurs, and a hat as big as a barrel head covered his hair. He looked keenly from Joe to Slim, as though trying to decide which man was the manager of the station.

"I'm Hadley." Joe left it at that, waiting for the other man to introduce himself.

"Hello, Mr. Hadley. I'm James McKinley. We were hired by Ned Baldwin to see that these vehicles arrived safely at the stations, and to help you in any way we can while we're here. Most of these men are carpenters or loggers by trade. Baldwin has given us a week to build some kind of shelter to house your coach, the black one. Then, we'll move on to Denver with the red coach. This gentleman is Bruno Smith, your driver, and the guard is Dakota. The short funny-looking dude is Rance Potter. He's sort of grown attached to the red coach; thinks she's his mother. He even sleeps in her at night. And the other guy is Thad Ray, who can shoot the eyes out of a hawk at fifty yards; he's Potter's guard."

They stepped forward to shake hands, and Joe introduced Slim as his veterinarian and animal handler. Joe spied Jeremiah and Peter returning from their fishing trip, their eyes astonished at the sight before them. Jeremiah slipped from his horse and broke into a run, leaving the older man holding the bucket of fish.

"Land sakes, Joe!" Jeremiah handed Joe his fishing pole and opened the door of the black coach and peered inside. His eyes gleamed. "Have you ever seen anything so impressive?"

His enthusiasm was contagious, and Joe set the fishing implement against the back wheel as he and Slim moved to look at the interior of the coach as well. It had maroon leather seats, with large windows on either side. The gold trim was repeated in several places. Wooden panels covered the sides and top. The windows had leather panels rolled and tied at the top, ready to be lowered in inclement weather. It truly was a splendid example of skilled workmanship and planning. When he drew his head back, Joe saw Hannah and Ruth on the porch.

"Come on down, Mama, Hannah, and see the new coaches."

Ruth whispered something to Hannah and went back in the house. Joe was disappointed for he wanted his mother to see the fine new coach.

Hannah whispered, "There are loaves of bread in the oven that can't be left unattended." Joe understood and nodded. Hannah walked around the coach, exclaiming over the detailed and luxurious appointments.

"Oh. Look, Joe, how soft the seat is to the touch." She ran her hand along the gold-colored trim and her eyes sparkled with pleasure.

Jeremiah was now examining the interior of the red coach. Hannah moved to that one, followed by Peter, but Joe stayed with the men. He caught the glance of the guard Dakota watching Hannah, and he turned away with a frown.

"How was the trip through the sand, McKinley? I've

been concerned about the driver of the east-west bound stage, driving alone through the deep sand."

"The coach passed us on the way. The driver stopped. Rusty, is that his name?"

Joe nodded.

"He told us of the danger and sent us a little to the south of the main road. He sure admired these coaches. Said he would like to drive one himself someday."

Joe turned to Bruno Smith and his partner, and told them to bring their belongings, and he would get their room ready for them. He damned Buck Jones again, for he could sure use that tent tonight. He gave them the room used by Rusty and Grover the night before. He could see that they needed a separate bunkhouse for the drivers and Jeremiah and Slim, who would have to sleep in the barn again.

The men tramped into the Public Room, and Peter took Ruth outside to see the vehicles while Hannah reached for the coffee pot. She filled it with water and coffee and set it on the stove. Jeremiah handed her the string of scaled and gutted fish, and she brought out her largest skillet for frying. The smell of baking bread made Joe hungry, but he was a patient man. He started the other men talking while Hannah tended to her cooking chores. Ruth and Peter came in and Ruth sat down and began to peel potatoes.

As soon as the coffee was drunk, Joe sent the men outside. He began to work out a plan, although he would have to wait to speak to McKinley about it later.

Slim went to speak with the horsemen, explained that he was a licensed veterinarian, and asked if anyone wanted his animal checked out while they were there. Several spoke up at once, and soon he had enough work to keep him busy for a while. Joe and Jeremiah tended to the unhitching of the mule teams and were grateful for an empty corral to house them, knowing that the red coach would be leaving with horses, instead of mules. Joe assumed the extra mules would remain with the black coach, but he would ask Bruno when he came from his room. He wanted Slim to check them before putting them with the others.

The horsemen took some time to set up their camp, and Slim remained with them, tending to the sores or bruises of the animals. Tomorrow, he would set up the forge and start shoeing any that needed it. It wasn't until after supper that Joe got a chance to talk to James McKinley about his idea. They sat under the shade of a tree, watching the glowing light of the campfires.

"McKinley, did I hear you say that these men are carpenters and loggers, and you were instructed to help me in any way you can?"

"That's right, Baldwin said to do whatever you needed done, before we move on to Denver with the red coach. We'll stay at Rockland only long enough to change horses. What've you got on your mind?"

"Obviously, you'll want to build some sort of structure for the protection of the coach. That was why you were sent here with carpenters. But, what I'm going to need is more room to house the passengers, and that's what this stage business is about, right?"

"Right. I can see what you mean about that. You are full up right now. How are you thinking to relieve that?"

"The builders of the line designed the house for the manager and his family, and the drivers on their overnight stop. They built four bedrooms with an open inner courtyard. It's a general plan set up for almost all the stations, I discovered on my trip from Indiana, depending on location and special circumstances. We had a full house last night with no spares." Joe held up his hand and counted with his fingers. "My wife and I have one bedroom; my parents in another; Jeremiah and Slim have their room, but when we have visitors they are housed in the barn, and one room is set aside for the drivers. That's four rooms, leaving none for the passengers. Last night we had a family: father, mother and two children; and a single man. All the rooms were full with the workers sleeping in the barn."

Joe took a few paces near the tree in an earnest attempt to explain the situation to the builder. He squatted and picked up a stick and pointed toward the barn.

"I hope you'll take the time to look at the barn. It took us several weeks to build it out of bricks and mortar. The previous handler took care of the animals, while his wife made the bricks, and my hand and I built the barn. It's a much more secure building because it has less material to burn, but it should be larger."

"Are you saying, Hadley, that you want a bunkhouse for the drivers, so you'll have more rooms for the passengers in the house?" McKinley sat with his chin on his fingertips.

"Call me Joe. Yes, that's exactly what I need." Joe was glad McKinley was so perceptive. He'd thought he'd have to justify every request but it seemed the man was already with him. "If the drivers have their own room that they can decorate or lock behind them, knowing no one else will use the room while they're on a trip, they would be happier, don't you think? I have the only overnight stop on the line from St. Louis to Denver City and it's not large enough. If traffic picks up from Denver to the east there won't be rooms for everyone. If it's a matter of wages for your men, I'm willing to pay them for the extra work."

"That won't be necessary, although a bonus never goes without notice when a job's done right. I think it's an excellent idea, although I've never run across a problem like this before. Usually the schedules are set up so the drivers use the same room on different nights. I can see where it would be an advantage for the drivers to have their own rooms at their base station. I tell you what I'll do, Joe, since you're on the edge of the forest. I noticed that there's a pile of unprocessed timber near the spring. I'll have my carpenters put together a shell of a log cabin. It won't be finished out, but I'll make certain to build a substantial roof for you. It won't be fancy, and you might have to do most of the work yourself. But, be aware, my first priority is the coach shelter. If I can, we'll work on both. I'll draw up some plans tonight and speak to my head logger. We won't chop down any green trees if we can manage without them."

"I understand, and thank you, McKinley. My men can wrap up anything you can't get to. For some privacy, I think they'll be willing to put in a few hours of extra work." Joe laughed, relieved McKinley was so agreeable to his plan. It had been weighing on his mind, and now he could let it go. "Just so you know, the logs near the spring were left by the road builders when they were here in the spring; the rest are fallen trees left from an ice storm we had a few months ago. My hand and I've been working on them when we have the time."

"Company property. Good. We'll make fair use of them." McKinley nodded as if already planning the new structure in his head.

"And, I haven't forgotten. I'll still pay the men a bonus as I said. They deserve it on short notice."

They clasped hands and parted ways.

Joe was making his way back to the house when Standing Tree, struggling with a great weight, came out of the forest. He had the bulk of a deer on his back. Joe yelled for Jeremiah, who had been idling and talking to Peter under a tree. Together the three men ran to the old man and freed him of his burden while the horsemen stared in surprise.

Standing Tree heaved a sigh of relief and wandered over to his favorite tree trunk and sat down. He took no notice of the two coaches. He wrapped his blanket about him and was soon fast asleep. Joe went to check on him. He was breathing faster than normal, but seemed to be well.

The three men spent the next hour cutting up the deer. Jeremiah took some choice pieces to the men's camp. Hannah and Ruth cut some parts into small strips and soaked them in brine to be smoked on the morrow, for it was much too late in the day for that now. They protected the meat with paper and cloth and went to bed.

While the men were working, they heard Grover return with the farm wagon. His eyes almost protruded from his head with shock when he saw the two new coaches. He walked around and studied them with envy. He went to bed in the barn early and was soon asleep from exhaustion.

Fifteen

If the day before had been busy, this day was twice so. Everyone was up early. The camp was alive with men moving about on one task or another. It reminded Joe and Hannah of when they first arrived with Clifton Taylor, and Odell Graham camped near the spring. Frederick Jackson's road crew had been there, too. Joe marked the day the coaches arrived on his calendar: September 3, 1867. It seemed an important date to him, and he wanted it to be recorded for the future managers who might be sent to the station. During the winter months when he had more time, he planned to write an account of their first year at the station. He chuckled under his breath; it would be something to pass on to his grandchildren someday.

In the Public Room, Hannah and Ruth were busy with preparations for breakfast. The men left them to their toil and finished cutting up and salting the deer to be stored in the shed. Slim gathered the eggs and milked the nannies, so Ruth could help Hannah. He grabbed a dry biscuit from the day before and a quick cup of coffee and headed to the corrals to start his own chores.

Grover came from the barn in time to meet the other stage drivers and guards finishing their meal. "Come on, men, I've got a hankering to get my hands on those new coaches. Didn't get a good look at them last night in the dark. Grab a water bucket, and let's wash them."

They followed him out to the new coaches. Hauling buckets of water from the creek in relays, the five men proceeded to wash the dust off the coaches. As soon as they were finished, Grover ate his meal, saddled a horse and started his trip east, thankful that he would make no more trips to Buckboard Station in the wagon.

When they'd finished with breakfast, Ruth and Hannah set up a small corncob fire in the pit in the yard and strung the deer strips across a pole for smoking. Standing Tree came and gave his approval and wandered back to his tree, his pipe smoking like a chimney. Jack lay on the ground beside him, watching the activity around him with his soft brown eyes.

In the meantime, McKinley explained the projects he wanted completed. He told Joe that they'd first use the logs left by Jackson's crew, for if they'd intended to come back for them, they would've done so by then. The road to Denver was now finished as well as the two station houses. If someone from headquarters objected, then Joe should tell them that McKinley took complete responsibility in the matter.

Jeremiah later told Joe that all that work, pulling the logs from the barn and replacing them with the bricks, seemed a wasted effort.

"Just remember, my friend, how much experience we gained in building the brick barn." Joe understood Jeremiah's complaints, for he accepted—with some chagrin—that the bricks were a mistake, with so many trees at his disposal. Still, the barn was strong and secure from a forest fire or Indian attack, where the house was not. He felt justified in building it that way.

"Well, Boss Man, I could've done without the calluses on my hands and the pain in my back." His Southern drawl was most pronounced as he placed a hand on his lower back, massaging the affected region with great gusto.

"I know, Jeremiah. I'm sorry. We had to take the logs off anyway in order to finish with the bricks. The barn would've been drafty and unsafe, half brick and half logs. I'm proud of you. You worked hard, and I appreciate it, even if I didn't say so at the time. Let me make it up to you by helping with your education when you move on to Denver."

"No. You're right; I needed the experience in bricklaying and log cabin building. I've learned a lot since you took me in. It's experience that'll help me to understand the problems of my clients when I become a lawyer. My father was justice of the peace in our county, and he said that to understand a man's troubles, you have to walk in their shoes. I suppose that includes callused hands and aching backs, too. I shouldn't have complained, for you and Buck and Rosie worked as hard as I did."

"I'm glad you came to me with your thoughts. Now, the barn's built, and if McKinley uses Jackson's logs, it'll save time. Besides, think of the benefits. You want that bunkhouse, don't you? You can spread out in your own room with your books and clothes on the floor, and no one will disturb them. I'll see to it. No more sleeping in the barn."

"Thanks, Joe. It'll be nice not to have the passengers sleeping in my room." The men shook hands and went off to see how they could help with the labor.

McKinley sent his men with a couple of mules to the pile of logs near the spring to haul them closer for the start of the two shelters. Joe and Jeremiah went with them, knowing two extra hands would make the venture go faster. McKinley explained his plan to his carpenters, and they looked at the barn, and the house and the corrals for the best place for the parked coach. They toured the inner garden for ideas for the bunkhouse.

By noon, there was a substantial pile of lumber in the space between the spring and the house. While the loggers went for more trees, Joe, Jeremiah and the carpenters began peeling bark and sawing off limbs and branches. Jeremiah used the sharpening stone to whet the tools of the workers. Joe stopped and joined Slim in selecting horses in case the northbound stage came this day, as the calendar schedule indicated it might.

Jim Owens was sitting high in the box, with Fizzure Rodgriguez beside him. They came to a rolling stop, and Jim jumped down and ran to the two new coaches, leaving Fizzure to open the door for the passengers with the grace of a Spanish matador. Out stepped a short, buxom woman with brown hair, and her beautiful, blonde-haired daughter on their way to Denver to meet the husband and father who had sent for them. Joe set out to be the perfect host. He welcomed the lady, whose name was Matilda Burkhalter, into the house and turned her over to Hannah and Ruth.

Hannah showed the woman and her daughter, Meg, to her bedroom and made sure that there were clean towels and fresh water in her room. The station's newest visitor stayed secluded only long enough to see that her belongings were intact and to remove her hat and gloves, before rejoining Ruth in the kitchen. She sent her daughter off to play with Jack before moving to the massive cook stove, rolling up her sleeves and peering into the bubbling vegetable soup. She lifted the oversized spoon and began to stir as if it were her own home, drawing in a deep draught of aroma with a smile.

She noticed that Ruth was making pie dough, and instead of rolling it out in one large flattened blob, she was making small round balls.

"Are you making pie pockets?" Ruth and Hannah looked at her in surprise. "My grandmother was from Bavaria, a small village called Kronach, and she called them streusel. She rolled them in sugar, and the men got fat eating them." She laughed, and there was a twinkle of mischievous amusement in her eyes.

"Pie pockets? No, we call them fried pies. I'll put fruit in each one and make a pouch and fry them in lard. Is that the same thing? The men like them because they can carry them in their hands. It's easier than baking on a hot day."

"I'll try one during our meal. What do you say, Meg? You want a pie pocket?" The girl looked up from Jack and nodded her head, her smile showing a missing front tooth.

All in all, Matilda was a jolly, plump, whirlwind of activity. Her daughter Meg was settled at the table with her lessons, and she instructed her in grammar between stories of adventure and romance in the small town of Trinidad in southern Colorado. Her husband had gone to the city to find them a new home, she explained to her hosts. He was a tinker by trade and had the same idea as Joe. The city of Denver would grow much faster than the backwater that was their home. She laughed easily. Besides, she claimed, he had mended every pot and pan in Trinidad and was tempted to poke holes in one or two so he would have something to do.

Joe and Slim quickly changed the horses on the coach, and within an hour, Jim and Fizzure were on their way south. Jim was an exuberant driver who couldn't stop his admiration for the new coaches, especially the black one. If he could only get his hands on the reins, Jim was certain he would fly like a blackbird back to Trinidad, he told Slim.

Bruno Smith was not so confident of his ability to fly, for he had driven the coach from St. Louis, but just after dawn, he made the attempt on his first trip to Buckboard Station, with the grim, freckled face of Dakota beside him as guard. Hannah and Ruth said a cheerful farewell to Matilda Burkhalter and her daughter. They had taken a liking to the agreeable woman and had a dozen stories to laugh about in the next few months when they thought of her.

Joe approached Slim that night about making a trip to the box canyon and a try for the mustangs, since Peter and Jeremiah were at the station to care for the animals, and no coaches were expected for a week except the return of Bruno and Dakota. Slim had taken care of the major difficulties with the workers' horses and needed a break. He admitted that he was eager to find the mustangs. Joe squatted beside

Standing Tree on the ground and offered him a small pouch of tobacco for his new pipe. The men were silent for several moments. With his inexperienced Indian language skills he asked Standing Tree if he would join them in tracking some wild horses. He got an enthusiastic answer, the Indian's black eyes glowing in the evening twilight.

Early the next morning, Joe saddled Mack, his personal mount, Prissy the mare, and a bay for Standing Tree. The Indian appeared with his long bow in his hand, and his quiver of arrows on his back. Across his shoulder hung a beaded bag containing a small supply of jerky in case he got separated from the other men. He refused a saddle, riding with nothing but a blanket and rope for a bridle, the Indian way. Joe solemnly handed him a buckskin scabbard containing a skinning knife. Standing Tree looked at him closely and grunted his pleasure. Nothing better could have shown the old man that Joe trusted him. Joe wasn't sure of the old man's ability to ride far and fast, but they headed for the arroyos and scrub brush of the high country. Joe packed enough food and ammunition to last eight days, but didn't expect to be away that long. He and Slim both had their pistols and rifles.

The first day was lazy, warm and sunny, with a brisk breeze coming from the south. The men jogged along at a steady pace, and set up camp in a sheltered spot along a fast-moving stream that had carved an ancient canyon through the huge boulders. Joe found three slender cottonwoods growing side by side, bent them and tied the tops together to make a sort of tent. With that finished, he piled up a mound of bushes, sod, grass and leaves to protect their backs somewhat from the wind. He dug a small pit and started a fire. Slim brought kindling and got out an old battered coffee pot that one of the loggers had loaned them. Standing Tree set off to find tracks of the horses.

Joe and Slim sat, drinking coffee and talking of the station and the new coaches. Slim told Joe something of his background, but nothing really personal. He remained some-

219

thing of a mystery to Joe. Standing Tree came back late talking excitedly in his own language. Neither man could understand him, but they received the message loud and clear. He had found signs of many horses.

They were up early the next morning, saddled the horses and circled the area looking for any indication of the animals. They were just outside the mouth of the box canyon when the first tracks appeared. Standing Tree held up his hand for silence. He muttered to himself and felt the ground with his hands. He bowed and put his ear to the grass. Joe was not an expert, and Slim could only guess, but it looked like about six or eight unshod horses had been drinking in a small coulee stream recently. Standing Tree held up both hands, fingers wide, an indication of ten horses, Joe thought. They were encouraged and began to cut bushes and branches from trees to block the entrance to the canyon if they could drive the horses into it. They headed back to their camp and went to sleep early. Before the night winds had calmed, Joe thought he heard about one hundred yards away the sound of hooves pounding the earth as if in a stampede. His first thought was of the renegade Indians that Sam Mozier had warned him against. He huddled in his blankets. Standing Tree, a few feet away from Joe, shivered with excitement, but didn't seem alarmed.

Making their circle wider, but staying as close as they could to the box canyon, the men picked up fresh sign about midday. Joe watched his Indian friend closely. When he held up his hand, they stopped. He pointed to the north, got down from his horse and walked, following the tracks. Joe took the reins of the old man's horse. Joe and Slim dismounted and walked slowly behind him. Standing Tree quickened his pace and set out toward a grove of piñon pine and Douglas firs in the distance about one hundred yards from their camp, walking in a north to northeasterly direction, about where Joe imagined he had heard the stampede the night before.

Giant red rock formations jutted toward an azure sky.

The trail seemed to follow an ancient pass through a rugged valley of trees and shrubs. As they paused a moment, a startled hawk flew from a jumbled nest in a tangle of high branches and soared into the heavens. The sun was warm on Joe's back and shoulders. A gentle breeze rustled the nearby tree limbs.

The Indian took the reins and swung gracefully onto the horse's back, his quiver shifting fluidly with his movements. Joe and Slim mirrored his every action. About half the distance, Joe estimated, the Indian slowed his pace, and got down to walk again. Joe and Slim watched in silence. Again, Standing Tree held up both hands, fingers stretched apart. The same as before, Joe thought. They must be the same horses. A few steps further, he stopped again; this time going a few yards to the west then retracing his steps going to the east. He gestured something that Joe couldn't interpret then pointed toward the mustang tracks. He held up four fingers. Joe frowned. Did he mean there were only four horses? Had the herd gotten their scent and scattered?

Standing Tree pointed at Joe, then Slim and to his own face. He rubbed his check and said something in Arapahoe.

"What does he mean, Slim?"

"Danged if I know, Joe."

"White men. Maybe four, five." Standing Tree pointed toward the northeast. "White men chase horses."

That was clear enough, but Joe knew of no one who might be interested in the horses. Then intuition hit him like a lightning bolt. Patterson! He had taken Patterson with him on that first ride to the box canyon. Was it possible that Patterson had come back to capture the horses?

"I think it might be the fellow that came with me the first time to look for mustangs. His name was Patterson; on Jackson's crew that built the bridge over the river and the road through the forest. I don't know what we might be up against; could be bad trouble. Do you think we should go back to camp? Or give up the idea all together?"

"You're the boss. I'm game if you are. We came for horses. The stage line needs fresh horses bad, and from what I've learned at the station from Jeremiah, that's what you signed on to do. But if you want to back off and come another time, I'm with you on that, too." Slim loosened the gun holster on his belt and felt the security it gave him.

Joe watched several emotions cross his face, then turned to the Indian. Standing Tree gave no indication that he understood Joe's words. His face was as expressionless as the boulders that surrounded them.

Joe took a moment to think it through. They might not get a better chance at the horses. Once the loggers and carpenters were gone, there would be four men at the station. If he challenged Patterson for the horses, one of them might be killed or injured. Was it worth the chance? He pictured John Dempsey's face in his mind when he was telling him how badly they needed the horses. It wasn't just the horses themselves, but the new bloodlines they would bring when mated with the animals he had. He leaned over and patted Mack on the neck.

Joe looked at Standing Tree. "Circle around and track the four white men. Find out what you can. We'll wait for you over there." He pointed at a stand of trees a few yards away. "Understand?" He used sign language as best he could to indicate that Standing Tree was to bring him back information. "Follow white man, and come back."

Standing Tree grunted and brought his horse's reins to Joe. "I go. You stay. White men follow horses. Standing Tree follow white men. Come back to Yo Hadley soon, maybe." He turned and walked away.

Joe and Slim rode the few yards to the stand of trees and dismounted. He ground-hitched the horses and sat on the ground to wait. They didn't say much while the Indian was gone. There wasn't anything to say. They could either go back to the station, or make a try for the horses. Joe wasn't sure about the better course of action. Dempsey had told him to try to catch the free-ranging animals, but he didn't mean for him to risk his life or the life of his animal handler, especially one as important as Slim, a veterinarian. If it were just him and Standing Tree, he'd go for the horses, in spite of the danger, but he couldn't risk Slim in the attempt. The responsibility hung heavily on his shoulders. He began to think back to the war years. He had been a corporal. He didn't make the decisions. He did what he was told. Suddenly, he heard a sound like running feet. It was Standing Tree.

"White men gone. Go west in hurry. Horses run like thunder. Chase white men. One white man fall, no get up. Dead."

Joe looked at Slim who was staring at Standing Tree.

"I heard what sounded like a stampede last night. Do you think the men got too close to the horses, and they stampeded? One of the men was killed falling off his mount, it seems to me like he's saying. Do you get the same message?" Standing Tree was nodding his head.

"I get the same, Joe. Now's our chance. If we can round up those horses and push them toward the box canyon before the men come back, we'll have them. No telling if the men'll even return; depends on how badly Patterson wants them. I've seen some mighty greedy men. He knows you'll be looking for them soon. It's getting toward winter, and if you don't catch them now, you'll have to delay it until spring. That's what he's counting on. I reckon he knows that you've been working on building a barn to shelter any of these wild horses you can manage to wrangle. I say we go find those mustangs."

Joe was surprised at the man's change of heart. He'd seemed only lukewarm to the idea earlier. He looked at Standing Tree and saw confidence in his eyes. The box canyon seemed unnecessary now.

"I think we'll forget the box canyon idea. It was only suggested as a way to trap the horses. With the three of us, if we can circle around behind them, and push them toward the station, sort of hurrying them along but letting them set their own course toward the direction we want them to go, we might get home by late tomorrow night. What do you say, Standing Tree? Can we get around on the other side of that band of unshod ponies?" He hoped the Indian understood him, because he didn't think he could interpret it in sign language and simple sentences. He could see by the excitement in his eyes that the man had followed him well enough.

"You get horses, Yo Hadley. We ride." Standing Tree mounted his horse and led the way to their camp. Joe and Slim quickly packed their saddle bags, and the three men wiped out all signs that they had been there, then rode northward, keeping their mounts to a steady, fast-moving trot. About a mile from the herd, Standing Tree indicated they should separate in the manner that Joe had said, and they spread out, Joe to the center, Slim to the left and the Indian shifting far right. They made a wide circle and came upon the horses grazing in a small meadow between stands of trees. Joe looked to Standing Tree and then Slim to get an idea of their position. He gestured to the Indian, and they moved closer until just yards behind the animals.

With a loud, rebel yell, Joe rode at a gallop toward the herd. Slim and Standing Tree followed suit. The startled horses stampeded in the general direction of the station. The men let them run until they were tired, and backed off to give them a rest, but kept them moving until nightfall. The herd stopped and nibbled on the grass. In the night they moved to a small stream and quenched their thirst. The men stayed alert and watchful during the night, sometimes drowsing and jerking awake, listening to the night sounds, but the animals remained calm. As a dim light was showing on the eastern horizon, the animals began to move. The men rode slowly behind, not letting them drift to right or left but pushing them steadily on.

By full light, Joe counted ten head, as Standing Tree had said. There appeared to be one dominant black stallion and a white female with spots, maybe a couple of yearling mares, and several younger, smaller animals, but he was too far away to tell and didn't want to get close enough for them to catch his scent. In the afternoon, they began to run into more trees, and he knew they were coming to the forest where it would be harder to keep them bunched together. He let them have several rest stops, and when they crossed a stream, the men gave them time to drink their fill. Joe took a couple of strips of jerky and nibbled on it and drank from his canteen, and hoped the other men took the time to eat and drink, also.

In mid-afternoon, the stallion jerked up his head and stood perfectly still, listening or sniffing for a predator. Joe hoped he hadn't gotten their human scent. He kept his horse steady and quiet with a tight grip on the reins. He looked to the right and to the left and knew the other men had stopped, too. The black seemed to calm down and lowered his head to graze. The men waited patiently.

After what seemed like an hour, but was probably minutes, the mustangs were on the move again, slowly, the men cautiously following. The trees grew taller and thicker, the piñons and firs now interspersed with bristlecone pines and other trees, and Joe recognized the area and knew they were about a mile from camp. He kept a close eye out and recognized the moment the stallion caught the sounds and smell of humans. He reared up and gave a warning to his harem, but Standing Tree had also been watching him. He sent up a yell loud enough to start an avalanche in the mountains, and rode straight for the horses giving them no time to scatter. Joe yelled as though a troop of Yankee soldiers were after him and heard a similar shout from Slim.

The men chased the herd as hard as they could ride, right into the midst of the carpenters' and loggers' camp. Some of them jumped up and started shooting at the sky. The horses tried to turn to their left, but Slim set off a warning shot, and they ran into the station yard, where Jeremiah and Peter got into the action. Jeremiah shot a few times, and Peter waved his arms and shouted until the animals could sense their days of running free were over. The stallion circled his herd, blowing hard and nipping at ears and necks, but he slowly settled down and stood, trembling.

McKinley and a couple of his crew mounted their animals, and the horsemen kept them bunched until Jeremiah opened the gate to the corral and the men drove them in, the mustangs jostling with the old timers. Joe hoped the influence of the stage horses and mules would settle them down, but he feared it would be the other way around. He dismounted and took a deep breath. They had the feral horses, but what trouble would they bring him?

In spite of his tiredness and aching muscles, Joe unsaddled Mack and watched to see that Slim and Standing Tree did the same. Jeremiah took over the Indian's horse, giving the older man more time to rest. The animals were given extra care after their grueling ordeal, and led to their stalls in the barn.

Joe, Slim and Standing Tree went in the house, ate a small meal and slept the clock around. Standing Tree slept under his favorite tree, oblivious to the noise around him, as the men put the finishing touches on the shelter for the coach, now standing in great splendor near the house, the red coach nearby.

Joe groggily came to life again. He doused his head in a bowl of water on the table by his bed and shaved his scraggly beard. When he stepped outside, twilight covered the land and sent dark shadows across the yard and corrals. He started walking and came to a dead stop when he saw the cabin attached to the barn. Built of logs, the structure was about forty feet wide and fifty feet deep, with a slanted roof. He stepped inside the open door and found Jeremiah playing with a deck of cards, and Slim cleaning his fingernails with the edge of his knife. Standing Tree was sitting on the floor wrapped in his blanket.

"Howdy, Boss. I see you found your way back to the

land of the living. We thought we'd have to throw a bucket of water on your head to rouse you for supper. How do you like our new home?" Jeremiah's voice echoed in the vast space. It was empty with no furniture except the small table and a couple of chairs brought from one of the bedrooms.

"New home?" Joe was still half asleep, and the significance of the words wasn't clear in his mind. He looked around at the bare walls and high beamed roof. The floor was dirt and straw. A huge rock fireplace was at the opposite end from where he was standing, one the masons must have taken great pride in building. It was unlit.

"Sure, Joe, don't you remember that you asked McKinley to build a bunkhouse for the drivers? Here it is, all nice and comfy. Of course, it'll be better when we have some bunks in here to sleep on, but at least it'll be out of the wind and rain when we get a door." Jeremiah tossed his cards on the table. He rose and motioned to Slim. "Come and see, Joe." He led Joe to the other end of the room and extolled the virtues of every detail: the beamed roof, the four corners, the crude log walls, some still with bark on them, the magnitude of the fireplace, the dirt floor, the open door, as though he were a curator at a museum. Joe was amused.

"Ah, you all are so slow! Come on outside, Joe." Again Jeremiah called out, insisting, as he cajoled the others, teasing them mischievously, as if he knew a great secret that he had to share. "The men have outdone themselves to please you." He led, and Joe and Slim followed.

Turning his attention to the source of Jeremiah's excitement, Joe found beside the new bunkhouse a tall shed with the large black stage coach inside. It had a roof and two sides, one being the wall of the brick barn, and the other side the bunkhouse wall. Joe gasped with astonishment. He hadn't noticed it when he came across the shadowed yard. He could see now that it was open at both ends so the coach could be driven in from either end and parked where the rain and hail wouldn't damage the painted doors and roof. The men had built the shell of a bunkhouse and extended a roof from one building to the next, leaving enough space for the coach between the buildings.

"Are the carpenters and loggers finished, then? Why're they still here?" He had seen the glow of the camp fire and men walking to and fro as they ate their evening meal.

"No, they've a few more minor details to complete. They want to caulk between the logs again. They waited until the first mortar dried out. Then they have to fix the door. I spent a few minutes with McKinley earlier, and he said one more day should wrap up the particulars if he puts several carpenters on it. The loggers are finished, though. They left a few logs for us. McKinley said we'd have to build the furniture and beds ourselves. He was only contracted to stay a week, and it's one day short. They'll be moving on to Buckboard Station on Tuesday."

Joe turned to Slim with a question in his eyes. He queried, "Are the saddle horses well?"

"I've been awake only a short time, myself. I plan to spend tomorrow with McKinley's crew and their animals, if that's all right with you. Peter and I checked the saddle horses in the barn a few minutes ago to see that they had plenty of water and hay. I'll stand the first watch; I feel kind of restless."

Joe nodded his approval and smiled at his animal handler.

"Say, Boss Man, those horses you brought in are mighty fine animals, but noisy. They pawed and neighed most of the night so a man couldn't sleep." It was said tongue in cheek, for the horse wranglers had slept as though dead. The noise hadn't disturbed them, having gone over thirty-six hours without sleep on the move with the animals.

The men were walking toward the corrals as Jeremiah spoke. They stood at the corral gate and watched the restlessness of the animals: stage horses, mules and mustangs all bunched together in the small space. He had no other choice but to put them together since the goats were in one enclosure, and the horses and donkeys in the other. Joe would see tomorrow about separating them, and after the McKinley group left, he and the other men would start to break the mustangs to the saddle or to pulling the wagon or coach. He was simply too tired to care about it tonight. He watched the black dancing nervously near the mules. He would start with that young, temperamental stallion.

Supper was a rather subdued affair. The women were glad to see the men back safely. Peter caught the horse wranglers up on the news while they were gone.

Bruno and Dakota had made one more trip to Buckboard Station and back with three passengers, all miners. In their estimation, business was picking up east to west, but there had been no coach from the south this week. Dakota admitted in his droll way that he was a pretty good horse trainer. He'd like a try at some of the mustangs if Joe would let him train them. Maybe one day they could have a race between Joe's saddle horses. The men were discussing the merits of the two saddle horses, Mack and Prissy, when McKinley came in.

Joe and McKinley spent an hour talking about the buildings and mustangs. Joe admitted he'd never seen such a fine log bunkhouse, not even in Indiana.

"McKinley, you've done a good job for me. I'll give you a draft on my Denver bank for that bonus we talked about earlier." He pulled out his wallet and removed a piece of paper that he had prepared for this moment.

McKinley drew back and protested that it was too much, but Joe insisted and handed it to him. It was for an amount equal to each man's monthly pay to be distributed when they reached Denver or left McKinley's employment.

"I have one stipulation, however." This was important to Joe, and he hoped the man would respect his wishes.

McKinley, holding the check as though it were a bag of freshly minted gold coins, held his breath. He looked keenly at Joe's determined face.

229

Joe coughed in embarrassment. "I'd appreciate it if you wouldn't use my name when you distribute the cash to the men. I don't need any hullabaloo about generosity and kindness from the men. They've worked hard and deserve the funds. It'll be better received if they think it's come from the company, rather than an individual. Let them think that the company appreciates their work and maybe they'll stay on to help some other station manager when he needs it."

"Hadley, you're more than generous. Frankly, I didn't believe that you'd come through with your promise. I've dealt with a few men, especially during the war, who've skipped out without paying the men their regular wages. It's been a pleasure to work for you. I'll see that the men receive the money, I promise." He shook hands and strolled from the room.

Joe stood at the door and watched the building contractor until his dark silhouette was seen against the glow of the campfire. He felt pleased that he had used Hannah's money for a good cause, but still there was a tiny doubt in his mind that the men would use the bonus wisely. He'd seen too many soldiers waste their pay on gambling, drinking and womanizing. It was out of his hands, though. He closed and locked the door behind him, checked the stove and fireplace one last time, and went to bed.

Sixteen

Two mornings later, McKinley and his men swung into their saddles behind the recently washed red coach driven by Rance Potter, dressed in his fanciest attire, with Thad Ray the guard sitting beside him looking sinister and solemn, his coach gun in his lap. Only his companions and Joe's family knew that the guard had a soft heart, loved animals, and was an expert carpenter. With the outriders as protection, and their supply wagon trailing them, Potter gave a shout of jubilation and drove away. Joe rather envied them their freedom. To ride high above that magnificent coach must be the ultimate in pleasure and commitment.

The four men used some of the leftover logs to build a temporary corral for the stage horses and mules, leaving the stronger, older corral for the mustangs. Twice the black stallion tried to escape but was held back by the barricade of timber and rope. Joe decided to call him Samson for his size and stubbornness.

The mares and their young continued to show their nervousness, and Joe decided to give them a few more days to get used to human sounds and smells. He walked among the animals and took a tally. There were six older mares, one colt and two fillies. Counting the stallion, that made ten feral horses.

Slim suggested the white mare might be an Indian paint by her coat coloring, and Joe named her Delilah. The colt appeared to be her offspring. The others seemed to be a mix of chestnuts and sorrels. He put the youngsters in with the horses and donkeys temporarily, and they began to calm down. One or other of the men kept a keen eye out for the animals during the night. He suspected that once Patterson knew they had captured the mustangs he might try to steal them. As the days wore on toward October, he began to relax.

The men spent some time each day in the next weeks with the animals, and the result was that four mares became accustomed to the harness, with the fifth being trained. Joe was gratified that there were no more attempts to break out once the stallion was left alone in the corral.

Dakota and Joe worked for days to train the stallion to accept its fate. Every morning and evening, Joe visited the corral, speaking softly and tempting the animal with apples and brown sugar lumps, until he finally came to the fence rail in curiosity. Dakota bragged endlessly on his skill as a rider, to the point of saying that he'd be damned if anyone was keeping him off the horses, until Joe relented and let him try the white mare. His skill and daring thus proven, Dakota began to work with the leader of the herd.

A roar of revelry pierced the late afternoon air as Dakota swung into the saddle atop the stallion for the first time. As soon as he dug his spurs into the black's hide, he began to buck and kick. He leaped high in the air and plunged to the ground with a teeth-rattling dive, but the rider hung on for several minutes before crashing to the earth with a loud thump and cloud of dust. Slim and Jeremiah raced to grab the horse's reins and unsaddled him.

Dakota groggily rose to his feet, cursing and stunned by the impact, and walked toward the rail where he had left his holster and gun. He strapped his weapon around his waist and walked to a cluster of trees, where he sat and brooded while the other men calmed the frantic animal and left the corral. He held a stick in his hand and from time to time thrust it into the ground, giving Joe and the stallion menacing looks.

Bruno Smith, the stage driver, turned and walked to the bunkhouse, where he lay on his bed and considered what to do about the guard's raging temper. He'd seen a hidden danger in the eyes of the man after his fall from the horse. Twice while at the Buckboard Station, Dakota had been rude and short with a passenger. Bruno suspected his interest in the mustang stallion was a personal one. Maybe he was wrong, and he'd keep his suspicion to himself for now.

The rest of the month was spent in hasty activity, for the mornings were cooler and the rain sharp and biting to the face and neck. Joe left the mustangs to the other men, who soon had them as tame as the goats. He and Peter spent time building partitions in the bunkhouse, with the occasional help of Jeremiah and Slim. Dakota spent most of his time with a deck of cards, or practicing his skill with rifle or pistol in the open field, sulking over his humiliation at the hands of the stallion. He fashioned a target on a tree and persisted until Joe told him to take his practice further into the trees so the women weren't disturbed by the noise. Joe suspected trouble from the man; but he'd been hired by Baldwin for his weapon skills and acute intelligence, not his forbidding manner and scowling face.

The women sewed mattresses for the bunkhouse beds and gathered straw and grass for the stuffing. Hannah wanted to leave her good feather mattresses for the guests. The men objected at first, but Hannah was insistent that the passengers were the reason they had their jobs. Ruth backed her up; and Peter and Joe supported Ruth. In the end, the feather mattresses stayed in the station bedrooms. As the season changed and the nights drew darker, Hannah and Ruth began to spend more time with their stitchery. Hannah was almost finished with the table cloth, and Ruth was sewing a new shirt for Peter's birthday.

Jeremiah and Slim spent more time together, both being young and ambitious. Slim had no experience of the law, but he'd been to university, and so he began to tutor Jeremiah in mathematics, Greek and Latin, knowing Jeremiah would need those skills as an attorney. Baldwin had sent books from his college days with the last wagon of supplies, and they used one of Hannah's tablets to practice his mathematical proficiency. Joe encouraged them in this endeavor as long as they didn't neglect their other duties. They worked two hours each night on Jeremiah's studies. Joe figured it was time well spent, although Jeremiah received a considerable amount of teasing from Bruno, until one night, something in the Latin text interested him. From then on, Slim made an effort to choose the lessons to interest the driver.

Dakota wasn't interested and spent more time alone, fingering his pistol and taking it apart and cleaning it. One night he fired his weapon into the log wall of the new bunkhouse, waking everyone. He received a reprimand from Joe and Peter, who accepted his explanation that it was an accident, but Joe continued to be nagged with trepidation over the man's increasingly hostile behavior.

In the last week in September, Hannah put fresh wood shavings together with three pine cones in the stove, stirring the blackened coals until they glowed. When smoke began to curl, she added two small, split logs and headed to the outhouse. There was a fine sprinkling of snow on the ground, and it was still falling. It had come down so silently and softly that they hadn't heard it. She went back in and called to Joe.

"Joe, darling, it's snowing." She shivered from the damp flakes in her hair and on her coat. She kept her coat on as she turned the damper on the stove. She filled the coffee pot and the kettle with water. She felt like a nice soothing cup of tea this morning, and she knew that Ruth liked tea better than coffee.

"It's snowing?" Joe came into the Public Room in his stocking feet. He skidded to a halt and almost stepped on the dog. Jack started barking. He had been interrupted from a deep sleep. He ran circles around Joe and tried to nip at his heels. "Hannah, get this damn dog before he trips me."

She scooped up the dog and put him in the inner garden, where he frolicked in the snow and chased a bird off the well.

Joe put on his boots, hat and heavy coat and went out. He observed the snow in wonder as the white flurries drifted about with no particular direction. It was dark, with over-hanging clouds, and no light could be seen in the bunkhouse. He decided to gather the eggs and milk the nannies to save his mother the trip in the cold and wet. He went back for a lantern. He thought of Standing Tree, who liked to sleep under the tree in the open air. He took the lantern and shook the old man on the shoulder to wake him. The Indian was instantly awake and on his feet.

"Wake up, old man, it's snowing. Go in the house where it's warm."

Standing Tree looked about him and laughed. It was so unusual for the Indian to laugh that Joe joined in, and they danced a jig in the white, puffy powder that covered the ground. "Go on, now. Get in the house before you freeze, you silly man." It was doubtful if Standing Tree understood him, but he knew that it was cold and there was a warm fire inside the house. The old man shuffled toward the lighted windows of the domicile, finally reaching the door, and leaving a bevy of tracks in his wake. Hannah let the dog back in, and he ran to the Indian. Hannah shooed him away and handed Standing Tree a warm blanket she'd brought from a bedroom. She took the damp one from him to dry by the fireplace. She set the kindling to blazing, and Standing Tree sat down in his normal place. The dog came and sniffed at his feet, then lay down to take a snooze.

Hannah heard a sound and turned to see Ruth coming

out of the passageway followed by her husband. "It's snowing, Mama. Better put on your heavy coat to visit the outhouse. Don't worry about the chickens or goats. Joe's gone to tend to them."

"What's this? You say it's snowing? Wait, Ruth, I'll walk out with you." Peter walked back to their bedroom and brought wool coats and scarfs for them. "I always liked the snow in spite of the extra work. The farm animals don't seem to mind, although it's harder for them to forage for food." His voice drifted away as he and Ruth disappeared in the gloom.

The next day was bright and clear, and the snow was melted by midmorning, except for the shadowed cracks that didn't get the sun until afternoon. The men got on with their work, and as Joe was coming from the barn, he heard the northbound stage arrive. He wasn't expecting it, so they must have an important passenger, he supposed. The driver was Paul Ward with the guard Manning, his shotgun in his arm.

Ward stepped down in time to open the door for a sprightly, middle-aged man with a goatee and mustache. He was dressed in overalls and worn boots, but he didn't look like a farmer, Joe thought. Manning stood as though at attention in his usual silent manner.

"Got a special guest for you, Joe. He came all the way from Walsenburg, but not on the stage. Started out on horseback, he said. Caught the stage at Pueblo. His name's Jameson. We can't stay long, just time to eat a bite and be on our way back south. The fellow paid for the trip, but it's not our regular run. We got to get back so we can keep to our schedule if it don't snow again." The stranger moved forward to shake Joe's hand, and Ward gave them a wave and headed for the house and some strong coffee. Manning moved off toward the corrals to look at the mustangs. He was an unusual man, who kept his thoughts to himself.

"Hadley, I'd like to take a look at those mustangs of yours, if I can. Ward told me you'd brought in a band of wild horses. I admire a good horse when I see one. My grandfather told me these wild ones are descendants of animals brought from Spain by the conquistadors centuries ago. I don't know if I believe that tale, but the animals are known far and wide for their stamina and endurance."

They'd arrived at the corrals, and Joe noticed that Manning gave the passenger a strange look, as though assessing his character. Joe suggested he might like to get some coffee and doughnuts Hannah had cooked that morning. He went toward the house without a word.

"Strange man; doesn't have much to say for himself, does he? I've seen a lot of those fellows since the war. Never talk about their background or families. I suspect he was in the war, but whether for North or South, I can't say. He spoke hardly a word on the trip. Hadley, tell me about that black."

Joe gave him a shortened version of the roundup, giving Standing Tree most of the credit for bringing in the mustangs without trouble. He told him of Dakota's special skill with taming horses. He was trying to understand why the stranger had made the effort to come from Walsenburg to see him, but didn't want to be rude and ask. He figured the man would tell him when he was ready.

Slim looked up from the pen where he was tending a mule with a small cut on his left front shoulder. He came over to see what was going on.

"Jameson, this is my animal handler, Slim Grimshaw. He's a trained veterinarian." The men shook hands.

"Slim, Ward and Manning want to leave as soon as possible. How's the mule this morning?"

"He's better, but I want to keep him under observation for another day or two." Slim moved into the pen and started selecting and bringing out fresh horses for the stage coach.

The two men left alone stood watching the black for a while without speaking.

"Are you planning to use all these wild horses for pulling coaches and for breeding?"

"No, I think one or two might make good saddle horses. The stallion especially, looks like he has good bloodlines. He's been ridden several times and is settling to his fate. It'd be a shame to hitch him to the vehicles for a life of drudgery. I want to breed him with my mare if I can. I've been giving them some time to get used to humans and their newly restricted life.

"If you look to your right, you might see that white mare with the two small black spots on her neck and the larger one on her back and leg. She looks like she might've been an Indian pony, and got away from the tribe somehow. She must have come upon these others and joined with them for protection. I think she'll make a good saddle horse. I watched them on the trail, and they both seemed adaptable to riders, if I can get the wildness out of them. I've got a number of mares with the donkeys for mules. We use mules on the route east of here because of the deep sand in places. Most of the mares will be trained to pull the coaches. Come into the barn with me, if you like to see good horses."

Joe led the way and opened the door to the barn. It was dim inside even with the door open, so Joe grabbed a lantern beside the door and lit it. He led Jameson to the stalls where he was greeted by a neigh from Mack. The chestnut leaned his head out of the half door to receive a scratch on the head.

"Sorry, old man, I didn't bring any apples with me today. I'll try to bring two tomorrow." He turned to Jameson. "This one and the mare next to him are my personal mounts and have no connection to the stage line. I haven't got around to it yet, been busy building up the place and the coaches that come in once a week, but I plan to breed these with some of those others you saw in the corrals."

Jameson patted the horse's head, and Joe moved on to Prissy. They stood admiring her for a few minutes.

"I named the mare after one of the passengers that came through named Priscilla. It seems to fit the old girl. Mack and

Prissy ought to give me some fine offspring in the course of time. I didn't set out to be in the horse breeding business; it just seemed to happen that way. We have to look to the future." He turned and started back to the door without showing the other animals in the barn.

"I'm glad that you brought that up, Hadley. I didn't come to talk of horses. I came to see you about an entirely different matter, but the animals seemed to be a good way to get your measure. If we could have a place to sit and discuss what I came for with some privacy, it would be appreciated."

Joe blew out the flame in the lantern and hung it in its place by the door. He gave a sideways glance at the stranger, but said nothing. He closed the door to the barn and set out walking to the house.

"Come up to the house. I suspect there's a room full of people waiting for their supper, but we can go to the garden and talk, if you like."

Slim was standing by the coach, giving it a cursory look. "Joe, everything's ready, if you want to look her over." He gazed closely at the stranger.

Joe walked to the coach and did his usual thorough inspection. He asked several questions as he encircled the vehicle. He went to the animals and approved of Slim's choice for the trip south. He praised him for his effort and turned as he heard the sound of voices. Peter and Jeremiah came from the house with Ward and Manning. Jeremiah was doing the talking, and the men were listening closely. They came to a halt as they approached Joe and Jameson standing by the coach.

"Joe, that was sure a fine meal your wife gave us; you better watch her good. I might want to steal her away from you some dark night. She's a mighty excellent cook. Her doughnuts are light as a feather. She gave us four to take with us. You might have to settle with stale bread for your dessert." Ward laughed and made his own tour of the coach and horses, while Manning stood near the front wheel, ready to mount to his seat. He gave Jameson that frozen stare again.

When he finished, Ward shook hands all around, and vaulted into the box. Manning clambered aboard, and they moved at a fast clip down the road to the south. There was a collective sigh of relief from the men left behind.

Joe turned to his guest. "Jameson, this is my father, Peter Hadley, and my help, Jeremiah Fuller. You've already met Slim Grimshaw, my veterinarian." The men shook hands with the stranger, and Joe walked toward the house. They followed him like a parade of ducks in a row. He went in and crossed to Hannah, giving her a peck on the cheek. He turned in time to see the look of shock on Jameson's face. He figured it was almost certainly Hannah's scar that had startled him. He moved to the stove where Ruth was tending a pot of vegetables and kissed her, too.

"This is my wife, Hannah, and my mother, Ruth. Over there squatting on the floor is Standing Tree, my Arapahoe friend." He sat down at the table, and the other men joined him. Jameson gave the Indian a glancing look and sat at the end next to Peter. Standing Tree rose, and keeping his blanket tight around his shoulders and waist, took his usual seat next to Joe. His black intelligent eyes squinted at the strange man, but he said nothing.

Cups were already on the table, so Hannah poured coffee for everyone. She moved away and brought a huge pot of soup to the table. Ruth placed the platter of meat in front of Joe to be carved. They were having a venison roast with potatoes, onions and carrots. Between the two women, bowls of vegetables, bread and baked apple dumplings soon appeared on the table as if by magic. The men were quiet at first, digging into dishes and swallowing their food, but soon talk began about Ward and Manning and whether they would hit rain before nightfall. Slim reported on the progress of the mule he'd been doctoring, and Jeremiah told a funny story about one of the goats. Jameson cast his eyes on each person at a time, his glance falling on Standing Tree the longest.

240

Standing Tree ignored the stranger. He had been at the station long enough to know that the passengers came and went, but if he had sensed a threat to his loved ones, he would have swung into action with his skinning knife in an instant in spite of his aching bones and aging joints.

Finally, the appetites of the men were satisfied, and they moved from the table. Slim and Jeremiah headed off to studies in mathematics and languages. Peter volunteered to bring in more firewood and water, but first he wanted a cigar. Hannah and Ruth began to clear the table.

"That was a fine meal, ladies. I thank you." Jameson watched as Standing Tree wrapped his blanket around himself and headed out for his nightly smoke with Peter.

"Jameson, if you'll come with me, we can have that conversation now." He strolled to the hallway door and entered the passageway, turned at the end door and thence to the inner garden, not looking back to see if the man was following. The garden only slightly resembled the place that Hannah had first seen, except for the well in the center. The saplings that Peter had planted were a few inches taller, their leaves beginning to change color for the cooler season. Two brightly painted jars held the remnants of green plants that Ruth had placed there, but they hadn't survived the snow of the previous day.

A handmade table with a slight wobble of the legs stood in one corner, with two equally unstable chairs near it. They had been Jeremiah's first attempt at making furniture, and kept in the garden since Hannah had deemed them unsuitable for the guests, even though she was as proud of them as though they were made in an eastern factory. There were several candles and holders on a nearby shelf, and Joe lighted one since the high walls kept the twilight sun from reaching the corners. He invited the guest to sit, and took the other chair. He waited patiently for his visitor to begin the conversation.

"Hadley, I'm here under false pretenses. Although I

came from Walsenburg, that's not my home or my place of business. I currently live in Denver, but my home is New York City. I have a wife and three children there. My business is with the United States Mail Service. I work for Wells Fargo. You may have heard of it. They have recently taken over the running of the former Butterfield Stage Mail Service from St. Louis to San Francisco. You might say that I'm your competition."

Joe brushed away a moth drawn to the flame of the candle. He looked up at the sky and viewed a single bright star almost overhead. The wind had stilled, but he felt the damp night air closing around the station. He wrapped his coat more closely around him. He felt guilty for bringing the man out in the cold, but it was the only place that he thought they might have privacy. He pulled his mind from his discomfort to the conversation.

Jameson continued, "It's my job to search this country of ours, looking for new routes and new customers. Now that the war is over, people will expect a faster, safer way to travel from coast to coast. The small villagers and farmers will expect their mail to be delivered in a timely manner. Since the days of Benjamin Franklin, the mail delivery has been sporadic at the best of times, and nonexistent in the worst of times. We intend to remedy that problem."

Joe began to suspect the man's motive for coming, but he waited for him to state the obvious. His apprehension grew.

"I've heard good testimony about you and your station. I sent spies pretending to be passengers to test your skills as a manager. You might recall two of them. Priscilla St. John is my stepsister. Matilda Burkhalter is my cousin. They're two different personalities with the same mission, to check you out. I received glowing reports from both women. You might be surprised to know that my sister was quite impressed with your handling of the situation that she deliberately put you and your wife in for the purpose of my information."

Joe was angry. He rose to his feet, his discomfort now obvious. He'd been fooled, and he didn't like that. A basically honest person, he couldn't abide dishonesty in another man or woman.

"Please sit down, Hadley, and hear me out. I'm here to offer you a position with the Wells Fargo Company, either as station manager such as this one, or an office job in Denver as my associate. I'll be returning to my home soon."

"No." Joe turned to go into the house.

"But you haven't heard my proposition. You'll have an increase in salary and benefits. Doesn't a large home in Denver appeal to you? You and your family can live in luxury and enjoy the advantages of schools, theaters, and restaurants."

"Jameson, I have everything I want in life right here. I have food, shelter and the stimulation of a variety of people who come and go through my station. I've made friends with the coach drivers and guards. I have employees who are loyal and hard working. I need no more than that to make me happy." Again, Joe turned to go inside.

"Have you thought of the danger of Indian attacks or the elements, or overturned coaches? Diseases, maybe? Any number of catastrophes can happen in a wilderness area like this one." Jameson sounded desperate, and Joe wondered why he was so insistent when many men would leap for the chance he was offering.

"I've thought of all those things, but my answer is still no. I didn't fight for my beliefs and values in a lost cause during the war only to turn my back on the people who live in this land. All you've said is true. This country's growing fast. People'll need the services that you named, but that's all the more reason why I want to provide those services to as many travelers as I can with my limited skills. Sir, I wish you a pleasant night. If you have need of anything that the station can provide, please don't hesitate to ask."

Willard Jameson sat for a long while after Joe had gone

into the house. His sister was right, and he was a fool for not trusting her instincts. She'd said that Josiah Hadley was an honest man, and he wouldn't bend his principles for the sake of expediency or wealth. He needn't put himself out on his behalf. There were other men who'd be willing to take less than he was offering Hadley. He rose and went to the well. He stooped and picked up a pebble and dropped it into the darkness. He heard the splash of water. It gave him an idea. His own company could benefit from the planning of others. He'd suggest this setup to the contractors who built the wilderness stations. Yes, his trip hadn't been totally in vain. He took the candle to light his way to his room. He undressed and pinched the wick with his fingers to extinguish the flame, and crawled into the bed, where he could smell the subtle scent of lavender. His last thought was that Hannah Hadley was a very clever woman.

Joe watched the large black coach drive away with Bruno and Dakota aboard the high seat. Inside sat Jameson with a buffalo rug on his lap for warmth and a half dozen johnnycakes in a bag beside him, should he become hungry on his journey to Buckboard Station. Joe wondered if he'd offer the same proposition to Blessing. He turned away and went to the barn to give Mack and Prissy the promised apples. He laughed. Did Jameson realize that the horse was named for his sister?

Hannah threw a party for Peter's birthday. She made a ginger cake and presented him with a pair of woolen mittens. Ruth gave him the shirt she had made from cotton bunting. Joe gave him a pair of leather shoes he had Ned Baldwin send in the last shipment of supplies. He and Hannah hid them in their room so it'd be a surprise. Joe decided the men could take a day off from the heavy work, doing only the necessary chores. The men played poker in the bunkhouse, with the fireplace burning brightly.

That week Grover drove the stage from the Mozier station with a new man named Mandrake acting as guard.

244

Grover said that Rusty had come down with the croup. Since they didn't have Rusty's old trumpet to blow, the coach caught the station attendants unaware. Joe and Hannah hastened to the coach to extend their welcome to the guests.

The passengers were a couple from Atchison, Kansas, on their way to Ft. Collins. The man, Jason Lancaster, was a pompous, overbearing windbag, Jeremiah declared without contradiction from Joe and Slim. The woman was young, pretty and very tall, standing at least three inches higher than her husband. She stayed in her room most of the time, only venturing out for the evening meal. The man had come to explore the idea of a mail route from Trinidad in the south to Denver for the Overland Stage Line since the company already had the east to west route from Atchison to Denver. Joe kept quiet about his encounter with the competition from Wells Fargo. He didn't think it was any concern of his.

Coming back from Buckboard Station, Dakota rode on the inside, playing cards and drinking with the passenger, a miner from California on his way to Platte City, Missouri. Immediately upon arrival, Bruno came down from the driver's seat and began arguing with Dakota. Joe, as was his custom, came from the house to welcome their guests from Denver. He was taken aback when he discovered that Dakota was drunk, a violation of the strict stage company rules. Bruno landed a blow to the head, which sent Dakota reeling against the coach wheel, and setting the nervous horses to kicking and pawing the ground in fright.

Slim went to the front of the team to calm the animals, while the fight continued for over twenty minutes, first one man attaining the advantage and then the other. Joe didn't try to interfere, since it seemed to be a personal fight. What he didn't tolerate was the miner, named Oliver Tate, egging on Dakota. He seemed as drunk as the stage guard, so Joe pulled his pistol from his holster and told the man to go to the bunkhouse and sober up. Tate, surprised at the forcefulness of the station manager's demand, obeyed him.

The males of the household watched the fight until Bruno landed a final punch to the head that knocked the drunken guard out. Peter and Jeremiah carried him to the bunkhouse and put him to bed. Slim drove the coach to the shed and unhitched the horses.

"What was all that about, Bruno?" Joe didn't want to interfere in the man's personal business; but if it had something to do with the station, it became his business.

Bruno had a bruise on one cheek, and his knuckles were bleeding. He took out a handkerchief and wiped them clean. He scuffed his feet and looked at the ground. "That damn Blessing has partitioned his station and opened a saloon on one side of the house. Dakota was drinking all night with that miner and a few cattlemen who work on ranches in the area. He stayed up all night, and when I told him it was time to go; I had to force him to come on the stage. He wanted to stay with his new drinking buddies. I told him to ride inside, because I wasn't sure he could stay on top. I didn't know he brought a bottle with him until too late to stop the coach and take care of the matter. I had the schedule to maintain. Since we'd get here before afternoon, I'd planned to travel on with the miner to Mozier Station and spend the night there. Now it's out of the question."

"Well, I guess you did the right thing. Go and eat and get Hannah to put some salve on those cuts. They'll probably sleep all night. See Slim about the horses before you hit the bed." Joe watched Bruno go into the house, and walked toward the spring. Peter and Jeremiah met him, and they discussed what had happened. "I'm disappointed in Blessing. What the hell was he thinking, opening a saloon in a way station?"

"It's the extra money, son. He probably has a supplier from Denver who brings him the liquor. I wouldn't lose any sleep about it; I don't know the man, but I know what it's like to drink. He thinks to make a profit on the side. Come in the house and finish your meal. You, too, Jeremiah."

Joe looked back at the bunkhouse, shaking his head at the foolishness of men.

Bruno and Dakota started off early the next morning, with a very sober miner inside the coach, carrying less money in his pocket than he'd started the trip. Tate sulked the whole way to Mozier Station, hoping he could win back some of the funds before he arrived in Missouri.

Joe and Jeremiah took a mid-afternoon ride on the saddle horses, Mack and Prissy. The wind had shifted to the north, and the tree tops caught the breeze. The sun shone brightly overhead. They stabled the animals and were discussing the merits of breeding the horses with some of the mustangs, when the black coach arrived back at the station.

Joe could tell from Bruno's expression that the trip had not gone well. He pulled on the reins, and the wheels skidded a few inches. Before the vehicle was completely stopped, Dakota dropped from his seat with an already empty holster gracing one leg; the weapon that should have been inside glistened in his hand, wickedly catching the late afternoon sun. He pointed the weapon at Joe and trudged with an expression of fierce intent on his face toward the station manager.

"Joe, look out." Bruno shouted the warning and vaulted from the box, the reins falling slack on the ground.

Slim was already running to take care of the mules. It all happened in an instant. Jeremiah jumped in front of Joe, striking him down with a hard shove of the elbow, knocking the wind out of his lungs. Joe heard the shot as he fell and thought the pain in his chest was from the bullet. Jeremiah fell on top of him, and Joe heard a second shot as though from a far distance. He heard a female scream and knew it was Hannah.

Groggily, he sat up and pushed the weight of Jeremiah off him. He realized that the pain had been caused by Jeremiah's arm in his attempt to save the life of his friend. Joe stood as though in a daze and saw the blood on Jeremiah's crushed head. For a moment he was back at Morgan's Raid in Indiana, gazing at the mangled body of his boyhood friend, Tatum Greer. A loud roar sounded in his head, and his breath came short and shallow. Twice Peter spoke before Joe came out of his haze and looked around. He seemed surrounded by intruders. Bruno stood as though turned to rock, his smoking pistol still in his hand. Dakota's body lay nearby, and Joe realized what had happened. Dakota had attempted to kill him, but Jeremiah had taken the lethal bullet instead, and Bruno had shot Dakota.

The two hapless men were laid to rest underneath the towering pine boughs near the mound that contained the remains of Brody White, who was shot by Buck Jones. To Joe and Hannah, it seemed so long ago.

Joe and Peter took the wagon to the river bank and found a good-sized rounded boulder. They hefted it into the wagon and carried it to the head of the young man's grave. Joe didn't know the exact date of Jeremiah's birth, but he knew his age, so with a chisel and a stout hammer, he carved the following: Jeremiah Fuller died October 14, 1867 in his twenty-first year. RIP.

Bruno later explained that Dakota had planned to steal the mustang stallion, and sell him to one of his poker-playing buddies at Buckboard Station, who owned a ranch in that area.

On a cold, brisk, sunny day in early November, Joe sat at the table with a page from Hannah's lined tablet writing a letter to John Dempsey explaining what had happened and informing the supervisor that five new draft horses were trained for the coaches and would be ready for duty in the spring. He requested instructions on what to do with the animals. He had already written to Wallace Tisdale, the new Western Division Agent requesting a new driver and shotgun messenger, since Bruno had decided to move on to California.

Hannah poured him a cup of coffee and put it on the table in front of him. He noticed her sympathetic gesture, but his thoughts were far away. He was thinking of the young man from Tennessee whose dreams and hopes of becoming a lawyer like his father would never be realized. He closed the letter and sealed it with wax to be taken to the next station and forwarded to Denver, where he hoped it would reach Dempsey's office before spring.

Jack was trying to get Standing Tree to play with him. He pulled at the corner of his blanket with his teeth, but the Indian only grunted and spoke to him in his own language. Ruth lifted the dog in her arms and took him to the kitchen area and gave him a bone to keep him busy for a while. The smell of fresh-baked bread permeated the Public Room. The gray table cloth with the pretty embroidered corners was neat and tidy. Hannah smoothed an imagined wrinkle on the top, and placed a fruit jar with a green leafed stem covered in red berries on it. She walked to the northern wall and straightened the watercolor painting of a lilac bush she remembered from Peter and Ruth's home in Indiana. She had completed it only that week, bringing tears to her in-laws eyes. Peter glanced up from the week-old Denver City newspaper he had been reading.

Suddenly, the loud, melodious sound of Rusty Backgammon's trumpet interrupted Joe's thoughts. The familiar rumble of mules' hooves reverberated throughout the area, and the old brown coach rolled to a stop in front of the overnight way station. Josiah Hadley looked up at his wife's beautiful face and smiled. He left his letter and rushed to help Slim unhitch the team and water the animals. Standing Tree rose and slowly followed him, his new moccasins shuffling softly across the floor. The dog barked cheerfully and wagged his tail. Hannah and Ruth grabbed their heavy winter coats off the pegs and went out to welcome their guests to the Sweetwater Station.

.

www.ingramcontent.com/pod-product-compliance
Lightning Source LLC
Chambersburg PA
CBHW071302250626
47159CB00004B/1272